Victoria *must* wed . . . and immediately!

To rescue her family from financial ruin, lovely Victoria Shelby has no choice but to marry. Her options for a bridegroom are limited . . . until she remembers the shy servant boy next door. Then she discovers that her childhood friend is actually Viscount Thurlow—ruthless businessman, future earl, and a man whose family is shrouded in scandal!

After two rejected marriage proposals, David Thurlow needs a wife who will give him an heir, someone who will not only overlook his past but also be above reproach. Victoria is the ideal candidate—quiet, unassuming, and in desperate need of funds. But even as she strives to be the perfect wife, her calm demeanor masks a shocking secret . . . one that is overshadowed by David's slow, heated lessons in the art of seduction that threaten to transform a "convenient" marriage into a torrid and passionate affair.

By Gayle Callen

Gayle Callen

THE LORD NEXT DOOR

AVON BOOKS
An Imprint of HarperCollinsPublishers

AVON BOOKS
An Imprint of HarperCollins*Publishers*
10 East 53rd Street
New York, New York 10022-5299

To the wonderful people who helped me write The Lord Next Door:

To my editor, Erika Tsang, who always has brilliant insight into my work and helps me make it the best it can be.

To my agent, Eileen Fallon, who always sees what I can't see, and inspires me to dig deeper.

To my husband, Jim, who accepted several last-minute challenges to brainstorm for this book and helped me immensely.

Thank you all.

Prologue

London, 1828

Dear Tom,

This is my Private Journal—how dare you spy on me and presume to write in it! You may be ten years old, but so am I, and I would never be so rude!

Dear Victoria,

You left the notebook under a bench in your garden where anyone could find it. I live right next door, and from my window, I happened to see you

1

hide it. I didn't come any closer, I promise. Your bonnet hid your face, so I didn't see you. My mother always says my curiosity will land me in trouble, and here it has. I do not know much about music (which you seem quite fond of from what you wrote about your lessons) but I am certain we could find something in common. My mother is the earl's cook, and I have no father or brothers or sisters. I'm allowed to be tutored sometimes with the earl's son. Think of me writing to you as a way I can practice my lessons. Can't we be friends?

Dear Tom,

I've never had a boy for a friend. I suppose writing to you can cause no harm. But I can never meet with you. You would get into trouble if the earl discovered that his kitchen boy presumed upon the neighbors. And my father would take my journal away if he thought I was consorting with a servant. He says we always have to associate with people above us, but since we're below them in status, why would they want to associate with us? It's all so very confusing. My father is a banker who invests the money of wealthy people. Even the earl is one of his clients. I have a mother and two sisters named Louisa and Meriel. Louisa is two years younger than I, and she has very red hair that my mother says is unfashionable, but which I think is uncommonly pretty. Meriel is four years younger than I, and her hair is golden ringlets. My hair is just this pale yellow color that doesn't really look like much of anything.

Dear Victoria,

Don't worry about your hair—it isn't important what a girl looks like. It's what she talks about that matters. Someday I'll convince you to meet me so we can have a real discussion. You're lucky to have sisters. You always have someone to play with. What do you do all day? I help my mother in the kitchen but I can play outside as much as I want. I have a secret hiding place in the attic. It's where I keep all of my most important things, like special rocks from the garden and paper no one wants because only one side is used. I like to hide in there where no one can find me and think about important things, like sailing to India or to one of those islands by the colonies. I'm telling you things I've never told anyone. See, you can trust me.

Dear Tom,

I would never be brave enough to go on a long, dangerous voyage to India. But I'm glad you have so much time to think. Little girls have not so

3

much freedom. My father hired a governess so that I can be properly educated like a lady, but I think my sisters like that better than I do. At least Louisa does. French is very hard (and why do we need it if we just finished a war with them not so long ago?). Mathematics make my head spin. Meriel is lucky. She is still allowed to play much of the day. Though thankfully music and needlework are part of my lessons. I also have to learn all about rank, like earls and dukes, and who goes into the dining room first, and who escorts whom. Really, why do I need to know all about the nobility if they won't invite us anywhere? Mama says we have to be prepared, because she wants to make sure my sisters and I marry the right men. Doesn't falling in love make a person the right man? I like that you have a secret place to hide. I do, too. I call it Willow Pond, although that is not its real name. But I can't tell you where it is right now. It's a secret.

1829

Dear Victoria,

Your tears are getting the notebook all wet and dirty—don't cry! I keep telling you to explain to your mother why you don't like to dance. She'll understand and make that nasty governess stop. No one should have to dance. But if you need someone to talk to, I could meet you at Willow Pond. I know you only go there with your sisters. You always go on and on about that place being magical, but it's a corner of your garden, Victoria. Why won't you share it with me, too?

Dear Tom,

I'm not like my sisters. I'm not like any other girls, and there are days my father won't look at me because of it. I don't like the things ladies are supposed to like, like babies and husbands and dresses. I want to play the piano all day. I hear songs in my head that no one has created yet. I think of designs for my needlework because the pictures intrigue me, not because needlework is what a Lady Should Do.

1830

Dear Tom,

You've returned from the country! It was such a long three months. You have such an unusual situation—your mother traveling with an earl. Tell me everything you did, and don't leave any-

5

thing out—unless it involves the inside of a frog. You talk about that too much, and I don't care if you call it scientific research. I may not like the thought of traveling myself, but when you tell me stories, I can imagine it all and live through your eyes.

Dear Victoria,

Don't listen to your father. Men like ladies who think. My mother reads the newspaper and thinks a great deal. We have long conversations, but then I'm her only child. She says she appreciates my opinions. Have you tried talking to your parents? If they're worried about who you'll marry, tell them I will marry you. You don't think about balls and dresses like some silly girls do.

Dear Tom,

When you marry, I hope you find a lovely woman. But she can't be me, because my father would never allow it. That is truly sad, because you understand me more than any person in my life, except my sisters. So let us think of the Perfect Wife for you. She would have to be a grand adventuress, of course, and not mind riding on elephants in India. You'll probably earn your fortune there and come back as quite the wealthy gentleman. (Don't scoff! I know you care little for the nobility, but perhaps the gentry will make room for a fine man such as you will become someday.) The Perfect Wife would be very brave, of course, and able to speak passionately about what she believes in. She'll read the newspaper, and know about Parliament and wars and famous men.

1832

Dear Tom,

My sisters are very worried about me, but I am not like them. I will be content to be our parents' companion as they age. I love nothing better than to be at home with my music and my needlework. You know I hate to dance—what man would want a wife who can't dance?

Father is angry again. Only to you can I complain how unfairly he always focuses on me. He punished me again by locking the door to the music room. Why won't he tell us what he's angry at? We can never question him. I'm worried that Mama knows what it is. Yet certainly she would not keep something important from us.

1834

Dearest Tom, my secret friend,

Why haven't you written to me? It has been months, and I know the earl is in town, so you must be there somewhere. I heard that the countess died, and that must be a terrible strain on the household. I'm so sorry. Surely your mother was able to keep her position. Yet—you're almost a man now at sixteen. Did you feel the need to look for work? Wouldn't the earl keep you in his household? Or have I offended you? I look back over the past year's correspondence, and perhaps I asked for too much pity as I made a fool of myself at the dinners my parents insisted we attend. They have friends among our own class, wealthy people who believe they're the equal of any member of the ton. *But I sit there like a silly lump, with nothing to say, getting names wrong whenever I speak. Oh Tom, why is it so easy to tell you everything?*

I even promise to finally meet you in person, if only you'll keep writing to me. I miss you.

Ten years later . . .

Dear Tom,

I pray that you're still next door, that by some miracle after all this time you'll come looking for our Journal. My father is dead, and the circumstances of his death would shock even you. My sisters have left to try to make their way in the world and help Mama and me. But the small amount of money they send home is not enough, Tom. Even as I write this, I am listing what item I'll next sell to feed us. My mother and I will be on the streets in only two months' time. I'm so desperate. Oh Tom, will you marry me?

Chapter 1

London, 1844

Victoria Shelby closed her childhood journal, feeling utterly foolish for writing in it after so many years. As if a servant could help her now, when everything was so bleak. She'd thought of Tom occasionally through the years, wondering if he'd moved away, if he'd married. But for days now, she'd found herself thinking about him frequently, and at the oddest times. It was growing more and more difficult to banish him from her thoughts. And marriage? Desperation must surely be driving her mad.

She looked about her sparse bedchamber, bare of anything of value but her simple furniture. It had once been such a magnificent town house, and now it seemed so empty, just like the sedate future she used to imagine for herself.

She'd been a foolish, naive girl.

With a sigh, Victoria smoothed down her mourning dress and left her room for the uncertainty of the master suite, where her mother now lived alone. She paused in the doorway and met the gaze of Mrs. Wayneflete, their housekeeper and last remaining servant. She wore her usual uniform of black silk dress, lace collar, and close white cap. No matter their situation, Mrs. Wayneflete could always be counted upon to remain unflappable. Together, they turned to stare at Victoria's mother, who clutched a vase to her bosom and stubbornly turned her back on them.

"Victoria, I will not part with this," Mama said, her defiance a hollow, pale sound. Her eyes were now lined with dark shadows and looked at nothing most of the time. Sadness bent her shoulders and strands of gray hair escaped the pins. "Your father gave it to me for our anniversary. He brought it from—"

"I remember," Victoria interrupted gently. "But Father would understand that we need to eat."

Her mother had a strange tendency to forget their circumstances, and Victoria found herself growing ever more impatient. Didn't she realize that they had all sacrificed? Victoria had sold her beloved piano, and Mrs. Wayneflete had taken no wages in many a month. Mama was waiting for salvation, but there was no one left to save them. Victoria wished she could convince her mother it was better to face the future than wallow in the past. But since Father's death ten months before, her mother's spirits continued to sink, though Victoria's cheerful letters to her sisters did not dwell on that sad fact. There was no need to worry them any more than necessary.

Victoria sighed and turned a brisk smile to her housekeeper. "Mrs. Wayneflete, do you have another suggestion for an item that will keep us in food this week? I do believe that Mr. Tillman quite looks forward to haggling with me over a price."

"You're an easy woman to respect, Miss Victoria," Mrs. Wayneflete said with a fond smile.

"Then there is Mr. Billingsly, the merchant from Cheapside. I could pit the two proprietors against one another for a better price." Victoria's laughter died when she saw her mother staring at her.

"How can you find amusement in this?" Mama whispered. "Your father is dead."

"Oh, Mama, of course I know that. But *we* are not dead, and we owe it to ourselves to go on living."

Victoria pushed those sad memories away. Since that terrible day, she and her mother had

12

seemed to switch places, as her mother foundered under the knowledge that her own husband had left them penniless. The long overdue mortgage on the town house, their last remaining property, had been bought by a distant cousin, who had agreed to let them remain until he returned to England with his family—two months from now. Time was running out.

Her sisters were doing what they could, but their earnings barely supported themselves. Meriel had used her logical nature and excellent education to find a position as a governess. Louisa's sweetness and patience had enabled her to become a companion to an elderly lady. Victoria had thought she was doing her share by keeping their meager household running, for she had not her sisters' talents. Lately she'd felt the urge to do more, to prove that she was no longer that shy girl who used to think she deserved so little in life. Had all she ever aspired to be was her mother's companion and caretaker? Yes, it once would have given her the chance to immerse herself in her beloved musical compositions. But that silly girl had come to know firsthand the harsh realities of life without privilege. And it was time to do something more.

"I do believe there is a clock in Meriel's room," Mrs. Wayneflete said. "Quite an old, fancy piece. Would that do?"

"Of course." Victoria nodded briskly, having long since accepted that she was the one to make all the family decisions. "Mama, you can have the vase for a while longer."

"Something will happen, Victoria," her mother said, a look of shining hope in her dull eyes. "You'll see."

Victoria's thoughts were tinged with sarcasm that was uncalled for. It was so easy for her to lose patience with her mother these days, though good breeding kept her from expressing her opinions. Mama had once aspired to the highest reaches of society, as if riches could make the *ton* forget that Mr. Shelby had been their trusted banker, not their equal. It had frustrated her mother terribly that wealth had allowed her to live in the same exclusive neighborhood as the nobility, but not to mingle with them.

That unrealistic hope shining from her mother's eyes made Victoria even more determined. There had to be a solution.

She thought of Tom again, that boy she'd never met, but with whom she'd shared the intimacy of her every thought. She had to stop such silly daydreaming and get on with the day. She wrote the clock into her household journal, where she kept lists of the items they'd had to sell.

At Tillman and Sons, Mr. Tillman quoted her a reasonable price for the clock, and Victoria left feeling a moment's triumph, followed by the inevitable worry that never truly went away. As she walked slowly through the busy city streets, her thoughts dwelled inward, searching for a solution she could not find.

Distractedly, she turned down an alley, a shortcut from the shopping district to her wealthy neighborhood. She used it every week, yet she was still surprised when she found herself all alone. The sky was overcast with the promise of rain, making the coach houses and stables on either side of her seem full of shadows. She heard a strange crack behind her and looked over her shoulder, but there was nothing. She picked up her pace.

Before she reached the halfway point of the alley, she felt certain she was being followed. She'd left Tillman and Sons with an empty satchel—anyone could figure out that she now carried money with her. And she was a woman alone. Why had she chosen the luncheon hour for her shortcut, when all the coachmen and grooms were obviously inside enjoying their meals? She increased her pace, debating whether a confrontation would deter a thief.

She was only two blocks from home!

So she picked up her skirts and ran. She heard pounding steps behind her almost immediately, but she didn't risk looking over her shoulder until she came out on the street. As she made the turn to stay on the pavement, she saw a dirty, skinny little boy, not more than eight, dressed in ragged clothing. He seemed even more desperate than she was, for he continued to follow her. Two men walked a block ahead of her, and she felt safe enough to fumble in her reticule. She grabbed the first coin she found—a shilling—and threw it over her shoulder. With a glance, she saw the boy fall to his knees and scramble for the money.

Only after Victoria had crossed the street and left him behind did she allow herself to slow down and catch her breath. A year ago, she would never have been able to run like that. Helping Mrs. Wayneflete with the cleaning had obviously improved her stamina.

The little boy had disappeared, and she hoped he would buy himself a hot meal. Biting her lip, she couldn't help shuddering. Would his life soon be hers?

She passed the home of the Earl of Banstead, right next door to hers. The house lived under a cloud of scandal many years old, but one that Victoria had been deemed too young to hear about. She'd given up questioning her housekeeper about the servants' gossip years before.

She couldn't imagine that Tom still lived there—surely she would have had some word from him.

16

She came to a stop and stared up at the huge town house with its gleaming windows and impressive entranceway. Was the answer to her problems in there?

But she had never been an impulsive woman, so she resumed walking home to help Mrs. Wayneflete with dinner—and came up short before she reached her property. The idea rolling around in her mind was so wildly impulsive that she felt the need to give in to it immediately, before she could change her mind. Her heart pounded, her gloves dampened with perspiration. Was Tom the answer to her prayers?

Would he marry her?

Oh, what was she thinking? A kind man like him, twenty-six years of age, would surely be married already. That was probably why he'd stopped writing to her. He'd met a girl and—

But what if he wasn't married? She could be a servant's wife. She'd become quite the frugal housekeeper, and she knew she could be content with Tom. She hadn't wanted to marry. It had been too difficult to flirt with men. Since she loved nothing better than to be alone with her music or her needlework, she had thought that would content her. It had been a relief when her mother had given up on marriage plans for her, when her father's disapproving looks had turned to indifference. He had always made sure Victoria knew it would be difficult to find a husband for her.

But now marriage might be the only answer. Could this actually work? Could she save her mother—and herself?

She marched up to the Banstead front door and knocked before she could change her mind. Too late, she realized she should have gone around to the servants' entrance in the back. But someone was already opening the door.

An imposing butler, wearing black livery and a white wig, bowed to her. "Good afternoon."

"Good afternoon. Forgive my impertinence, but I am looking for a manservant who once worked for you—and might still work for you, of course."

The butler stepped aside, and she entered the two-story entrance hall. A graceful marble staircase curved up one wall, a corridor led to the rear of the home, and several closed doors hid other rooms.

The butler studied her. "The servant's name, miss?"

"I never knew his last name," she said, "but his mother was once the cook here. The boy's name was Tom, and he would be twenty-six years old by now."

"Miss, I have been with the earl for nearly thirty years, and I can assure you that—"

A door suddenly opened, and a tall man

stepped into the hall, quite taking her breath away with the power of his presence. He was dressed in somber colors with the most expensive fabric and cut. He had dark brown hair, cut close to his head as if to hide wayward curls he couldn't control. Though some might not call him handsome, his face with its intimidating cheekbones and dark, heavy brows was definitely striking. But it was his eyes that had unnerved her. They were the palest blue, frosty with intelligence, a winter glance in springtime.

He studied her more intently than any man had the right to do to a stranger. She lifted her chin and tried to appear calm, when inside her every insecurity was bubbling to the surface.

The man turned to his butler. "I'll handle this, Smith."

"Very good, my lord." After giving a bow, Smith left the entrance hall and motioned the footman to leave with him.

This could not be the earl, who Victoria knew was an elderly man, so it must be his son. She'd always gotten the impression from Tom that the young viscount was often away at school, for he seemed to have not overly influenced the household. Unless he was part of the scandal . . .

"I am Viscount Thurlow. And you are . . ."

Memories came flooding back of countless parties where she stuttered talking to every man, but she forced them away. She wasn't that girl any-more. "Miss Victoria Shelby, my lord. I live next door."

"I know the family name."

"You do?"

"You live next door," he said dryly.

She tried to smile. "Oh yes, of course. My lord, I am looking for—"

"A servant named Tom," he interrupted. "I overheard."

"Does he still live here? If not, perhaps I could speak with your steward for a forwarding ad-dress."

His examination made her feel uncomfortable and even annoyed.

"Miss Shelby, there is no other way to say this except to be blunt. I'm Tom."

Chapter 2

David Thurlow was ready for any reaction, from hysterics to satisfaction, but Victoria Shelby just blinked up at him slowly, her face draining of color. He felt a stirring of something, a jolt of emotion that escaped his usual iron control. He hesitated, for once unsure what he should do.

And it cost him, for she suddenly whirled away, flung open the door, and ran down the front steps. He stopped at the doorway and watched her run next door. With a sigh, he retreated inside. He had always worried that his lies would be taken as a betrayal, and evidently he'd been right.

Could this day get any worse, after the *second* housekeeper in two months had just quit?

He'd spent much of his childhood trying to meet Victoria Shelby in person. It had been a game between them, and she'd proved herself a worthy player by always managing to sneak away before he could catch a glimpse. The mystery of her had lured him on, as much as the kindness she'd shown to a lonely little boy.

She was . . . not what he had expected. She was a plump little hen dressed in unrelieved black. The hair peeking out from beneath her bonnet was a pale blond, as if it couldn't decide what vivid color to be. In those brief moments when their gazes had met, he saw big wide eyes, the most flattering of her features, the vivid color of amethysts, so violet as to seem unreal. They had flashed the powerful emotions of desperation and despair before she'd fled. What had happened to the optimistic young girl he once thought he knew? She'd been calm and sensible as a child, her words infused with a quiet joy. He'd admired her simple life and her siblings, and had read her journal entries to him with a voraciousness that even then he'd recognized as envy.

Whyever would she be looking for . . . Tom? He'd almost forgotten about the pretend life he'd created to escape his problems. He'd known even at ten years old that his father would be angry if

David had encouraged a real friendship. One simple lie had expanded each year into a larger web of lies. All because of his father.

David's whole life had revolved around his father's whims, and the old man was still exerting his control over the household from his sickbed.

Ever since his father's illness, and David's subsequent move back into the family town house, David's orderly life had spiraled out of control. He hadn't wanted to deal with his father, a man who for years he had spoken to only once a month concerning business matters of the estate. The earl had done enough harm to the family name and position, and it was time for him to retire to the country and do whatever bitter old men did.

Except the earl wouldn't go. It was as if he thrived on making David's life a hell.

David stepped back into his study, his personal retreat in the house. But even amid his favorite scents of old books and beeswax polish, he could not relax.

He glanced at the precise stack of mail that awaited him, and wished he hadn't. The top letter was addressed in the scrawled, sloppy hand of his cousin, the wastrel who would inherit the Banstead estate if David did not marry and produce an heir. He was probably wheedling for an increase in his allowance again. If only David could be rid of him. He could not let his own hard work be wasted. Marriage would seem to be the only solution.

He shook his head in resignation. Twice he had asked for a woman's hand in marriage, only to find that no one of the right bloodlines would have him. He'd made the mistake of fancying himself madly in love with the first woman, and though he thought she loved him in return, she hadn't fought to keep him when her family had refused their permission to marry. It was then that David had begun to realize that his father's scandals would continue to taint his own life.

David had approached his second attempt at marriage with a much more practical mind, knowing he would never allow his heart—suspect as it was—to be involved again. He had thought he'd planned the campaign well, choosing the daughter of a family that surely could not refuse a future earl. Noble yes, but the finances were not quite what they once were. But refuse him they had, leaving David full of anger and frustration. After that last debacle two years before, he had completely retreated from society's affairs until he was ready to plan a new strategy for marriage. He was glad to avoid the kind of parties where he'd been stared at, whispered about, and made the object of an occasional dare.

But there was still the puzzle of Victoria, and

what she wanted with Tom after all these years. He'd been a lonely child with an ill mother when, from his nursery window, he'd watched a little girl hide something beneath a bench in her family garden. He'd found that journal and written in it, meaning to tease her. The fictional identity he'd created of a kitchen boy suited his father's constant demand for privacy where the lower classes were concerned. It was also David's way of escaping his life. What started as a lark resulted in his only childhood friendship, since all the other boys of his age went off to school, and his mother's health would not permit him to join them.

Too late, he'd realized he could not undo his lies without hurting Victoria.

Now, ten years later, the revelation of his identity had obviously hurt her. His childhood curiosity came rushing back; he had to find out everything about her.

Victoria opened her town house door and slammed it shut behind her as her heart pounded and her breath came much too fast. She couldn't make sense of her racing thoughts, could only hear "I'm Tom," over and over again.

Oh God, she'd been such a fool.

"Miss Victoria?" Mrs. Wayneflete came into the entrance hall, wiping her hands on her apron. "Did everything go well at the shop?"

It took her a moment to remember her first reason for leaving the house today.

"Of course, Mrs. Wayneflete." How she managed to make her voice sound so normal, she couldn't explain. "Mr. Tillman gave me a fair price. I'll be down to help you with dinner shortly."

She hastily began to climb the stairs and pretended that she didn't see the housekeeper's confused frown.

In her room, Victoria closed the door and leaned against it, suddenly exhausted. She knew there were other items on her list to do today besides helping with dinner, but at just this moment, she couldn't think about anything but Tom—

Viscount Thurlow.

Why was she feeling so betrayed? They'd shared writing in a journal, not an undying commitment.

But she'd trusted him, confided in him, believed in him.

And it had all been a lie.

She'd spent six years writing her deepest secrets . . . to a viscount. Her face burned with embarrassment, and she couldn't stop feeling a rising tide of anger and despair.

Her last plan to save her mother winked out of existence.

Surely that was why she found herself crying. She pulled a handkerchief from a drawer and blew her nose, taking satisfaction in its unladylike loudness.

She could spend no more time dwelling on this mistake—oh, why had she even allowed impulse to guide her to his door?

It was done—no one need know of her foolish idea to marry Tom.

She washed her face in cold water, dried it, pasted on a false smile, and went down to the kitchen. If Mrs. Wayneflete noticed anything unusual, the dear woman said nothing.

It took until early afternoon the next day for David's curiosity to be satisfied. The investigator he'd hired presented his formal report at luncheon and went away paid handsomely. The money was worth it, for David never approached anything without knowing every fact.

He drank his coffee and opened the folder of papers. As he read, he eventually allowed his drink to grow cold. Victoria's mother had been widowed ten months before—which explained the mourning gown. Victoria's foolish father, once so successful in business, had let several bad decisions erase his empire. He'd left his wife and daughters with nothing but a mortgage that had since been purchased by a cousin, who was on his way home to England to claim the town house. The man had his own family, and did not want strangers—relatives though they were—to intrude on him. The Shelbys had no other family to take them in, and would be forced to support themselves somehow. He imagined shy Victoria confronted by the hard work required of a governess. She'd be overrun by the children.

And now she'd come looking for Tom. Why?

Because maybe he'd been her only childhood friend beside her sisters. Such thoughts made him uncomfortable, for he had to admit he'd considered her a friend, too. It was hard for him to remember how innocent he'd once been, before his father had ruined the family name.

As a child, the longer he had written to her, the more his fictional life had chafed at him. He'd wanted to tell her about his sick mother, about so many things that Tom the cook's son wouldn't know. But he'd been trapped in his lies. Then after his mother had died, he couldn't put into words the loss he'd felt, couldn't tell Victoria the truth, so he'd just stopped writing. He'd gone away to school after years of tutors, glad to escape from his father, whom David blamed for his mother's death.

David and Victoria had been so close as children. Would she come to him to help solve her problems?

There was a brisk knock on the dining room door, and Smith the butler entered. With a single look from Smith, both footmen bowed and left the room.

David sighed, already guessing the gist of what was to come. "What is it now, Smith?"

"The previous housekeeper"—the butler no longer said her name, as if she no longer existed—"has told the upstairs maids that they answer to the downstairs maid, and not to me. Forgive me for disturbing you with this, my lord, but my authority must not be questioned."

David sighed. "Please tell me you've placed an advertisement for a new housekeeper."

"Heavens, no, my lord. I will find the right employee without resorting to such public displays of our . . . problems. Now if you'd be so good as to meet with the maids."

David didn't need this. He had an important railway meeting to host soon, and since the directors' families needed to attend as a diversion, he'd been up to his elbows in party details that were normally a woman's domain. And he'd *thought* he could count on his housekeeper's help.

Bracing his forehead on his hand, David looked down at the report on the Shelby family. There was a housekeeper to find, a party to plan, his wastrel cousin to deal with, his father to placate—all the things a wife would take care of.

"Tom" could do nothing to help Victoria, but with one decision, David would solve *everyone's* problems.

He would marry Victoria Shelby.

She was not the woman his father would have picked for him, but that was almost a grim pleasure. Although she was not of noble birth, she was long bred for the duties required of her—he remembered her writing about her studies of the feminine arts. And the most important duty would be providing him with an heir to secure the family fortune with his own line.

For a moment, he felt like his father, who demanded heirs of his mother even though David had already been born. But this was not the same situation, and he could not allow himself to worry about Victoria handling a pregnancy. She was a healthy woman, one who couldn't refuse his proposal as other women had done. He didn't even feel guilty for taking advantage of her desperation. After all, it would not be difficult to be the wife of a future earl. Women lived to plan parties, didn't they?

He remembered Victoria as shy and kind, a girl who worried about hurting the servants' feelings as much as her family's. She had no great mission in life, as some women had, to reform society or negate poverty. She would cast little scandal on a family already brimming with its own. And Victoria could deal with his father and his household, leaving David free to pursue his business interests.

Everything figured out before dinner. The day

was looking up. Now all he had to do was tell the bride.

Victoria had to admit that the drawing room looked splendid, with a riotous bloom of flowers from their garden in a beam of sunlight. It was a simple way to make her mother feel better. One room in the house would look as normal as possible. She'd gathered their last decent possessions: the sofa from Mama's sitting room, matching tables from a guest room, the last of her sister Louisa's collection of clocks Father had brought her from his trips to the Continent. There were still so many paintings on the wall. She allowed herself to enjoy them for a few minutes, and then she began to catalogue their worth in her household journal. Much as she loved art, they would have to be sold soon.

Mrs. Wayneflete entered the room, and in a formal voice, said, "Viscount Thurlow is here to see you, Miss Shelby."

Before Victoria could say that she wasn't at home today, the viscount himself rudely appeared behind the housekeeper. He loomed large in the doorway, so very foreign in this household of women.

It had been only a day since Victoria had seen him, but her feelings of anger had not lessened, only waited to be roused.

"Mrs. Wayneflete, do tell His Lordship that I am feeling ill today." She wished she could have left the room, but he was blocking the only exit. So she simply stared at him, waiting for his good manners to assert themselves.

They didn't.

He handed his hat and gloves to Mrs. Wayneflete. "Do leave us alone, please."

"That wouldn't be proper, my lord," the housekeeper said stiffly. "I did not realize that Miss Victoria was unwell."

Victoria felt gratitude pour through her.

Lord Thurlow looked down at Mrs. Wayneflete with a respect that Victoria didn't trust.

"Your protection of your mistress is understandable, but we are childhood friends, and I need to explain something to her."

Victoria wanted to call him a liar, but she couldn't. And she couldn't leave her dear housekeeper in the middle like this. "Mrs. Wayneflete, you may leave us, but keep the door open."

The housekeeper curtsied, shot a curious look between the viscount and Victoria, and left the room.

Victoria faced the man and waited. She didn't have to make this easy on him. His presence was still just as intimidating, though he watched her almost warily.

"We need to discuss what happened yesterday,

Miss Shelby," he said, "and what happened all those years ago. I have no excuse for the lie about my identity. I was but ten years old, and can only blame my behavior on my own unhappiness at the time. I ask for your forgiveness."

Well, he wasn't going to get it.

"Thank you." She started to walk past him to show him down to the front door, but he caught her arm.

"I'm not finished yet," he said firmly.

She hardly heard his words. She was staring at his hand on her black sleeve, feeling the hot imprint of each of his fingers. He leaned over her; tall, powerful, a man who didn't know what it was like to wonder when his next meal would be.

"You may release me, Lord Thurlow. We are quite done."

His hand fell away, and he crossed his arms over his chest. "I have more I wish to say to you."

"What more could there be?" she asked, not bothering to hide her bitterness. "You have revealed your lies, and shown me what a fool I was."

"I didn't mean to—"

"Good day, Lord Thurlow. If you don't wish me to escort you to the door, then I assume you can find it on your own."

"Miss Shelby, I have a proposition that might help us both."

"I don't need your help."

"Of course you do. Your father is dead and you have no way to support yourself."

She pressed her trembling lips together. She never should have given in to impulse and gone to Banstead House. "So you already know every-thing about me."

"I'm sure it is not quite everything. But after you left yesterday, I was curious about your motives. I discovered your regrettable situation."

"Discovered?" she echoed.

"I hired a man to look into the situation."

"You had someone *spy* on me?" She didn't think she'd ever be able to breathe again. She looked about the room as if she expected to find a man hiding behind the draperies.

"Of course not," said the viscount. "He looked into public records. My sympathies to you and your family on the death of your father. I was in the north at the time."

"And you would have come to his funeral?" she said, appalled at the bitterness that filled her every word. She had sworn she wouldn't allow her des-perate circumstances to change her so very much, and she regretted it. "Forgive me, my lord, that was uncalled for."

"You do not need to apologize to me," he said in the mildest voice she'd yet heard from him. "You have been through enough."

Oh God, did he know the truth about Father's

death? Was he even now going to shout her deception to the world? She'd never thought that the
man she'd known as Tom the cook's son would be
capable of such a thing. But this was Viscount
Thurlow, a man whose family was no longer respected by the *ton*, their own class of society.

"You *are* a survivor, Miss Shelby," he continued.
"I am impressed at your thought to come to me."

"I didn't come to *you*," she said, swallowing back
her relief. Surely he would have said something if
he knew her secret. "I came for Tom's help."

"But I'm Tom, and I have a proposition for you.
Marry me."

Victoria stared up at the viscount, feeling the
blood drain from her face. Surely he was making a
terrible joke at her expense. She looked for a sly
expression, but found none. He was watching her
impassively, and there was nothing to indicate
that he was even attracted to her.

Because, of course, he wasn't. He had his own
plans, just as she did. Stepping away, she put
down her notebook and really looked at him: a
successful, handsome nobleman asking a poor,
maidenly commoner to marry him.

A buried part of her was weak enough to want
to shout "Yes!" with terrifying relief. Thank goodness another, stronger part of her surfaced. "My
lord, this is terribly presumptuous on your part.
We don't even know one another."

"Don't we?"

His voice had deepened, softened, and for a moment she thought back longingly to lazy summer days spent reading his words and laughing, so anxious to write back. She stared into the viscount's eyes, looking for the man she thought she'd known. But he was a stranger.

"No, I don't know you," she answered firmly. "You may have written to me, but since you pretended to be someone else, everything you wrote is suspect."

"My true identity was a secret, but that did not mean everything was a lie."

He looked uncomfortable, as if he wasn't used to needing persuasion to get his way.

"But I'll never be able to believe that, will I?" Oh, where did her words spring from? In the end, what would she accomplish by this—driving away a rich viscount who'd asked to marry her? How could she let her pride stand in the way of her mother's empty belly—of the woman's very sanity? But if Victoria married him, how would her own name be tainted?

With a heavy sigh, she turned away from him and sat down in a straight-backed chair. She rubbed her arms as if she might never be warm again.

Without looking at him, she said, "Tell me why you wish to marry me—and don't say that you're rescuing me. We both know that that is not the reason."

"It's part of the reason. You came to me for help, and I'm offering it."

At least he didn't know that she'd been forward enough to come looking for a husband. "You can have any woman you want, my lord, and they would bring along fine dowries."

"I don't need money," he said shortly.

She studied him, trying to step away from her emotions to see what he was hiding. But he was too good at wearing a mask. After all, this was the man who'd lied about his identity from the time he was ten.

She had to make certain of his motives. "Then you need prestige, a woman who can bring you connections."

"I don't need that, either. I remember everything you wrote to me about your training as a gentleman's daughter. You will make a fine wife."

A fine wife. What did *that* mean? And most of Lord Thurlow's class would not call her father a gentleman. He was their banker, their trusted confidant where their finances were concerned—but not a gentleman, because he had accepted money for his services.

She tried to remember what girlish musings about her wifely education could have possibly impressed Tom—Lord Thurlow—but her thoughts were too jumbled with confusion. She needed to understand *why* before she accepted his offer of marriage.

Because, of course, she couldn't refuse. She could tell herself to be wary of his reputation, but in the end rumors mattered little compared to a harsh life in poverty.

"I need more of an explanation from you, my lord," she said simply, too tired for subterfuge. "Why me?"

"Because I need a wife, and you need a husband," he said briskly, beginning to pace as if he didn't want to truly see her. "You came to Tom because you thought the two of you got on decently together, am I right?"

She gave a reluctant nod.

"And I think the same thing. Yes, I could choose some pretty chit fresh into her first Season, and I might be lucky—or not. They seem so very young lately. But with you—"

He paused, and she thought she almost detected a hesitation in his gait.

"But with you," he continued smoothly, "I have a better idea of the woman I'd be marrying."

"Do you, my lord? We have never spoken, and haven't written to each other in ten years. You think you know me so well?"

"I would never presume such a thing, Miss

Shelby. But I know the kind of girl you were, and that is enough for me."

But she wasn't that girl anymore. Life had changed her. It had certainly changed him. But in what ways?

Victoria's mother chose that moment to enter the drawing room, draped in a black gown that hung on her thinner frame. Mama stared between her daughter and the viscount in obvious confusion. Victoria's resignation faded into tender worry. She rose and took the woman's cold hand in hers.

"Hello, Mama. I'm so glad you came. I'd like to introduce you to our neighbor, Lord Thurlow. Lord Thurlow, my mother, Mrs. Lavinia Shelby."

Confusion clouded her mother's eyes, but then a tentative smile touched her pale lips. "Are you the little boy from next door?"

Victoria smothered a gasp, staring at her mother in shock. Had Mama read Victoria's journal all those years ago?

Lord Thurlow bowed over Mama's hand, watching the older woman as if he sensed nothing amiss. "I am, Mrs. Shelby. Have we met?"

"Once on the street my bonnet blew away, and you ran and fetched it for me."

"Ah, I see," he said. "Forgive me for not remembering."

"You were quite young, but very polite."

She looked around, and Victoria saw her gaze take in the moved furniture, and regretted the confusion it caused.

"I don't believe you've come to call before," Mama said.

Victoria frowned at the viscount, warning him not to speak of what was not yet settled between them.

"And it was past time I did visit," he said. "We are neighbors, after all, and such bonds carry a certain . . . weight."

Victoria didn't know what he was implying, and it was obvious her mother was even more confused. Victoria slipped her arm into Mama's, and she almost flinched away. The rejection stung, and Victoria felt the unwanted start of tears. She wouldn't cry in front of Lord Thurlow.

Victoria guided her to the door. "Why don't you find Mrs. Wayneflete, Mama? I understand that she wanted your opinion about the dinner menu."

Without even acknowledging the viscount, her mother wandered out of the room. Victoria turned and looked at Lord Thurlow, waiting for what he would say. Would he change his mind and leave her to poverty? Or would he stay, which was frightening in itself?

Suddenly she couldn't stop thinking of the intimacy involved in a marriage. She would have to let him . . . touch her.

He clasped his hands behind his back. "I'm sorry to see how difficult your father's death has been on your mother."

He was watching her too closely, and it unnerved her. She turned away, waiting for his rejection.

"Our marriage would help your mother, too," he said.

She let out a deep sigh. "Why are you trying so hard to convince me to marry you, my lord? You know how difficult it would be for me to refuse. Tell me what you require of me as your wife."

He'd begun pacing again; she could feel his movement behind her. It made it easier for her to turn and face him.

"My requirements are quite simple, Miss Shelby. You will run my household, and the household of my family seat, where we'll spend several months of each year. I shall need an heir"—that part was rather rushed—"and of course, I would need my wife to be above scandal at all times."

Inside a coldness began to grow within her.

"Scandal, my lord?" she said, trying to sound unperturbed.

"Yes. I have a career in the House of Commons—and someday the House of Lords—to think about. Members listen to the opinion of a man they can respect."

He didn't quite meet her eyes, as if he wasn't telling her everything. Was that what he longed for, respect? What had his father done to make the name of Banstead something that harmed even the next generation?

Yet she could not find fault with Lord Thurlow's honesty, when her own was suspect. What would he do if he discovered that her father, a man who was well known within the circles of the *ton*, had killed himself, and that she and her family had hidden the truth?

But she would live with the guilt of her crime, rather than ruin this opportunity to keep her mother safe.

Chapter 3

David found himself studying Victoria's every emotion, so openly revealed on her face. She was worried about his marital requirements, but he couldn't decide if it was the thought of sex, or how she could carry off her position as a future countess. He didn't know whether to be flattered by her concern or annoyed.

He still couldn't forget the horror in her expression when he'd revealed himself as Tom. She certainly had a way of taking him down a peg or two without even trying.

He was having to *convince* her to marry him, she a poor spinster with no other prospects. He had thought he'd gotten used to women rejecting him because of his father's notoriety, but Victoria's reservations seemed even more personal. He refused to continue thinking of it that way. She was a scared woman taking care of an ill mother, with little choice left in her life.

"So do my conditions for marriage meet with your approval?" he asked.

"You know they do, my lord. I would ask nothing less of myself as your—as a wife. But if you don't mind, I have conditions of my own."

He raised a brow in acknowledgment of her courage. "Please speak them freely."

"I ask that you make a place for my mother in your household."

"Of course, Miss Shelby."

She went on quickly, as if she hadn't heard him. "I promise I will take care of her, and she would cause no—" She stopped, and her wide-eyed gaze found his.

He was feeling properly insulted. "Did you think I would turn your mother out on the street?"

"Forgive me if I gave such an implication, my lord," she said quietly. "It was not my intent. But my mother has not been well since my father's death, though she is showing signs of improvement. I felt the need to make everything clear between us."

"There is nothing else you wish for yourself?"

"Just that my sisters be allowed the occasional . . . lengthy visit, my lord."

"Of course. You are a rare woman, Miss Shelby. In the interest of making everything 'clear,' allow me to assure you that I will provide you with a comfortable life, including an extensive wardrobe and spending money of your own."

Her complexion had deepened to scarlet throughout his speech. It was obvious that she was a proud woman, unused to having to ask anyone for anything. He wondered how well he would have handled her situation were he in her place, how it must feel to be condemned not to work by society. He knew some of that feeling, of course, because his business dealings crossed the line into commerce, something that would be frowned upon by other gentlemen if it were common knowledge. Other than investments and land dealings, gentlemen did not lower themselves to trade. Being told how he could earn his money did not sit well with David, but it wouldn't stop his railway venture.

Victoria had no way to earn money at all as a gentlewoman unless as a companion or governess, which her sisters had done, two positions that demanded the utmost work and the utmost in humbled circumstances.

"My lord, your generosity is appreciated," she said. "If there is anything else you wish of me, please say so before we agree on this arrangement."

"Arrangement," he said in a chilly voice. "This won't be an arrangement, Miss Shelby, but a marriage, a real one in every way."

In two strides he was right before her, and she stared up at him with wide, beautiful eyes. But she didn't shrink from him, and for that he was grateful. He reached for her hand, deftly unbuttoned her glove at the wrist, and slid off the offending accessory. She inhaled sharply. Her hand was not as soft as that of every other lady of his acquaintance. This woman had worked hard to feed and shelter herself and her mother. And he admired her.

He brought her trembling hand up and bent over it, never taking his eyes off hers. For just a moment he let her see the sensuousness in his gaze. He pressed his lips to the back of her hand, lingered, inhaled the elusive scent he couldn't quite place. Ah, the smell of flour and baking, a woman who helped prepare meals. He found her practical nature and his lack of familiarity with it almost erotic. He dipped his tongue against her skin to taste her.

Her strangled gasp satisfied him in a very primitive way. She was not so immune to him as she tried to pretend. He released her, and though she dropped her hand, she bravely stood her ground.

"My lord, we don't know each other well." Before he could speak, she quickly added, "As adults. I ask for your patience to allow us to become reacquainted."

"My patience?" he echoed in a low voice, beginning to understand where this might lead.

"Yes. We would have a real marriage, of course, but could we not . . ."

Her face flamed red and her gaze centered squarely on his chest. She pulled her glove back on.

She bit her lip. "That is, could we take our . . . relationship . . . slowly?"

She was asking for a reprieve on their wedding night. He understood that she was a virgin, and some delicacy on his part was required. But the longer she withheld her affections, the greater the risk that their marriage would fail. He could not allow that. He would have to think of a solution that would satisfy them both.

"I understand and accept your terms, Miss Shelby. You will marry me?" He posed it as a question, instead of the statement of fact they both knew it to be.

Her gaze never left his, and her words, though softly spoken, were firm with intent. "Yes, my lord. And I thank you."

He wanted to tell her not to thank him yet, not until she'd met his father and seen his disorganized household, but the reality of that could wait for another day.

"I'll have the banns read," he said. "The wedding will take place a month from today. You will have time to have a gown made. Does this meet with your approval?"

"My lord, I am not quite out of mourning yet, so my gown will be—"

"I request that you not wear black, Miss Shelby. I'm sure that your father would understand, and wish you to celebrate our marriage."

"But my lord—"

"Humor me in this, I beg you. Mourning attire is not something I would wish for my wedding day."

She studied him. "Do men have dreams of their wedding day?"

He was startled. Dreams of a wedding *night* might be more accurate, but he could hardly say that, not after her recent request.

"Perhaps I didn't have dreams, Miss Shelby, but I know a wedding day only comes once to a couple, and it should mean something."

There was a wry twist to her lips, but he did not remark on it. Theirs would not be a normal marriage, he knew.

"Go to your mother now, Miss Shelby. Please send Mrs. Wayneflete to discuss the wedding details with my steward."

He bowed over her hand again, but this time did not kiss it. He hoped she regretted the omission.

Victoria stared at the receding back of Lord

Thurlow, running her fingers absently over her hand, the one he'd kissed just a little while before. It still felt . . . burned, not as if he'd hurt her, but as if he had marked her in some way as his.

His. She would be that now, under the care of a man she truly didn't know. Did he have a music room? Would he care about her dreams beyond their wedding day?

Or their wedding night. She shivered and tried to make sense of what she'd felt as he'd pressed his lips against her skin so intimately. When he'd opened his mouth and touched her—she squeezed her eyes shut, feeling uncomfortable and hot and confused. He wanted a baby. And she had some sense of how one achieved that. Yet he had agreed to take his time.

Victoria walked into the hall. "Mrs. Wayne-flete!" She came up short as she found the house-keeper leading her mother back toward the drawing room.

The housekeeper threw up her hands. "I am so sorry, Miss Victoria! Mrs. Shelby was helping me prepare tea, and then she was gone—"

"Your worry is all for naught, Mrs. Wayneflete," Victoria said. "Lord Thurlow did not mind Mama's interruption."

Her mother peeked into the drawing room. "Did he leave? I'm sorry I didn't get much of a chance to speak with him."

That sounded more like the mother she knew. "You'll have plenty of opportunity to get to know him, Mama. The viscount has asked me to marry him."

Victoria had not expected great rejoicing, but Mrs. Wayneflete's obvious trepidation was a little frightening. Even her mother frowned. Didn't she understand what Victoria was doing to save the family?

She regretted her selfish thoughts. She turned to her mother. "You never allowed me to hear of the scandal surrounding the Earl of Banstead. Perhaps I should hear it now, even though it's too late."

Mrs. Wayneflete and her mother exchanged a glance, but it was the housekeeper who spoke.

"I don't know the details, Miss Victoria. Though servants gossip, even the Banstead maids seemed embarrassed by their master's behavior. There were parties at Banstead House, miss, the kind no one of good society would go to. And they started within a month of the countess's death."

Victoria sighed. "That's all you know? I always thought you were withholding something due to my young age."

"No, miss. But the servants' silence made me realize something scandalous had to be going on there. Are you sure marrying the viscount is the correct decision?"

"How could I say no, Mrs. Wayneflete? We'll have a place to live, food to eat. And I'm marrying the viscount, not the earl himself. We can't blame a man for his father's actions."

"But we don't know what those actions *were.*"

"Don't worry, Mrs. Wayneflete. This is the best I could do. Will it bother you if I try to find a position for you in the Banstead household? But of course if you'd rather not work there—"

"Oh no, miss, it would be a great relief for me to be able to look after you and Mrs. Shelby," she said, dabbing her tears with her apron. "I am relieved that you've found a man who wants to marry you."

"He has taken pity on me," Victoria correctly her dryly. "And I sense that we will be helping him as well." She couldn't put her suspicions into words.

"We have so much to do," Mrs. Wayneflete said, leading Victoria and her mother into the library. "Let's make our lists. When will the wedding take place?"

"In one month."

"Heavens, Miss Victoria, that will barely be enough time!"

"The first wedding in the family." Mama suddenly smiled.

When a tear slid down her mother's cheek, Victoria wanted to melt.

"It is what your father and I always wanted for you," her mother said softly.

But it wasn't what Victoria had wanted for herself.

When David arrived back at Banstead House, he had already decided to face the most difficult task first: telling his father about the upcoming marriage.

He walked down the hall on the ground floor to his father's bedroom. He knocked briskly on the door, and his father called for him to enter.

Alfred Thurlow, the Earl of Banstead, was sitting in his wheelchair in his usual place, staring out the window at the garden. There was a book beside him on a table, but David knew he seldom read—he seldom did anything but brood on his illness and ever progressing infirmity.

And take out his misery on the entire household. The maids were often crying from his verbal abuse when they were only trying to clean his room. David had finally given strict orders that no one was to even attempt to clean unless his father was somewhere else. But that was less and less often. The man's greatest joy seemed to be making housekeepers quit.

The earl looked up at David with flashing blue eyes, obviously ready to yell at the intrusion. But he caught his breath when he saw who it was and only grumbled something before looking back out the window. His white hair was longer than it should be, but the earl didn't care about such things anymore. It was hard enough to get him to bathe regularly. His face was lined more with anger and bitterness than age, and those once broad, imposing shoulders were bony and bent. But the earl had made sure by his intolerable behavior that no one offered him pity anymore.

"Good afternoon, Father."

"Not so good here" was all the earl said.

David clenched one fist behind his back. "I won't disturb you for long. I wanted to tell you that I'm to be married in a month's time."

That brought the old man's head around. "You negotiated such a thing without consulting me?"

"I'm twenty-six years old, Father. I am quite capable of procuring a bride."

"You hadn't been able to prove *that* before."

And whose fault is that? David barely stopped himself in time. Too often, he sank to his father's level, but not today. Today he would wallow in the satisfaction of his accomplishments.

After a length of silence David refused to break, the earl glanced at him—showing no remorse or guilt, naturally.

His father said, "It's about time you provided the earldom with an heir besides that useless cousin of yours."

David stiffened. His father's endless quest for children had been what killed his mother. She'd endured pregnancy after pregnancy, all ending early or with a stillborn child. The town house had always been draped in black crepe, and David had worn mourning clothes for much of each year.

But still the old man had spent David's adult-hood hounding him about an heir. Was Father oblivious to what he'd done?

And again, David found himself experiencing a passing feeling of worry about Victoria, but he pushed it ruthlessly away. The earldom needed an heir.

"Did you negotiate the terms with her father?" the earl demanded.

"He died ten months ago. I negotiated with the bride herself."

"Unheard of!"

"But necessary. I'll speak to my lawyer about the papers tomorrow."

"Who is this girl?"

"Miss Victoria Shelby."

"I know that name," the earl said, his brows lowered in rising anger.

"You should. The family has been our next door neighbors my entire life." *The people you insisted we ignore socially, because you said they weren't good enough.*

"One of the Shelby girls?" his father cried.

"Victoria."

"But their father was in trade!"

"He was a wealthy banker, Father. You yourself did business with him."

"But he was not a gentleman!"

"Perhaps not by your definition. But his daughter has been raised well. I've already asked her to marry me."

"She will bring nothing to this family in politics or land. If you would have consulted me, I could have told you—"

"It's interesting how you follow the dictates of society only when it pleases you. Regardless, there is nothing you could have said to change my mind."

"Tell me you're not in *love* with this girl!"

David was about to make a disparaging comment—their arguments followed such a predictable pattern—but something in his father's face stopped him. It wasn't anger there now but despair, as if he'd thought love was a tragedy not to be experienced because of the pain.

David's mother knew all about that.

But he couldn't say the words that would hurt the old man, not when he already looked so devastated. Did the earl stare out over his garden and remember all his mistakes, the way he'd treated his wife?

David didn't want to feel sympathy for him.

"Father, in one month, Miss Shelby will be living here, as the new lady of the house. You will conduct yourself properly."

"I am the earl!" his father thundered. "She will have to—"

But David had already walked out of the room.

Night after night, Victoria lay sleepless in bed and stared at the shadows on the ceiling, wondering if Tom was still there somewhere inside Lord Thurlow. Or was she being naive? Her underlying sorrow wouldn't go away. Except for her sisters, Tom had been her closest companion, her staunch ally, a sounding board when times were difficult. But to remember those times now only made his betrayal sharper, sadder. She finally resolved the Tom debate in her mind by putting it aside for now, pretending that she was just like every other woman about to marry a stranger.

Two weeks before their wedding, her future husband surprised her by coming to call on her unannounced. Mrs. Wayneflete came to find Victoria, who was sorting through her belongings for the move. Victoria followed the housekeeper down through the house, asking twice if her hair looked presentable.

"Surely I have cobwebs or *something* in it!" Victoria said with exasperation.

Mrs. Wayneflete patted her trembling hands. "You look fine, miss."

And then they were in the drawing room, and *he* was standing there, so tall and very foreign in such a feminine room. His gaze swept over her, making her wonder what he thought about her appearance. She should not care, because their bargain had already been made. But . . . he smelled of fresh air and cologne, a masculine mixture, and it made her shiver, though she was not cold. The engagement—the very thought of marriage—still seemed so unreal.

He had his hat and gloves in his hands, and Victoria wondered why Mrs. Wayneflete had not taken them from him.

"Good afternoon, Miss Shelby," he said in that deep voice.

"Good afternoon, my lord."

"Would you care to take a carriage ride with me?"

Was he actually . . . *courting* her, when it no longer mattered? She felt ridiculously warm at the thought of such flattery. "I—of course. Just give me a few minutes to prepare myself."

Then she and Mrs. Wayneflete went looking for a bonnet and shawl and gloves. Soon she was sedately walking down the front steps to the pavement, her hand just resting on Lord Thurlow's bent arm. At the edge of the street waited an elegant phaeton, with its top down, led by a matching pair of white horses. If he was trying to impress her, he was doing a decent job of it. Behind the main bench, a maid perched on a small seat.

Victoria smiled at her, and the girl shyly smiled back. She was surprised by the chaperone, being that she and Lord Thurlow were an engaged couple—but she was certain he did not want even a whiff of scandal. She tried to put aside her unease.

He held her hand as she stepped up into the carriage, then he climbed in beside her and lifted the reins. He took up much of the bench, and his shoulder brushing hers made her feel rather strange inside.

She was not surprised to find that he was an excellent driver. He'd always been the kind of person who achieved whatever he put his mind to.

Or had he changed? She didn't know what to make of him, how to bridge the ten-year gap in her knowledge of him. People could change so much when the responsibilities of adulthood settled in. A conversation would help, but he seemed to be concentrating on his driving and his occasional nod to people who called out his name with a wave.

No matter what his father had done, Lord Thurlow still had a place in society; he still had friends, if only in politics. All people whom she'd have to meet. She'd never imagined herself in such company.

But if Lord Thurlow was not going to talk, she herself could not sit here silently, each minute growing ever more awkward. As he guided the carriage into Hyde Park and down the Row, she wet her lips and tried to think of a topic of conversation.

"My lord, I hope you won't think this a prying question," she began.

He glanced at her. "We are to be married. Ask whatever you wish."

"Most boys of your class went off to school at a young age. Why didn't you?"

He concentrated on a sudden slow down of carriages. She almost thought he'd forgotten, until he said, "My mother was often ill. She did not wish to be separated from me, her only child. My father hired tutors."

"I see." That left him plenty of free time to tease a lonely little girl next door. She kept reminding herself that he'd been very young when he'd lied to her, but that could not erase the feelings of betrayal deep in her soul. She thought they'd been sharing . . . everything.

Had he enjoyed writing to her? She glanced at his profile, so stern, yet handsome to her in an unusual way. She kept expecting a mischievous smile, for that was how she'd always pictured

59

him. But his face was like a mask that hid all the truth behind it. Why couldn't she know what he was thinking, as she once knew Tom's every thought?

She sighed. "At least now I know why you never spoke of yourself."

"Pardon me?"

"Your real self. I knew the earl had a son, but since you—since Tom never mentioned him, I always thought he—you were away at school."

"You make it sound more complicated than it was. Except for the change in my name, it was always me writing to you."

"Then why did you stop?" Oh, that was far too personal a question. But she couldn't take it back. She wanted him to tell her everything, but he no longer seemed the kind of boy—the kind of man who would reveal intimacies about himself.

He kept looking straight ahead, guiding his magnificent horses, a man at ease in at least this part of his world.

"We were both almost grown," he finally said. "I was sent off to school."

"So there was no time for a brief explanation?"

He glanced at her, his eyes narrowed, and though she wanted to back down, she couldn't. She stared at him, silently demanding the truth.

"I'm sorry I hurt you," he said. "I was a stupid

boy who got caught up in the excitement of finally being allowed to escape that house."

"What did you have to escape? It seems like a perfectly acceptable house." But it wasn't the house—she knew that.

"I chafed at not being allowed to be with other boys my age. I was simply glad to feel like I was growing up."

She knew that that was only part of the truth. His writing would have revealed a need to be gone, and there had been none. But she could hardly accuse her future husband of lying once again. After all, how could she trust her own judgment where he was concerned?

In silence they drove out of the park, then turned away from the street leading back to their homes. Victoria frowned and looked up at him, but felt foolish asking where they were going. After all, he'd only offered her a ride.

Gradually the buildings grew closer together, bland brick buildings of commerce rather than the pleasing architecture of the West End of London. They finally came to a stop before a building with a sign proclaiming SOUTHERN RAILWAY. A boy came bounding out of the door to steady their horses, as if he'd been waiting for Lord Thurlow.

Victoria could hold her tongue no longer. "My lord?"

He set the carriage brake and glanced at her absently. Had he forgotten she was even there?

"Miss Shelby, I must deliver some important papers. I'll be but a moment."

She opened her mouth to protest, but he had already dropped to the street, a leather satchel under his arm. He took the stairs two at a time and disappeared inside.

Victoria glanced over her shoulder at the maid, who was looking around them with wide eyes. Victoria gave her what she hoped was a reassuring smile. It was not that the street was in a decaying neighborhood of London, but it was obviously an industrial area, where few women were seen, to judge by the stares she received from passersby. Even Lord Thurlow's sleek white horses looked like something out of a fairy tale compared to the draft horses pulling heavy carts through the streets. Men in plain tweed coats and trousers tipped their hats as they walked by. One man, without a coat to hide his shirt and suspenders, whistled as he looked over the horses.

"Liedy, whot a fine matched pair they is," he said.

What was she to say to that? "Thank you, sir."

More and more she was feeling as if Lord Thurlow had forgotten her. He should have at least invited her inside to wait, away from the dust and noise of the streets!

The door finally swung open, and he emerged. She saw the surprise on his face before he tucked it away.

He *had* forgotten her. After all, he must have had this errand planned, and taking her for a ride fulfilled two purposes for this trip. How convenient for him.

The horse admirer hurried on his way, and Victoria noticed that even the little boy holding the horses seemed relieved at His Lordship's presence. Lord Thurlow swung up, and as the carriage tilted beneath his weight, she gripped the rail behind the bench. To her shock, his . . . hips grazed her as he sat down, pinning her hand between him and the rail. Blushing furiously, she yanked hard to free herself. Lord Thurlow shifted and eyed her beneath one raised eyebrow.

"Miss Shelby, have you ever ridden on a train?" he asked as he flicked the reins to guide the carriage into traffic.

"I have not," she said tightly.

"It is an exciting experience."

"I've heard it is very loud and very dirty."

He shrugged. "Perhaps. But the railway is England's future. Haven't you noticed how in just the past few years, the price of coal sharply dropped and food from outlying farms became fresher?"

She stared at him. "No, my lord, I have not."

"Of course, of course, your father would have dealt with such things."

She lifted her chin. "The prices must have already lowered since I began overseeing our household purchases less than a year ago."

He studied her intently, and she wished he would watch the traffic instead.

"I had not forgotten your recent accomplishments," he said in a lower voice. "I admire you for them."

She wished it wasn't so easy to be distracted just looking at him. She wanted to stay angry. "I was not looking for admiration as I kept food on our table."

"Of course not. But the railway will make everything easier, not just travel. It's a new era, where men who control the flow of goods and services control industry—and the future of our country."

She stared at him in confusion. He sounded like a little boy obsessed by the roar of a passing train. Memories flooded back of the detailed observations he'd written every time he discovered a new frog or snake. Had trains become his new interest? Many peers became railway shareholders, of course, or so her father had once tried to explain to her. But how many delivered their own paperwork? Lord Thurlow was such a puzzle to her.

They drove in silence for several blocks, until

the streets began to widen, and the carriages turned elegant.

"Miss Shelby," Lord Thurlow said, "would you do me the honor of accompanying me to a luncheon next Wednesday? I would call for you at one o'clock. There will be several couples in attendance, so you will not feel so alone should the other gentlemen and I have business to discuss."

Her entrance into society had begun. Her stomach seemed to turn over as she remembered every dreadful luncheon she'd ever attended—and there had been many. But she had never been to the *ton*'s events. Her mother had once resented that she herself could not break into the *ton*, and had thought to do so with her daughters. Victoria and her sisters had been expected to shine at parties, to eventually marry well, and the pressure had weighed on her.

She could never put into practice the skills her mother drilled into her. She had barely been able to meet a stranger's eyes. After one dance with a man, tripping all over his toes, she was not asked again. She was never at ease in conversation—except writing to Tom. Toward the end, she sat more and more with the chaperones and wallflowers, content that her mother had finally given up on her.

She wanted to refuse Lord Thurlow's invitation,

but she felt so petulant and childish, so she only said, "Of course, my lord. I'll be waiting for you."

They finally drove past Banstead House, her new home. She stared up at it, worried for the future, frightened of her new duties as viscountess, yet allowing her relief to take precedence. She had a place to live.

Outside her town house, he drew the horses to a stop.

Victoria glanced over her shoulder, smiling distractedly at the maid, but still looking at Lord Thurlow's home. "I didn't get a chance to see much of Banstead House on my visit a few weeks ago."

When she turned to face him, he was holding a flat, rectangular box toward her. "Let me present you with a gift in honor of our engagement."

She reached for the box, then opened it. A lovely diamond necklace nestled within. She stared at him.

"For the wedding day," he said.

He climbed down from the carriage without another word, as if he hadn't just offered her a fortune in jewels. She pressed her lips together to hold back a slightly hysterical giggle at the thought of what she could have done for her household with the money this cost.

"Thank you for your generosity, my lord," she said, closing the box and slipping it into her reticule.

He helped her to the pavement. "As for Banstead House, I will be honest with you, Miss Shelby. I am in the process of hiring a new housekeeper, and my butler would be appalled if I invited the future lady of the house at such an unsettled time."

Lady of the house . . .

That almost distracted her from the important part of his speech. "You need a new housekeeper, my lord? Could you perhaps consider Mrs. Wayneflete for the position?" Before he could answer, she hurried on. "Our house will be handed over to my cousin, but I know Mrs. Wayneflete would prefer to remain with my mother and me. She's been with us my whole life."

"I would be happy to interview your housekeeper, Miss Shelby. Do send her by to speak with my butler."

Not a definitive answer, but it would have to do. Lord Thurlow escorted her up to her door, then turned to face her on the top step.

She wanted to move away but restrained herself. Was he going to take her hand again? The memory of his mouth on her skin still arose at the most inconvenient times.

Lord Thurlow wore the faintest smile, as if he knew what she was thinking. Would it always be this way, he full of awareness, she ignorant of everything he was contemplating?

"Hello!" came a sudden call from next door.

Victoria and Lord Thurlow both looked toward Banstead House, from where a man was just leaving. As he came closer, she saw that he was very blond and pleasant-looking, smiling at her as if she should know him. Twenty-six years of maidenhood, and on the same day, two different men at her door!

Chapter 4

Only through good breeding did David keep from swearing out loud. What the hell was his friend Simon doing here on Victoria's doorstep?

"Hello," Simon said again in that cheerful voice that verged on annoying.

Simon's speculative glance was all for Victoria as he looked between them from the bottom of the stairs. For some unknown reason, David wanted to clench his teeth together. Instead he lightly rested his arm around Victoria's waist. She gave a little start, then held unnaturally still. She felt very warm, very soft.

"Miss Shelby," David said, "may I introduce Simon, Lord Wade."

Victoria's face took on another rose blush as Simon took her hand in both of his.

"Miss Shelby, it is a pleasure to meet David's betrothed at last."

"Thank you, Lord Wade," Victoria said, "but it could not have been that long since you first heard of me."

David felt an absurd feeling of satisfaction. "I told him of the engagement two days ago, Miss Shelby, but as you can see, he has the patience of a mouse."

"Is that a slur, Thurlow?" Simon asked in mock horror. "Will you not even invite me in? Your staff went to all the trouble of telling me where you were."

Simon was obviously spending too much time at Banstead House, if the staff was talking to him so freely. "I was just leaving, Wade. You can accompany me."

"But I could further my acquaintance with Miss Shelby. After all, I will be an integral part of her wedding."

"You must be Lord Thurlow's best man," Victoria said.

"Indeed he is," David said, before Simon could speak. "Although I'm not sure if he's the best, he'll have to do. Good day to you, Miss Shelby."

She nodded to them both and stepped inside her town house, closing the door behind her. David dragged Simon away by the arm.

Simon laughed. "This is quite unnecessary. I assure you I mean no ill will toward your lovely future bride. Although I must admit, I'm rather . . . surprised."

David pulled him out onto the pavement and turned toward Banstead House. "And what do you mean by that?"

"Just that, in my brief few moments with her, she seems rather . . . young."

"She's twenty-six." David released his friend when two elderly ladies peered at him suspiciously through identical monocles.

"Then I'll amend that to naive. Shy and naive. Does that sum her up?"

"Of course not. But she has a rather shy nature I admire." And he admitted to himself that the gray gown was a vast improvement, making her hair less washed out.

"Not exactly like your mistress, eh?"

"That's not a topic to be mentioned in public," he said shortly, opening the town house door and leading him inside. "I won't bring scandal on my bride."

"It's hardly scandal to—" Simon broke off when he looked into David's face.

David thought he saw pity in Simon's eyes, and

71

he didn't want it. Simon must have known what the earl's scandals had cost David, but in the spirit of friendship, he'd never brought up a subject David didn't want to speak of. Simon had been a friend since schooldays, one of the few who hadn't deserted him when the earl had ruined the family name.

"So how did you meet her?" Simon asked, trailing him into the library.

"She's been a friend since childhood."

"So have I. Why have I never heard of her?"

David smiled. "Because her friendship goes back to when I was ten years old, nearly half a lifetime earlier than I met you."

"That doesn't explain why you never spoke of her," Simon chided, pouring them each a glass of brandy.

David stared down into his drink. "Maybe because I never actually met her. She wouldn't allow me to."

Simon sank into a leather wingback chair before the hearth and waited expectantly. David was forced to explain the journal writing he and Victoria had shared, and that he'd stopped writing once he went off to school.

"So you know a lot about her already," Simon said. "No wonder you've settled on her as a wife."

"It comes at a fortuitous time. The railway directors are demanding that we meet more often as the deadline approaches, but we can hardly meet in public, so we're going to include our families as a reason to socialize."

"Why can't you meet in public? The scandal of a peer doing more than investing in the railways would hardly rival your father's notoriety." Simon eyed him thoughtfully. "But of course, you want to draw no attention to your activities at all. It's a fragile game you play, David."

"It's not a game," he said as he sat down in the opposite chair. "Much of my capital is tied up in this venture—if it fails, it would be an even bigger scandal than my father's. I won't let that happen."

"You'd hardly be on the streets."

"No. But there's power to be had in guiding England's industrialization. Men come to me for advice, and they don't care about my father's scandals. I like the feeling of shaping a new course for the country, Simon, but I know I can't be open about it with the *ton*. I've been ostracized enough—I won't do that to my children. Someday, men of any class will be appreciated for their vision, and when that happens, I'll already be ahead of everyone, making the name of Banstead important once more."

Simon smiled. "I thought you were doing that in Parliament."

"I am," David said with satisfaction. "But a man can spread out his bets, can't he?"

Simon shook his head in a rueful manner. "So you're marrying for business reasons only?"

"Of course not. I need an heir," he said bitterly. "And let's not forget she'll have to deal with my father."

"It sounds like she'll have a lot to do." Simon lowered his voice. "Are you certain you can make her happy enough that she'll want to help you?"

David frowned as he drained his glass. "She and I are helping each other. It will work out to both our satisfaction."

Though he looked troubled, Simon raised his glass in a toast. "To your success in securing a wife."

David clinked his glass. "At last."

A week later, Victoria was waiting in the entrance hall for her betrothed. She would have chewed her lip incessantly if Mrs. Wayneflete had not caught her in the act.

"It will be all right, miss," the housekeeper said kindly. "You'll do fine."

Victoria took a deep breath. "I tell myself that. I know I am not the same frightened girl I used to be when I attended these events, but . . . what if I embarrass him?" she finished with a whisper. "What if he realizes our engagement is a mistake, that I'll be nothing to him but one scandal after another?"

Mrs. Wayneflete took her quivering hands. "You

are perfect just the way you are, Miss Victoria. You found me a position, you saved your mother, and you've given your sisters a safe place to call home. Hold your head up and show him what it means to be a Shelby."

Victoria gave her a tremulous smile.

Lord Thurlow arrived exactly on time, with the same maid sitting in the seat behind his bench. As he came up the front steps, Victoria waited as Mrs. Wayneflete insisted on opening the door. He stepped inside, bringing in the wind and the smell of the rain that clung to his broad shoulders and dripped from the top hat he put under his arm.

Though she had told herself to be prepared, Victoria was still shocked by the thoughts that chased each other through her mind as she stared at him.

He was going to be her husband. And Mama and Mrs. Wayneflete had just last night stumbled through a recitation of a typical wedding night, which even now left her cheeks aflame as she imagined herself and Lord Thurlow in such close proximity.

Once again, she expected his indifference—he had left her on the streets just last week!—but he surprised her, looking her over with an interest that made her glad she had worn the half-mourning color of lavender. When his gaze lingered briefly on her breasts, she wanted to whip the shawl around her immediately. Instead, Mrs.

Wayneflete reached to help her until Lord Thurlow took the shawl away.

"Allow me," he said, his voice perfectly polite.

Biting her lip, Victoria turned her back and
waited with something approaching trepidation
as the material settled around her. His hands
reached over her shoulders to enfold the shawl
about her, and she quickly stepped away.

"Thank you, my lord."

As they walked through the doorway, he pro-
duced an umbrella and held it above her until she
was safely under the hood of the carriage. She remembered to brace herself before he climbed up
beside her.

He drove only several blocks away, then pulled
up before a town house on Belgrave Square, an
area of London not quite as fashionable as it used
to be, though still filled with elegant town houses
of the wealthy.

"My lord, who are we visiting?" she asked,
when it was obvious he hadn't thought to tell her.

He took her hand to help her down. "Mr. Lionel
Hutton and his wife."

She glanced up at the three-story home. "I
know that name. I think my father did business
with him."

"Surely your father did business with most of
the wealthy people in London, Miss Shelby."

But she couldn't stop frowning. It still unnerved

her to meet people who had known her father. She was almost relieved when the maid followed behind them dutifully.

Once inside, they were greeted by Mr. and Mrs. Hutton, both smiling in a parental way, as if Lord Thurlow was their son.

"So good to meet you, Miss Shelby," Mrs. Hutton said. "We were so pleased upon hearing of your engagement."

"Thank you, Mrs. Hutton," Victoria said, trying to relax.

Mr. Hutton cleared his throat. "Are you the daughter of the late Mr. Rutherford Shelby?"

Her insides went tight with panic, and it took all her courage not to glance worriedly at Lord Thurlow.

"Yes, I am."

"A shame about his passing," Mr. Hutton said, shaking his head. "And to think—a fall from his horse can take a man just like that."

Victoria's practical sister Meriel had thought of that lie should anyone glimpse the bruising at their father's neck during the funeral. But no one had noticed—that they knew of.

"Now Mr. Hutton," his wife said in a scolding tone of voice, "let Miss Shelby enjoy the day without reminding her of such tragedy. Lord Thurlow is giving her the chance to begin a new, exciting life!"

After their maid had gone off to the kitchen, Victoria and Lord Thurlow were led upstairs to the drawing room, where every inch of wall space sported a magnificent painting and every table overflowed with collections of bric-a-brac.

Two couples rose as they entered. There were plenty of curtsies and bows as introductions were exchanged, and finally they all sat down on the comfortable furniture, facing one another. Both sofas were already taken, so Victoria found herself in a chair alone.

As they talked, the men monopolized the conversation with their discussion about the railways, a discussion that surprised her at an elegant luncheon. It didn't take Victoria long to realize that the men were investors, as Lord Thurlow obviously was. Miss Damaris Lingard, the only other unmarried woman in attendance, spoke just as freely as the men, and Victoria admired her knowledge of business.

"Lord Thurlow," said Mr. Staplehill, a younger man dressed in the very height of fashion, "do you really believe there's a market for a railway line so deep into Cornwall?"

Victoria watched the men defer to the viscount in a way that seemed beyond his noble title. Was it the fact that he was a future member of the House of Lords, whose patronage would help their business interests?

"In the Commons," Lord Thurlow said, "we had a discussion of this subject, when members of that very shire brought us letters of complaints."

Good heavens, she'd forgotten that he was already in Parliament.

She felt like a fool, and wished she could think of a thing to say. Besides Miss Lingard, none of the ladies interrupted the gentlemen's discussion. Victoria found herself wishing she knew something of the subject. But all she could do was look at her betrothed, so very comfortable among businessmen not of the *ton*, and worry. She had thought she was leaving this society behind, and had been glad because of how she had embarrassed herself in the past, and the secret that weighed on her soul.

But by this mysterious involvement in the railway, he was creating a new scandal of his own. And he'd worried about *her* starting one?

When they all went into luncheon, Victoria found herself seated with young Mr. Staplehill on one side, and a Mr. Blake on the other. Mr. Blake concentrated solely on his food, and Mr. Staplehill turned his back to listen earnestly to something Lord Thurlow was saying farther down the table.

Victoria sighed and looked down at her carrot soup.

"He can be a bore, can't he?" Miss Lingard said politely from the other side of Mr. Blake.

Surprised, Victoria leaned back, where she could meet Miss Lingard's friendly eyes behind Mr. Blake. "Who can, Miss Lingard?"

"Why, Mr. Staplehill, of course. Not you, Mr. Blake," she said to the man who continued eating as if he hadn't seen food in several days.

Miss Lingard studied Victoria. "Did you think I meant Lord Thurlow?"

Victoria slowly smiled. "Not really, because I don't consider him a bore."

"Very admirable," the woman said dryly.

She was very pretty, with a tall elegance that Victoria had always admired in woman.

"But you have to say that, don't you," Miss Lingard continued.

"My betrothal would not bind me to speak lies," Victoria said mildly.

Behind Victoria, someone laughed loudly, and she looked over her shoulder. She saw Lord Thurlow's attention settle on her. He studied her with narrowed eyes, then relaxed and turned back to Mrs. Hutton.

And it was in that moment that Victoria knew he was not marrying her just to rescue her or to give him an heir. He needed her for situations like this, where he would not have to be a single gentleman anymore. She sensed mysterious undercurrents to him, but how could she question him about his business dealings?

"So are you attending the dinner?" Miss Lingard asked.

Victoria gave a start and turned back. "I beg your pardon?"

"All of the railway directors that Lord Thurlow has assembled for the Southern Railway will be attending a dinner at Mr. Bannaster's home next week."

Victoria smiled. "I'll be married by then, so I imagine I will accompany my husband."

But more and more she found herself unsettled. Why was Lord Thurlow so immersed in the world of commerce? She would not ask Miss Lingard, only to look like a fool whose betrothed didn't confide in her.

But that was exactly what she felt like. A woman easily forgotten.

She was determined to speak up and question Lord Thurlow—but not until after the wedding.

"I still can't believe it," Meriel Shelby said after taking a sip of wine. "Our Victoria getting married."

"And to that man next door," Louisa added in her demure voice, her demeanor always so at odds with the flame red of her hair. Her eyes fixed on Victoria. "Though he'll be an earl someday, I can't help worrying."

Victoria sighed. It was the day before the wedding, and they were celebrating the reunion of their small family at a special luncheon prepared by Mrs. Wayneflete. Victoria's sisters, whom she hadn't seen in six months, were making her the center of attention.

Victoria was the eldest, but always she had gladly stood in their shadows, allowing them to face the world while she had immersed herself in her music and her needlecraft. She had enjoyed the stories of their friendships and parties and adventures, and had not realized how much she would miss their companionship until they'd gone.

"You didn't explain anything in your letter about how you managed this feat," Meriel scolded. Her golden curls did not seem tame enough for how Victoria had always pictured a governess. "Did she tell you, Lou?"

"She said nothing to me, Mer. Vic, surely you must confess everything."

Victoria smiled with relief at their childhood nicknames, and was glad to see her mother smile in return.

Victoria put down her fork after finishing her stewed apples. "You must promise to keep it a secret. I don't wish my . . . betrothed to be embarrassed."

"Mrs. Wayneflete, perhaps *you* should tell us," Meriel insisted. "You'll say more than Victoria. Didn't you warn her about—"

The housekeeper put up both hands. "I have dishes to see to. You young ladies talk. You too, Mrs. Shelby."

Victoria shook her head. "There really isn't much to say. Do you remember the boy I used to write to?"

"How did that lead to an earl?" Louisa asked.

"A viscount," Victoria corrected.

Meriel groaned. "Future earl. You're trying to distract us."

"No, I promise I'm not. For strangely"— Victoria took a deep breath and looked at her mother, who was watching in bewilderment— "Viscount Thurlow was Tom all along."

There were gasps from her sisters, but her mother simply looked stunned as she said, "Victoria, you intruded on an earl's family with letters?"

"I didn't know his father was the earl," Victoria said. "He lied to me. I thought he was the cook's son. And it was a journal we shared, not letters."

Meriel frowned. "So he lied to you even then, proving himself just as dubious as his father."

"Tell me what you know about the earl," Victoria said. "There's always been talk of scandal, but nothing in fact."

Meriel and Louisa exchanged glances, which only made Victoria angry.

"Why would you two know something and not tell me?"

"Because we really know nothing," Louisa said softly.

Meriel took over. "All of our friends knew a scandal had happened within the *ton*, at the earl's house, but none could give any details. We whispered over it, but the subject soon died down as far as we were concerned."

"I keep telling myself that unsubstantiated rumors are not a reason to condemn a family," Victoria said with frustration.

Meriel gave her a guarded look. "I hope you have considered that he can't be trusted."

"I considered that, yes. But it could not play much into my decision, now could it?" she asked pointedly. "If he knew everything, he could say the same about me."

Her sisters exchanged a glance, and Victoria knew no one wanted to speak about their father in front of Mama.

Louisa sighed and spoke in her soft voice. "Our positions are at least temporary, but marriage is permanent."

"I know," Victoria said, attempting a reassuring smile. "Lord Thurlow explained to me that he'd been ten years old when he'd thought of the lie of his identity, and that later he couldn't find a way to tell the truth without hurting me."

Louisa looked about the table at her family. "Perhaps he cares about your feelings."

As usual, she wanted to see the good in people, and Victoria appreciated the comfort of that.

Meriel was still scowling. "Not enough to tell the truth. You must have been horrified."

Victoria hesitated. "It was . . . a sobering experience. But it has all ended well. He asked me to marry him, and he will welcome Mama into his home."

Their mother should have looked relieved, yet there was still so much worry in her lined face.

"Why did he ask you to marry him?" Meriel asked.

Victoria was beginning to regret her sister's logical nature. "Because he needed a wife. He remembered me from our journal, and felt that gave him a good idea of the woman I was."

"But you bring him no dowry or bloodlines."

"He says he has enough money, and doesn't care about the other. And he's already escorted me to a luncheon where my purpose as his future wife was made very clear. I make a suitable dinner companion."

"But surely you asked him about the scandal?"

"Meriel, of course I could not do such a thing. Don't you think I say these things to myself every night while I lie in bed?" Victoria's voice had begun to shake.

Louisa's eyes shone with tears while Meriel just looked worried.

"I refuse to regret this decision," Victoria said firmly. "Don't you see? It solves all of our problems. Banstead House is so enormous, that I'm certain Lord Thurlow would allow both of you to live there."

There was suddenly an uncomfortable silence, and Victoria's secret hopes began to fade. "Don't you understand? You could both cease working."

Meriel began to cut her meat with determination. "I can't abandon my pupil just yet. He has no mother, and his father—" She broke off, taking a bite of lamb and chewing vigorously. "His father is not much help."

"But you could stay until you find someone worthy for the position," Victoria insisted. She'd never imagined that her sisters wouldn't come back to London to live with her.

Meriel shook her head, meeting Victoria's eyes with regret. "I can't do that to a little boy. He needs me." She lowered her voice, as if someone might overhear. "There's something about his father that seems . . . unusual to me. He's a duke, but he's ill at ease, though I don't understand why. I certainly can't leave until I'm positive little Stephen is protected."

"Meriel," Victoria said firmly, "you always see plots where there are none. You should have been the writer in the family."

"I'll leave that to you, Vic," Meriel said.

Her smile seemed forced, and she wore her most closed-off expression. Nothing was going to change Meriel's mind. Victoria turned to Louisa, who gave her a gentle smile.

"I'm sorry, Victoria, but I, too, must stay where I am for a little while. Lady Margaret is depending on me. She is quite ill and confined to her bed. And I am the only one she has to talk to."

"Constant talk, from what you've implied," Meriel said, her brows lowered in a scowl.

Louisa sighed. "She's a dear old lady, whose children do not visit her enough. I promise, if the viscount will have me, I'll join you when I'm able."

"But Louisa, living here would give you the chance to meet society," Victoria said earnestly. "You would surely meet a suitable man to marry. Hasn't that been what you've always wanted?"

Louisa's distress was palpable. "Please don't make this any more difficult than it already is," she whispered.

Victoria sat back in her chair, knowing that she had to accept her sisters' decisions. Louisa and Meriel were adults with responsibilities they couldn't abandon—which they didn't want to elaborate on. Victoria realized that by trying to persuade them to live with her, she was selfishly making herself another responsibility to them.

She wouldn't do that anymore. She would be the mistress of her own household now, responsible for herself.

But the worry that was never far from her thoughts crept closer. She would just have to concentrate on the fact that Mama and Mrs. Wayneflete would be with her.

And Lord Thurlow.

She shivered and presented a bright smile to her family.

On the eve of the wedding, Victoria retreated to her room after convincing her sisters that she needed her rest. She stacked her notebooks on her desk: a book on her latest artistic endeavors, so that creative ideas wouldn't leave her mind; a household journal, where she wrote out the daily things she had to accomplish; and a journal where she wrote her most private thoughts. It was this last one she opened now. She hadn't written in it since the day Lord Thurlow had proposed. She'd been too busy with all the preparations.

Now, as she stared at the blank page, she realized that she didn't want to see her fears put into words. She would wait until after the wedding.

Then she opened the lowest desk drawer and withdrew her childhood journal. Something had been bothering her about it all day, and the reason kept eluding her.

Victoria touched the words written in Lord Thurlow's boyish hand.

Now that she knew his true identity, she could see the gaps in his writing, the way he'd avoided the subject of family, except for his mother. She had always thought it simply meant he was almost alone in the world.

She felt her uneasiness rising, and once again she forced away thoughts of betrayal. She was just as guilty of lies now as he was, and it did not sit easily on her conscience. So he was going to use her as his partner in social events—every wife fulfilled that function.

She closed the book and put it in a crate to be moved to her new home.

Home. She couldn't imagine another one than this, but she reminded herself that she hadn't always been happy here, that it was no idyllic place she'd pine for.

Could she make a *new* home? Would Lord Thurlow welcome her, give her a real chance, or would he treat her like the property she'd become upon marrying him?

Of course, marriage took two people, and it was equally up to her to contribute to its success. She wasn't sure how to do that; she'd spent so many years settling into the role of spinster that tomorrow's ceremony seemed like the start of someone else's life.

And she would *be* someone else—Lady Thurlow.

Victoria could make Lady Thurlow's life a success. She was no longer that naive girl who'd written in that childhood journal. She had experienced hard realities, and knew how close she'd come to seeing poverty firsthand.

And she'd survived. She'd fed her small family, kept them warm and clothed for as long as she could. And then she'd found a man to marry— well, he'd asked *her*, of course, but that didn't negate the fact that she'd initiated it. Even a year ago, that would have seemed impossible.

And now she had to keep a secret from a man who was trusting her in marriage, a man whose own father had tainted their family heritage. She had promised Lord Thurlow that she would commit no scandals during their marriage. She rationalized to herself that this was the truth, that she'd told no lie.

For how could she risk that her father's remains be moved to unholy ground because of suicide? How could she risk the *ton* thinking their finances must have been mishandled, since her father was so obviously mentally unbalanced? There were good reasons to keep this terrible secret.

But there was also the sanctity of a marriage— and she was betraying it.

Chapter 5

In the vestibule of the church, Victoria fingered the diamond necklace that Lord Thurlow had given her. Outside a light morning shower was turning steadily heavier, denying her cheerful sunshine on her wedding day. Her sisters had gathered in front of her at the partially opened door and peered inside the church.

"Can you see him?" Louisa asked.

Meriel gave Louisa an unladylike elbow. "I could if you'd move your big head."

Victoria waited behind them for their judgment. They were suddenly very quiet, then turned to stare at her in unison.

Oh God, had the bridegroom changed his mind? Had he remembered that she would never be the Perfect Wife of their childhood imaginations?

Victoria was looking for something to brace herself on, when Louisa began to nod.

"He's quite handsome," Louisa breathed, reaching back to squeeze Victoria's hand.

Victoria gave a sigh of relief.

Meriel frowned. "He looks overpowering. Is he as large up close as he seems from back here?"

Not trusting herself to speak, Victoria just nodded and waited for the light-headedness to pass.

Louisa put an arm around her. "It's normal to be nervous, dear."

"It's not normal to be frightened," Meriel said. "You don't have to go through with this, Vic. We'll tell him you changed your mind."

"No." Victoria gently pushed Louisa away and stood on her own. "I'm fine. I know him; I trust him."

"You know his lies," Meriel pointed out.

Victoria stared at her and softly asked, "Why are you saying these things?"

Meriel bit her lip, such a familiar gesture in their family. "Because I feel terribly guilty that you were driven to something that you never wanted in the first place. It's not right."

"But it feels right," Victoria insisted, more for her own benefit than her sisters'. "It is as if . . .

God gave him to me for a reason. I'm not fleeing. Mama is already inside."

"But—" Meriel began.

"Hush," Louisa said, her hand on Meriel's arm. "Her decision is made. Are you ready, Victoria?"

"I'm ready. Do I look suitable?"

Victoria wore a cream-colored gown draped with lovely bridal lace. The color managed to make her hair look more vivid than it normally did, and hide the paleness of her skin.

"You look beautiful," Louisa whispered.

Victoria squeezed their hands. "Thank you. Now you both go on ahead."

They opened the inner doors to the church and walked down the aisle. Lord Thurlow didn't smile, but he studied her in a way that could not be termed dismissive. She had noticed that he didn't seem to mind looking at her, and it made her feel rather . . . good.

The best man at his side, Lord Wade, gave a cheerful grin when he saw her sisters, and something inside Victoria relaxed the tiniest bit. Lord Wade seemed like a man who accepted life as it came to him, and didn't worry overly much about anything. If he was a common example of the *ton,* she should not be so anxious. There must be something good-natured about Lord Thurlow, to have such a happy friend.

And then it was her turn, and she walked up the

aisle alone. She was the focus of every stare, few in number though they were. She'd once spent her whole life hiding from such notice, hugging the walls at long-ago parties, retreating for hours alone in the music room. But not anymore. She would be the wife of a viscount, and she would not embarrass him.

Her sisters looked determinedly cheerful, her mother worried. There was an older gentleman in a wheelchair who watched her with a scowl, and she knew that this must be the Earl of Banstead, Lord Thurlow's father. He was thin, hunched, pale with the pallor of sickness, not looking like the inspiration for so much gossip.

And he was obviously angry about the wedding. Of course he disapproved—she brought nothing to the marriage but herself. She tried not to look at the old man, but his feelings were palpable, pressing in on her. She would be living in the same house with him.

The ceremony itself was brief and echoed strangely in the empty church. Victoria remembered little of the words; all she could do was stare into the impassive eyes of her betrothed— her husband.

Then it was done. He kissed her cheek, and she was married.

The two of them rode alone as husband and wife in Lord Thurlow's enclosed carriage back to

Banstead House. Victoria held her pink roses and stared blindly out the window, thinking about that simple kiss, and how inhaling the scent of him had actually been pleasurable.

He cleared his throat. "I am pleased that your sisters could attend."

"So was I," she said, glancing at him.

He was watching her with a look she couldn't decipher. Was it . . . relief? That didn't make sense.

"You'll have to forgive my father," he said. "He is an old man whose pain has clouded his thinking. It was wrong of him to display his unwarranted feelings."

She would start out her marriage with as much honesty as she could. "My lord, he has every right to be angry. I am quite certain I am not the sort of woman he planned for his son to marry. Perhaps you kept me away from him deliberately?"

"Does that bother you?"

"It is understandable. Being told the truth up front would have helped." She waited for a response, but he said nothing. "Did he try to talk you out of the marriage?"

"Yes."

She winced. She had wanted honesty, after all.

"He may be the earl, but I make the decisions about my future," he said.

"Then yours is an unusual relationship, my lord."

He only frowned.

At Banstead House, the servants gathered in a long line to greet her, and it was a relief to see the friendly face of Mrs. Wayneflete. The other servants were a bit more reserved, but surely Victoria could win them over.

After the servants had all filed out of the entrance hall, Victoria looked about her as Lord Thurlow led her up the stairs to the drawing room. Everything was of the utmost elegance, with damask draperies, velvet cushions, and marble-topped tables, but there was something . . . cold and impersonal about it all. That was when she realized that a woman's touch was missing. There was not a memento or a vase of flowers to be found, though dozens of expensive paintings made it seem like a museum. And everywhere the draperies were only partly drawn, as if the sun was unwelcome.

Meriel and Louisa, already waiting for her, gave her cheerful smiles that seemed forced. Lord Wade sat across from them, and Mama stared about her with that same sad, worried expression. Why couldn't she understand that everything would be all right now?

The earl was not in attendance, and Victoria admitted to herself that she was relieved. She would have to face her new father by marriage eventually, but she didn't want her wedding day marred.

The breakfast was cordial, even cheerful, with Lord Wade guiding much of the conversation with the amusing doings of the *ton*. Victoria noticed that Lord Thurlow did not contribute much to the gossip; in fact, he seemed to disapprove.

But hadn't he used to tell wonderful stories, back when they wrote in their journal? Sometimes he'd created fantasy tales of adventure, and other times he'd made the realities of an earl's household seem amusing. Now, as she listened to him discuss a horse race with Lord Wade, she studied him intently, looking for the boy in the man, but she didn't see him. He had changed so much.

Of course, he was now a grown man. She hadn't realized how much she would notice such a thing. But his very maleness seemed foreign to her, and her fascination with his physicality embarrassed her.

He turned and caught her staring. She blushed and sipped her wine and tried to pretend that everything was all right, when it wasn't.

"Lord Thurlow," Meriel said, "Victoria's things will have to be moved into Banstead House. Since we do not know your schedule, is there a time that would suit you? Or do you plan to be traveling?"

Victoria was grateful for Meriel's practicality, since she hadn't even questioned her husband about the first days of their marriage. She'd been too focused on the actual ceremony!

Lord Thurlow turned to look at Meriel. "Any time will suffice, Miss Shelby. I have too much business in London for a wedding trip."

Railway business, Victoria was certain. Another sign that he would not leave his investments to be handled by someone else.

After breakfast, Lord Thurlow rose to his feet. "If you'll excuse me, Lady Thurlow—"

She looked about for a moment, and he waited with an air of amusement until she realized he had meant her.

"Oh, do forgive me, my lord," she said in a faint voice, listening to Lord Wade laugh good-naturedly.

Her husband inclined his head. "I have a meeting that I could not reschedule. I'll be back for dinner."

"Oh." She rose to her feet, but didn't know what to do. Should she accompany him to the door?

But he turned and left the room.

Lord Wade rescued her from awkwardness. "Lady Thurlow, have you seen the grounds yet?"

The afternoon flew by in a relaxed and easy manner. Lord Wade gave them a tour of the gardens, then they all played croquet after eating luncheon on the terrace. Out on the lawn, smelling the grass and flowers, Victoria quite forgot her worries until she looked up as the sun lowered behind the trees. Her husband stood on the terrace, looking at them.

Looking at her.

Oh goodness, the night was almost upon her.

David did his best to encourage Simon and the Shelby family to stay for dinner, but everyone was determined to see the newly married couple alone for the evening. The sisters said their mother was tired and needed to rest, so they took her home for the night, promising to return on the morrow.

He watched the good-byes dubiously. There was much kissing on the cheek and hugs and worried looks they obviously didn't want him to see. From the way the Misses Shelby were acting, it was obvious they thought he was about to drag their sister off to his lair and pounce on her. By God, people got married every day.

But surely they knew of the rumors circulating about his family, and were now regretting that their sister was trapped.

But it was too late for any regrets.

David watched Simon escort the women home, and then he closed the door and turned to look at his new wife. She stared at him solemnly before she remembered to smile.

"Shall we go in to dinner, my lord?"

"Give me a moment to file this afternoon's papers. I'll join you in a few minutes."

But a few minutes ended up being a half hour, and he hurried up to the dining room, where Victoria sat amid fresh flowers and candles.

"I'm sorry for the delay," he said.

Victoria closed the notebook she was reading. To his satisfaction, she did not berate him, only smiled as she said, "It was not an imposition. Will your father be joining us?"

"Since the table is set for two, I assume not. He doesn't leave the house much anymore, so the ceremony this morning probably exhausted him."

She said nothing to that, and he wondered if she believed him. She'd be right not to.

After the first course was served, he watched Victoria quietly sip her turtle soup, her eyes downcast, her manner demure. He was rather surprised by how easy it was to remain focused on her, when his thoughts usually drifted to practical matters he had still to accomplish that day. He watched her delicate fingers at work, and even the movement of her lips. He had thought her plain but for her violet eyes, yet the way she moved intrigued him, full of purpose, without the artifice so many ladies of the *ton* had mastered.

"Victoria, I know that becoming my wife has led to great changes for you—"

Her eyes fixed on him.

"But I promise not to interfere in whatever you choose to do during the day. I am often gone, or at work in my study. I will, however, try to be home as much as possible for the evening meal. The household is yours to run. You'll have no interference from me."

"But my lord, you've been a bachelor for many years—surely there are things you'd like done a certain way."

"Not at all," he said, taking a bite of his broiled pheasant. "I am relieved to hand over the household to you."

She frowned, and he knew "relieved" was a poor choice of words.

"If you have any questions, just ask," he continued. He didn't expect her to—after all, she had been well trained.

After the next course was served, she looked up at him expectantly.

"My lord, I do have several questions, about *you* rather than the household."

"Only several?" he asked mildly, trying to hide his discomfort. "Perhaps I answered most of your questions a very long time ago."

"You know that is not true. You could borrow our journal and see for yourself."

He raised a hand and shook his head. "No, that's all right. The past is dead and gone. I don't need to relive it."

She studied him, and he wondered what he'd just revealed to her. He didn't like to think, let alone talk about that time in his life so tainted with constant loss.

"Very well, since I have your permission," she said, "what do you do with yourself all day?"

Her fingers touched the notebook like a lifeline in a storm.

"Much of my time is taken up with Parliament from January to August. I was elected a member of the House of Commons, although when I inherit the title someday, I'll move to the Lords. Since my father is so ill, I also deal with the running of our estates and our investments."

"Do you have many estates?" she asked.

"Besides our family seat in Kent, we own nine estates throughout England, and another two in Scotland. They all vary in size, of course."

Her mouth had fallen open, but she managed to repeat, "Of course."

Though her father had once been wealthy, it was obvious from her reaction that her family had not expanded much into land. Perhaps that was Mr. Shelby's main failing. Nothing to fall back on.

"You already know about my interest in the railway, but please do not discuss it in front of my father. According to him, and most of society, a gentleman is not in trade."

She gave a rueful smile. "That I already know."

"Of course you do."

"My father made himself wealthy, all through his own efforts. I always admired that."

There was an underlying bitterness that he couldn't decipher.

"You did not wish that he was termed a gentleman?" David asked.

"So that I could attend parties with people who thought themselves better than me? No, my lord."

"Well, don't worry that your days will be filled with the *ton*'s events, Victoria. I don't care for such things myself."

And they went on with their quiet dinner. Again, David was surprised to find how often his gaze settled on her. Surely it was because she was a new facet of his life that he would have to work around.

After they'd finished their custard, David pushed back his chair and cleared his throat. "I've already hired a lady's maid for you. She will escort you to the master suite. I'll join you soon."

Her face went pale.

Chapter 6

Victoria stood very near her new husband; he loomed over her, so much broader and taller than the men of her acquaintance. He took her hand and she tensed, knowing how damp her palm was inside her glove.

He placed a chaste kiss on her knuckles that she felt even through the fabric.

"Until later," he murmured.

When their eyes met, when he really, truly *saw* her, there was a connection, a heat between them she had never experienced. She could feel him watching her even as she followed the maid to the second floor.

Before she knew it, the maid opened a door and led her inside a spacious room, lit with candles, and decorated in green and red and gold. There was a large four-poster bed and chaise, but also, to her relief, a desk. Another door on the far side of the room must lead to Lord Thurlow's chambers.

Well, she would simply not think about that yet. Her own small assortment of garments had already been put away in the drawers and wardrobe. There was a hip bath steaming before the hearth, and she was glad for the chance to relax.

After introducing herself as Anna, the maid left and Victoria was alone, soaking in the tub, trying to dissolve away the day's tensions. But she couldn't stop looking at the door to Lord Thurlow's room. He had every right to just walk in, surprising her in her bath, or while she was dressing. Would he? After all, what did she even know about him as a man?

But no one disturbed her. She finally got out of the tub, dressed in a silk nightdress and matching dressing gown, then sat before the hearth and brushed out her hair, drying it by the warmth of the grate.

She couldn't stop thinking about what her mother and Mrs. Wayneflete had told her about a woman's wedding night, even though Lord Thurlow had promised to wait. Both women had stumbled over their words with embarrassment. Finally

Mrs. Wayneflete had told her that a man put part of himself inside her, and that although it would be awkward, it was necessary to make a baby. To Mama's shock, the housekeeper had insisted that her "dear Harold" had made sure she enjoyed herself.

That had actually made Victoria feel better.

As if she'd mentally called her husband, his door vibrated with a knock.

She cleared her throat. "Come in."

The low candlelight made him seem darker, even more a stranger. Her pulse fluttered in her throat and sounded loud in her ears as she stared at him. He still wore trousers and a shirt open at the neck, but he'd wrapped a robe around himself in place of a coat. It was strange to see his throat looking so bare, strange to be in a man's presence wearing so little herself, although she was as covered as she would be by day. But without a corset and petticoats, she felt positively unencumbered.

He stopped to stare at her for a moment, and she remembered that he'd never seen her with her hair down. But he didn't say anything, just brought a bottle of wine and two glasses to the little table near the hearth.

After pouring for each of them, he lifted his glass. "To our marriage."

She gratefully took a sip of wine and tried to

imagine that it flooded her stomach with warmth and courage, overshadowing this cold feeling of worry that never left her anymore. She was married; she had helped save her family. If he had changed his mind about their wedding night— even if he'd simply "forgotten" their agreement— she would accept it.

Lord Thurlow sank down in the chair opposite her, his legs parted, his body more casually relaxed than she'd ever seen it. He was still watching her with those pale eyes, assessing her. What was she supposed to do? Wouldn't he tell her?

He glanced at the brush in her hand. "I didn't mean to interrupt your preparations. Please continue."

Her eyes widened, and she almost wanted to giggle with nervousness. He was going to sit there and watch her brush her hair?

But he did. She combed through the damp strands, holding the curls out to the heat of the grate, while her new husband stared at her, sipping his wine occasionally. Her hands trembled so much, she didn't dare lift her own goblet again, for fear of spilling it all over the new nightclothes Mrs. Wayneflete had insisted she purchase.

"You don't need to be so frightened of me," he finally said.

Her gaze met his. "I'm not frightened of you,

my lord, but I will admit to nervousness about the unknown."

With his elbow on the arm of the chair, he propped his chin on his fist. "Did your mother tell you what usually happens on a wedding night?"

She felt heat rise up her face. "Some, my lord. Mrs. Wayneflete helped as well."

"Your housekeeper?" he asked, raising a brow.

"She has always been more than that to me. You'll never know how much I appreciate that you've employed her."

"Smith says she is an excellent worker, and already the household seems to be running smoothly." He leaned forward. "You don't need to keep calling me by my title."

She frowned. "How would you wish me to address you?"

"My name is David."

And suddenly, it was as if he'd brought up the memories of another time, when he'd called himself by another name. The deception hung between them, and bitterness made her worry about what kind of life they could have together. How was she supposed to forget such a betrayal?

Yet he'd saved her family. And now she was the one doing the lying.

He pressed his lips into a thin line. "Call me whatever you're comfortable with."

"Thank you, my lord."

"But I shall call you Victoria."

Because I never lied about my name, she thought with heavy sadness.

"Is your hair dry?" he asked.

She wet her lips and nodded. He took the brush from her hand and set it down, then encouraged her to take another drink of wine.

He twirled his own glass between his fingers and watched it. "I know why you asked that I should take my time with you. This is truly awkward between us, since we did know each other once upon a time. Now we're newly married, yet . . . with so little time for you to grow used to the reality of being alone with a man."

"Is it the same for you, my lord?"

"Pardon me?" His heavy brows lowered in obvious confusion.

"Are new husbands . . . nervous?"

He opened his mouth as if astonished, but nothing came out, and he finally refilled his glass and took another drink before speaking. "No, I'm not nervous, but then husbands tend to already know what's involved in a wedding night."

"Why?"

Was he blushing?

"Victoria, unlike women, most men have already—" He stopped and frowned. "I have already . . . participated in the act."

The act? she wanted to repeat incredulously.

That's what he called the most intimate part of marriage between a husband and wife?

"You had a mistress?" she asked. Her sisters had told her that men did not have to wait for the sanctity of marriage, that no one assumed they would. Victoria had always thought that seemed rather unfair.

"Yes, but rest assured, I have one no longer. I would never dishonor our marriage like that."

She wondered why that didn't reassure her. Perhaps because it sounded as if he was more worried about how the "marriage" appeared than about hurting her feelings? But he was a man, and she knew men did not think of emotions as women did.

"So you have . . ." She waved vaguely toward the bed. ". . . done that before."

He tilted his head, his eyelids lowered as he studied her. "Yes."

"Mrs. Wayneflete said that I might enjoy it, though perhaps not the first time."

"I would make sure you enjoyed it."

His voice had deepened, roughened, losing some of the civilized, so-in-control sound. It did something to the inside of her, sent a strange, hot feeling shooting down into her stomach, down even lower, where it lingered with a heat that was almost . . . moist.

How could he make her feel this way?

Lord Thurlow put his glass down, and she gave a little start.

"But I don't want you to be frightened when I touch you," he said briskly, "so I have an idea of a way to introduce you to the intimacy of marriage."

"Besides taking our time?"

He gave a small smile. "Besides that. Being that we don't know each other as adults, and have not had much time for actual courtship, I propose that each night we go one step further in our intimacy."

Was he trying to alter their bargain? "My lord, I don't understand what you want of me."

"I don't want much, Victoria, but I'll be grateful if you learn not to flinch when I touch you."

"But I don't—"

"Yes, you do."

She remained silent then, knowing he was right. He held out his hand, and she stared at it.

"Hold my hand, Victoria. I am a man, not some monster you need fear."

She bit her lip. Was that how she made him feel? Inside her, something softened. Gingerly, she reached out and put her hand in his.

She had only once felt a man's bare skin, when he'd kissed her hand several weeks ago. She'd been too flustered to think about anything but his lips. Now she realized that his flesh was warm and dry, rougher than hers across his palm. His hand was so much bigger than hers, making her feel fragile and small.

They sat unmoving before the hearth for several minutes, staring at each other. For the rest of her life, she would be with this man, and she must make the best of it. She must learn to forget her hurt feelings, to focus on the fact that his offer of marriage had saved her. He hadn't needed to do it; it would have been nothing to him to offer her a little money.

Then he gave a tug and slowly pulled. She leaned forward from her chair; he leaned forward in his.

"A simple kiss," he whispered, his breath now a warmth on her face, "on our wedding day."

She should resist. He'd already kissed her cheek just that morning. And he'd promised not to rush intimacy. But as she looked into his eyes, so bright and almost fierce with purpose, her resistance began to melt, though she frantically called it back. He was more handsome than any man who'd ever looked her way, and such beauty could be mesmerizing.

Their lips met softly, and her wide eyes stared into his. She'd never been kissed before. And then it was over before she could think what to do. He leaned back, and the extent of her disappointment shocked her. Lord Thurlow released her hand and rose to his feet. She followed, and they faced each other awkwardly. He took his glass and bottle of wine and walked toward the door to his room.

"Good night, Victoria," he said, without glancing back at her.

"Good night." She stopped herself from calling him "my lord," but could not bring herself to substitute his Christian name.

And then he was gone, and she was alone, not quite sure it was relief she was feeling. She sat down at her desk and opened her personal journal, because writing helped everything make sense.

David barely restrained himself from slamming the door. Nothing had gone as he'd meant it to. Whyever had he asked her to call him by his name, as if he somehow wanted to be close to her again?

Instead he'd allowed his virgin wife, who asked intimate questions of her *housekeeper*, to question him about his *mistress*, for God's sake. He had nothing to be ashamed of. He'd been more kind and understanding than most husbands would be on a wedding night.

But when she'd trusted him with her hand, full of a strength he hadn't anticipated, something had happened inside him, something he didn't understand.

And then he'd wanted to throw out all his plans, to sweep her onto the bed and take her immediately, as was his right.

113

What was he, a feudal knight? He didn't think he'd ever skirted the edge of restraint like that. When she'd looked at him as if she might trust him again, it had almost been his undoing. He'd thought to satisfy himself with a chaste kiss, and even that had set his blood burning. Her lips were soft, silken . . .

He had to get control of himself, something he always prided himself on. There was never a business arrangement or an argument in the Commons of which he did not have complete mastery.

But his new wife, his childhood friend, had been afraid of him, and he'd only wanted to make that emotion go away.

He would not live his life like this. She was his partner in marriage, not his reason for existing, as in a foolish romantic poem. They each brought their skills to the marriage like a business arrangement. They could coexist quite nicely, and no one would suffer any pain.

He took off his clothes and went to bed, satisfied in mind, but not in body.

Victoria awoke as the sun streamed in her window, and she realized with a start after glancing at the clock that she'd slept almost half the morning away. She pushed aside the blankets, prepared to help Mrs. Wayneflete with breakfast, when she remembered her new situation.

She was Lady Thurlow, and she had servants to do all those tasks now. Very slowly she leaned back on her elbows, took a deep breath, and let some of her worry go. There would be food on the table that she didn't have to sell a family heirloom to buy. She would never have to watch her mother grow thinner again.

There were tears streaming down her cheeks before she even realized it. She didn't know where a handkerchief was, so she wiped her eyes with shaking fingers and let the relief flow into her. She'd accomplished something she'd never believed she could do.

She got out of bed and went to the window, where she could see the gardens they'd wandered through yesterday, and then in the distance the back of another grand town house. She felt calm today. Maybe it was knowing that her husband was content to wait for intimacy until they knew each other better. Surely most other husbands didn't have the patience for that. He had once been a kind boy, hadn't he? She remembered him writing forlornly after his puppy had been killed by a carriage.

She'd thought that little boy had long since disappeared, but last night had shown her that she might be wrong. Maybe when they'd started writing, he'd just been a lonely boy who'd felt he couldn't reveal the truth of himself.

These last few weeks she'd worried she was marrying a man like her father, cold and aloof. Yet she didn't dare hope that Lord Thurlow wanted a real marriage, the kind with fondness and concern between husband and wife. No, he was too focused on his railway business, and on how she could prove useful to him.

After she dressed for the day in her new blue gown—how wonderful it felt to wear colors again!—Victoria went downstairs to the dining room, ready to join her husband on the first day of their marriage.

But there were only two footmen in powdered wigs and livery, waiting patiently beside the sideboard with its covered tureens of food. They informed her that His Lordship had long since eaten and left for the morning.

Of course Lord Thurlow was an early riser, Victoria scolded herself as she scooped eggs and ham onto her plate. She normally was, too, but after the stress of the last few weeks, she'd slept long and soundly in her comfortable new bed. From now on, she would have to awaken early every morning to eat with her husband. She at least owed him that respect.

Though she had grown up in a wealthy family with several servants, she had never been watched by footmen while she ate. She was used to going through her notebooks and planning out her day.

But this morning she was self-conscious, so she finished eating quickly.

She heard someone clear her throat, and looked up to see Mrs. Wayneflete standing in the doorway. The housekeeper looked her over worriedly, but seemed to relax when Victoria grinned.

"Come talk to me," Victoria said. "We didn't have much chance yesterday."

Mrs. Wayneflete smiled. "I wanted to tell you that I sent a breakfast basket to your family this morning, so you needn't worry about them all alone in that nearly empty house."

"Oh, Mrs. Wayneflete, you're such a comfort to us. Thank you!"

The housekeeper waved away Victoria's praise. "The girls sent a note back that they would be visiting you later this morning."

"Wonderful. I want to see them as much as possible before they leave tomorrow." She hesitated. "So how have your first days here been?" Her curiosity was twofold; what was it like to work for Lord Thurlow? Surely the other servants talked.

The housekeeper looked over her shoulder, then lowered her voice. "The household was in a bit of an uproar, but that could be expected, what with no housekeeper for a month. Everything seems to have quieted down, but almost like they're waiting, if you know what I mean."

"Waiting for what?"

"I don't know. I've heard bits and pieces about the old earl, but he hasn't set foot out of his room yet."

"No talk of scandals?" Victoria whispered.

"None."

"Well that's good then. Please let me know if there's anything I should deal with."

"Of course, my lady."

"Could you arrange for me to meet with a different servant every morning? I'll feel better when I know everyone."

Mrs. Wayneflete nodded with understanding.

"I'll want to go over the menus with you, and see the household accounts, but for now, would you mind taking me on a tour of my new home?"

The housekeeper beamed. "I'd be happy to."

The tour itself proved to Victoria how big the town house really was. There was even a second, larger drawing room behind the first. "For dancing," Mrs. Wayneflete added, and Victoria felt a little pang in her stomach at the merest thought.

Above the second floor of bedchambers, there was a floor for children, and then another floor for the servants.

The earl's suite was on the ground floor in the rear of the town house to accommodate his wheelchair.

Mrs. Wayneflete kept her voice low as they stood in the corridor. "My lady, only this morning the earl threw his breakfast tray at the maid, saying it wasn't cooked to his exact specifications."

"How inconsiderate of him." Victoria wondered if a man with notoriety attached to his name would even bother to care what people thought anymore. "But he is dying," she said aloud.

"We all die, my lady," the housekeeper said, shooting an irritated look at the closed door. "Some of us do it graciously. Though the earl seldom leaves his room, when he does, he finds fault with every servant he encounters. I've heard stories of maids crying, footmen quitting, and housekeepers finally refusing to deal with the extra work. Those women came so highly regarded, they knew they could get a plum position in a better household, regardless of how much the viscount paid them to stay."

Victoria stared at his door with worry. "We must do something about this, Mrs. Wayneflete. The last few months, my mother has shown a disturbing tendency to sleep too much of each day. I won't watch two elderly people confine themselves to their rooms and be miserable at the end of their lives. There has to be some way to help them both."

Mrs. Wayneflete nodded, though her expression showed her skepticism.

Victoria went back to the music room on the first floor overlooking the garden. A piano was the centerpiece of the room, flanked by cabinets full of musical scores. A covered harp rested quietly in one corner, and a cornet and a violin sat on a shelf in their cases. There was a large desk near the window, and Victoria could see herself there, working on her music.

She found her favorite compositions among the sheet music, soft, quiet tunes that should bother no one in the household. Eventually she grew bold, playing ever louder until the room swelled with music, and her ears rang with each reverberation. As always, she poured her worries and fears into the music, letting it release in glorious sound. She had forgotten how much better her music always made her feel.

With a happy sigh she let her hands fall into her lap. In the peaceful silence, she thought she heard the front door close. No one came looking for her, but an uneasy feeling rose within her, a prickling at the base of her neck.

Perhaps Lord Thurlow had come home for luncheon. She walked into the corridor and looked over the railing into the entrance hall below. The voices were louder now, coming from the library, a woman's—and Lord Thurlow's.

Victoria gripped the railing and considered what she should do. He could be speaking to a maid, after all. Victoria would just walk down to the kitchen—past the library—because she still had to discuss the day's menu with Mrs. Wayne-flete. When she reached the ground floor, she paused. The library door was partly open, though she could not see inside. The woman's voice was not that of one of the maids, yet Victoria knew it from somewhere.

Lord Thurlow's tone was solemn. "Forgive me. It was rude of me not to tell you about Victoria immediately. Things just happened so quickly."

"Forgetfulness is often your excuse, David," said the woman in a sad voice. "How many nights did I wait for you, delaying my own plans, because you said you were coming to me?"

Victoria felt gooseflesh sweep over her skin, and she shivered. This was Lord Thurlow's mistress! She was brazen enough to come to Banstead House in broad daylight!

"You're right, I have treated you poorly," Lord Thurlow said.

"No, you have always been a good man, and that is why this is so difficult for me. Why couldn't it have been me?"

"I beg your pardon?" he said.

Victoria held her breath, guilt long since faded away. She *needed* to hear this.

"I always thought you would marry a woman of your own class, so I never had hopes for myself." Her voice broke. "But you married a commoner, just like me."

"Damaris, you must understand—"

Victoria gasped and backed away from the library door. Miss Damaris Lingard was her husband's mistress? And he had allowed the two women to attend the same luncheon, hurting Miss Lingard and making a fool of his own betrothed?

Chapter 7

Victoria's sisters and mother arrived a half hour later, and Victoria had the butler show them into the drawing room. Victoria had dried her tears and washed her face, determined to speak to her husband about his mistress before the day was out. Until then, she could do nothing about the horrible cold feeling in the pit of her stomach. Was he already lying to her? Did he have no plans to end his affair?

When the butler had left them alone, her sisters' faces showed puzzlement as they stared at Victoria, and then growing concern. No matter how hard Victoria had tried to keep her expression merely pleasant, her sisters had already seen that something was wrong.

Victoria did *not* want to talk about it.

"Good morning, Mama," she said, kissing her mother's cheek. "Is everything ready for you to move in here?"

She'd obviously said the wrong thing, for her sisters winced and her mother looked mutinous.

"Am I missing something?" Victoria asked as they all sat down.

Meriel sighed. "Mama is sad to be leaving home."

Their mother rolled her eyes. "You all seem to think it should be easy to leave the place where I built a life with your father."

Louisa slid closer to their mother on the sofa and put an arm around her. "We don't think that at all, Mama. But you won't be far away. I'm sure our cousin would love to have you visit occasionally."

Meriel gave her a warning glance over their mother's head, and even Victoria realized they couldn't know such a thing for certain.

"Mama," Victoria said, "I thought you would be happy not to see me working so hard in the house."

She sighed. "Of course I am, dearest. Your marriage is something I've dreamed of for so many years. It's just—I wish I knew what was wrong with me." Her voice trailed off to a whisper.

Victoria felt her ever-present tears return.

"We've had a terrible year, Mama, and we all have to recover."

"Thank goodness for Viscount Thurlow," her mother said.

Victoria almost bristled. Didn't her mother realize that Victoria had sacrificed her freedom to make everyone safe?

Her own thoughts suddenly baffled her. How could she resent her poor mother, who'd suffered a terrible blow?

Then Mama looked at her sadly. "I'm sorry that this is so sudden for you, Victoria. I know you would have liked more time to prepare for marriage."

Surprised, Victoria could only say, "It's all right, Mama."

Mrs. Wayneflete entered the drawing room, smiling as she approached their mother. "I have your new room all ready, Mrs. Shelby. Why don't you come see it with me?"

The sisters watched sadly as their mother left, her shoulders still bowed.

Victoria sighed, then regretted it as both sisters turned to frown at her in worry.

Victoria lifted her hands. "I'm fine, I'm fine, just worried for Mama."

Louisa frowned at her, then turned to stare toward the door through which their mother had disappeared. "She seems no better."

"But she will be," Victoria insisted. "We've all seen to that."

"Mostly because of you," Meriel said. "Vic, you're not trapped in this house, are you?"

"Of course not."

"Then let's take a last walk to Willow Pond."

Victoria was relieved. She assumed Lord Thurlow was still in the house somewhere, and she did not want to see him. She might burst into tears in front of her sisters.

The Shelby gardens were not as extensive as those on the Banstead property, but they were as familiar as Victoria's own bedroom. She looked out over the grounds, letting bittersweet memories wash over her. She deliberately didn't look at the stables in the rear of the gardens. Her father had died there, and she needed no reminder of that.

Holding hands like children, the three of them wandered into the remotest corner of the garden, which had become even more overgrown in the last year without a gardener to tame it. They bent low under the hanging branches of the willow tree and found the little pond. No one had kept the fish stocked, no one had cleaned the creeping greenery that had spread across the water's surface, but there was still something magical about the place. With a high wall on one side, and trees and shrubbery everywhere else, the pond had made them feel that they were in the country, all alone. Roses of varying hues still grew in abundance, now wilder and more entangled than ever.

They'd told each other their deepest secrets here, had come out at night to escape the heat of midsummer, had hidden here when their father was angry with them. And they had always considered it so romantic, because their father had proposed to their mother right here, sitting on this very bench.

But now as an adult, Victoria saw her parents' marriage in the cold light of reality. And it had not been made of romance. Her own marriage was only a day old, and already it seemed to be following the pattern laid down by her own parents. She was still dwelling on the sadness of that when Meriel tugged on her hand.

"Is everything all right between you and Lord Thurlow?" her sister asked.

Victoria smiled. "Of course. Whyever would you ask such a thing?"

Louisa took her other hand. "Did everything . . ." Her voice died away, and she looked at Meriel with appeal.

"What she's trying to say," Meriel said forthrightly, "is was your wedding night . . . acceptable?"

Victoria sighed. She had known before coming here that her sisters would inquire. For the first time, Victoria felt that there were things she shouldn't confide in her sisters. The fact that Lord Thurlow had a mistress was something to be worked out between them privately. And she didn't want her sisters to worry more than they already were. She would discuss the wedding bargain, because it would make them go back to their lives feeling better about her situation.

"The wedding night was fine," Victoria said. "I asked Lord Thurlow for more time to get to know him. He agreed."

Louisa drew her breath in sharply. "You mean he didn't—you both didn't—"

"That's what she means," Meriel interrupted. "Not quite a true wife yet. Why would a man agree to such a thing?"

Louisa took Victoria's hand. "Meriel, I've never known you to be so cynical. Victoria's husband is treating her with kindness. What has happened to you since you left us?"

Meriel shook her head, looking toward the pond with a distracted expression. "You're right, I'm sorry. It is easier to see the worst in people, I guess."

Victoria's worry made her soften her voice. "Is it so terrible being a governess at the Ramsgate estate, Meriel?"

"No, no, really, it is tolerable. I am just not used to feeling so . . . helpless, so inconsequential."

"It is not inconsequential to see to the education

of a young boy," Louisa said. "Your calling is a noble one."

Meriel looked at her in shock, then began to laugh. "Oh, Louisa, how I've missed your optimism. You're right, I have to remember who I'm really helping." She turned to Victoria and took both her hands. "Forgive my pessimism, my dear. Your husband is being kind to you, which I'm certain is quite rare. He sounds like an honorable man."

David entered the dining room for dinner and found his wife waiting for him. She nodded graciously, and he gave her a short bow. Because of her—and her housekeeper—not a single complaint had greeted him when he'd walked through the front door. It was a refreshing, welcome change. One day married, and already things were running smoothly.

Things within the household anyway, he thought with a sigh.

As he seated himself at the head of the table, he found himself studying her now that she was wearing something other than black. Though he would have thought that color improved her complexion, she seemed pale. Had she already had an encounter with his father?

The ever-present notebook remained near her right hand, and he almost wanted to know why she felt it necessary to have it with her everywhere. But that personal a question could lead down paths he didn't want to go.

Victoria thanked the footman serving them, and the servant retreated to stand near the wall.

"That is a newly purchased gown you're wearing," David said.

"Yes, my lord."

"Surely you didn't have enough time to purchase a satisfactory amount of gowns."

Her polite expression faded. A compliment would have been the wiser choice.

"Not that it isn't a lovely gown on you, Victoria," he said.

"Thank you, my lord."

Of course she would realize that his praise was an afterthought. But thinking about her wardrobe made him realize that she would need to shop for more soon. The gown she wore today was suitable for his business acquaintances, but what if on her own—and with more money to spend—she chose garments that would make the directors' wives feel inferior?

"Victoria, tomorrow I am free after mid-morning. I shall accompany you to the dressmaker's."

Her eyes narrowed. "Surely that is too much trouble."

"No, I insist. It would give us the opportunity to be together."

At a dressmaker's shop? That excuse couldn't possibly make sense to her, but she only nodded her assent.

"My lord, your generosity is overwhelming," she said quietly.

"Generosity? But you're my wife. I promised you a wardrobe, and you shall have it. I hope you won't mind not having anything new for Bannaster's dinner."

She stopped eating. "Bannaster's dinner? Do we have an engagement?"

"Tomorrow evening."

"I heard about it at the Hutton luncheon, though not the exact date. If you don't mind, my lord, I'd like as much notice as possible when you've accepted an invitation."

He clenched his jaw, reminding himself that as his wife, she deserved more consideration. "I'll make sure my secretary discusses everything with you."

"You can't tell me yourself?"

"Of course."

"Thank you."

She lowered her gaze and continued eating, not even angry at his thoughtlessness. He realized that he liked spending time with her, that her conversation was never dull. But then again, hadn't he been enthralled by even the words she'd written in a book? Now he was able to regard her freely, and he found himself watching her lips. He'd kissed those lips last night, if only for the briefest moment. They'd been so soft, her breath so sweet. Like her disposition. Surely she knew that his family was not looked upon well, yet she didn't seem to judge him for it.

"My lord, forgive my mother for not joining us this evening," Victoria said. "She is feeling rather unsettled in a new house."

"I understand."

"Where is your father?"

"His illness often prevents him from leaving his room." David couldn't look too long into her eyes, knowing that his relief would show. Soon enough, she'd realize that the earl's absence made everything easier.

"How ill is he, my lord?"

"His heart is failing. He lost the use of his legs some time ago. He is not a well man, though doctors cannot tell us how much time he might have left. Don't be surprised if you don't see him all that much. He has his own nurse to see to his needs."

"But I am his daughter by marriage. I would enjoy getting to know him."

"Victoria, let me be honest. My father is unhappy with the decline in his health, and he has managed to make the household suffer for it."

"Oh surely—"

132

"He is the reason two housekeepers quit. He's not an easy man to get along with."

"I understand that, my lord, but I can't live in his house and not speak to him."

She moved food around on her plate for several minutes, but didn't eat it. David knew she was not finished with the subject, but before he could think of another one—even the weather—she spoke.

"Wilfred," she said to the footman, "that will be all for now."

David arched an eyebrow and waited.

"My lord, when you were pretending to be Tom, you told me you didn't have a father."

He stiffened. "As you just said, I was pretending."

"You could have given yourself a father—for instance, the butler—but you didn't."

He sighed. "Clearly it must be obvious to you that my father and I don't agree on much, Victoria. I disapprove of the way he's lived his life, and he disapproves of me."

Her eyes held an understanding that made him uncomfortable.

"My lord, if you remember anything about me, then you'll know that my father and I did not often agree with one another."

"He tried to force you to be what you weren't,"

David said. "But you don't need to draw comparisons between you and me, because there aren't any where our fathers are concerned. My father only cares about himself, the prime evidence being how he treats the servants. And when he is cruel to you, please don't take it personally."

"You don't think my father's motives were selfish?" she asked.

For only the second time, she allowed him to see anguish in her eyes, and he didn't know what to do, what she wanted from him.

"By the end," she continued, "he was a very selfish man. It is difficult when your own parent seems to disregard you. I tell myself that maybe I was only seeing my own side of our problems."

"Or maybe you were seeing the truth. You need to do what I did and just forget."

She stiffened. "Forget?"

"Yes. If you work at it hard enough, it eventually won't bother you anymore."

"But your father is right here, alive. How can you forget him? Why would you want to?"

His stomach clenched. "You try to forget his actions." *Or they pare away at your insides.* But he wasn't following his own advice. "Do you think the quail is too dry tonight?"

She put down her fork. "My lord, something happened today that I cannot forget."

"What did my father do?"

"It's something *you* did. I was walking by the library this morning, and since you did not close the door, I overheard some of your conversation."

He straightened in his chair and looked at her. "My conversation with Miss Lingard, the milliner?"

"Miss Lingard, your mistress." Her face was pale but determined.

In a low voice, he said, "I made no secret that I was with another woman before you, Victoria."

"But you told me it was over."

"And it is. I swore to you as your husband that I would honor you." And David had looked into Damaris's sad eyes and had not felt the need for a last night in her arms. Already Victoria held a power over him he had not anticipated.

"What I witnessed today is *honoring* me?" she asked.

"I'm not sure how long you stood there, but if you heard the whole conversation, Miss Lingard knows that my relationship with her is over."

Victoria took a deep breath. "You had a month to end it, and instead you *forgot*, and that poor woman was forced to come speak to you in your own home, risking her public reputation—or what is left of it."

"She owns shares in Southern Railway, which is

how we met. Our business together did not risk her reputation. Think of me what you will, Victoria, but I would not harm a woman in so callous a way."

"You don't think you harmed her?" she asked.

Her eyes were wide with disbelief. He didn't like that she was trying to make him feel guilty.

"Victoria—"

"You allowed the two of us to meet at a luncheon, when you had not officially told her your affair was through. You let me, your betrothed, converse with her unawares, making me look like the fool."

"But no one knew," he said, his anger beginning to thread through his voice.

"*She* knew. And now I know." Her disappointment was palpable. "How did you answer her question today?"

"What question?"

"She asked why you didn't marry her, a commoner just like me. I left the hall before I could hear your response."

"We did not suit," he said in a controlled voice.

"You were obviously suited in plenty of ways that I have not yet allowed you."

He stared at her, stunned. Was she threatening to leave him, have the wedding annulled before it had even begun? My God, he'd look like a complete fool. "Victoria," he said quietly, "what do you want from me?"

"Did you tell her that I was penniless, that you felt sorry for me? Is that what you've been telling everyone?"

Tears glittered in her eyes.

"I would never do that. We were friends."

"Do you hear yourself?" she whispered. " 'We *were* friends.' What are we now?"

"We are husband and wife—and it can be more than a friendship, if you'll give it time."

She stared at him, her shoulders bowed, her eyes sad. "Is that what you really want?"

"I wouldn't have married you otherwise. I admit, I've handled things badly. But I can make this better. Will you give me the chance?"

Her hesitation seemed to last forever. They were frozen, gazes trapped within each other, trying to read the truth by expression alone.

"Yes, my lord," she finally said. "I am your wife, and I do not take that lightly. I ask that you treat me with respect from now on."

"You have it," he said.

He watched her leave the room, her posture rigid, her face without emotion. When she was gone, he sat back in his chair and closed his eyes. He had almost ruined their marriage out of stupidity. He was a man who prided himself on thinking out every decision, but since Victoria had come back into his life, things seemed to happen spontaneously. And he wasn't handling them well.

*   *   *

Victoria found a bath already waiting for her, and she sank in gratefully. Every muscle in her back and shoulders ached as if she'd been beating rugs all day, instead of simply arguing with her husband.

She'd *argued* with her husband.

Only a year ago, she could never have imagined standing up to a man like that. But she'd done it because it had been necessary. She would not start out her marriage with secrets between them. She still didn't know if she could trust him, but at least he knew she was serious about trying. As far as she was concerned, his mistress was a thing of the past. He abhorred scandal enough to see to that.

But after their earlier discussion about the earl, she found it very sad that Lord Thurlow had no relationship at all with his father. She recognized herself in her husband, and it softened her toward him. She would have to do her best to see father and son reunited in the short time the earl had left. It was too late for her and her father, and she bitterly regretted that. She always would wonder if there was something she could have done to save him from the fate he chose for himself.

The water was growing cool, so she finished her bath quickly. Most likely she'd be going to bed alone, after their "discussion." Relief and disappointment mingled within her.

She was sitting before the hearth, her hair almost dry, when she heard the soft knock on the door between their rooms. She froze with her hand on the brush, then slowly set it down.

"Come in."

When he stepped inside, she realized they were both garbed just as they had been the previous night, dressing gowns belted in place. He watched her with a serious gaze as silence stretched out between them.

He sat down across from her, their knees almost brushing. Her throat went dry. As always, Victoria had no control over her skin; it heated into a blush that she knew could be seen by candlelight. She wanted to talk about everything, yet she didn't feel an apology was necessary. Yet how to make things right between them?

"My lord—"

"Victoria, we said everything that needed to be said. As I sit here looking at you, smelling you—"

She gasped at how sensuous that sounded.

"I find I'm not thinking of the daytime, of discussions and agreements and business. I'm only thinking of you and me alone together."

He leaned forward again, and this time their knees touched. He didn't move away, just put out his hand, palm up.

"Give me your hand, Victoria."

His voice was deep and hoarse, and made her

think of movement in the darkness, things better felt than said. She gave him her hand, and this time he cupped it in both of his.

"Kiss me, Victoria," he whispered.

Her gaze flew to his in surprise. Still holding her hand, he leaned back in his chair. Her arm was forced to straighten between them. She understood that he was challenging her, and she realized that she wanted to meet that challenge. She pulled on his hands, but he remained where he was, a lazy smile tugging one corner of his lips. He looked so . . . intriguing.

Slowly, she rose and leaned over him, bracing her free hand on the arm of his chair. His head was tilted back, and they stared at each other as if they shared a silent contest of wills. And to her shock, she didn't mind that he was winning this one.

There was something different about being above him, seeing him below her. It made her feel . . . powerful, in control, something she'd rarely felt in her day-to-day existence. But here, in the candlelit dark, he was letting her experience it in a very intimate way.

She lowered herself ever nearer to him, her gaze sliding to his mouth. Their lips touched, and her uncertainty began. What was she supposed to do—remain still?

Then his fingers began to slowly caress her hand, his thumbs brushing the back of her palm.

Her eyes slid closed. She never would have imagined that a man touching her hand could make her feel . . . fluttery, shaky, so very aware of their skin meeting.

Her attention was torn between the gentle pressure of his mouth and the movement of his hands. As she caught her breath at the sensation, her lips parted. His did the same, catching the fullness of her lower lip very gently between his. She shuddered at the exquisite rush of pleasure, so very new.

Her worries about her desirability faded. His questing fingers slid up her wrist, beneath the cuff of her nightdress. He rubbed her there, gently, and her soft gasp echoed in his mouth.

He broke the kiss. "Does that feel good?" he asked in a low, rumbling voice.

Straightening, she found her wits. "Yes."

"Then I'll leave you with that."

He released her and rose to his feet, so tall and near her that she wanted to step back, but wouldn't. His clothing brushed her body, making her tremble with a feeling of want. She wanted him to touch her, wanted him to kiss her. As he looked down into her face, she could tell he knew it.

"Good night, Victoria."

"Good night."

And then he was gone, and she was left to slump bonelessly in her chair, disappointed in his absence, but relieved she would not have to discover tonight just how much he could control her with a touch. Was that his true purpose, to show her who was in charge in their relationship, after she had challenged him at dinner?

Chapter 8

The next morning, Victoria persuaded her mother to leave her room. They were to meet Mrs. Wayneflete in the kitchen, and then go next door together to say their farewells to Louisa and Meriel. As they circled the stairs above the entrance hall, Victoria looked down and noticed that there was a silver tray on a table bearing the day's post.

"Just a moment," she said, hurrying down the stairs in curiosity.

She lifted an envelope or two, all of which were of course addressed to the earl or his son. Many of them looked written in a woman's flowing hand.

Were these invitations? Several bore a wax seal with an insignia proclaiming them from society's highest families.

Victoria felt her mouth go dry. These were vastly different parties from the ones Lord Thurlow had planned with the railway directors.

"Those aren't for you," said a cold voice.

Victoria gave a little start, sending the stack of invitations to the floor. She heard her mother gasp and come quickly down the stairs. From her knees, Victoria glanced up. The notorious Earl of Banstead sat in his wheelchair near the front windows in the library, which looked out over the street he seldom visited. His valet stood against the wall.

Lord Banstead watched her, and she recognized something of his son in those expressionless eyes. With Lord Thurlow, she sensed polite attention—at least when he chose to see her!—but with Lord Banstead, there was a bitterness that colored the edges of what he'd just said.

Before she could respond, Lord Banstead glanced with disapproval at her mother, who now hovered protectively at her side. Victoria rose to her feet and took Mama's arm.

She looked down at the invitations she was still holding, wishing this had happened after they'd at least been formally introduced.

"My lord, I know this mail belongs to you and your son."

"Then why are you touching it?"

"Because I saw several addressed in a woman's hand."

"And why should that concern you? You can hardly accuse him of an affair two days after your marriage."

"An affair?" she repeated in a quiet, stunned voice. Good Lord, did even his father know about his mistress? "I would never make accusations, my lord." She didn't need to.

The valet was looking pointedly at the floor, and Victoria inwardly winced that a servant had to overhear such a personal disagreement.

"Then why do you care who corresponds with him?" the earl demanded.

How could she tell him that she was still frightened by simple party invitations, that the thought of attempting to dance at a ball made her feel dizzy inside?

"I had assumed that one of my roles as his wife would be to look after the social aspects of our marriage. I thought the letters were party invitations."

"They may very well be, but he never attends anymore. If you married him for the rise in social class, you'll be vastly disappointed," he added with satisfaction.

She could not be angry with Lord Banstead—she'd married his son for something far worse: the safety bought by his money. She had no right to feel slighted because the earl didn't like her. Yet she couldn't think of a way to change his attitude.

Instead she let herself think about Lord Thurlow. So his father didn't know he'd begun to socialize with commoners. Yet Lord Thurlow never attended the events of the *ton*? She couldn't be surprised, because of the rumors of scandal attached to his family name. She imagined it was easier for Lord Thurlow to deal with wealthy railway directors, who cared more about his money than any gossip. No wonder he hadn't found a bride among the *ton*. His relationship with his own class seemed so very mysterious. Yet she still didn't feel comfortable asking him to explain everything. She sensed he was far too proud.

"My lord, a rise in social class is not the reason I married your son," Victoria said. "And since you are aware of my background, you'll know that society is nothing I'm accustomed to. I can't miss what I have never known." And she admitted to herself a feeling of relief that she would not have to find out. If Lord Thurlow did not wish to socialize with the *ton*, she was just fine with that.

"So you say," the earl said, glancing over his shoulder at his valet. The man came forward to slowly push the wheelchair toward her.

She held her ground. Her mother was staring intently at the earl, a frown spreading across her face. Victoria could not have Mama saying something they'd both regret.

"My lord, I will do my best to be the kind of wife your son needs."

The slow roll of the chair brought him past them.

"That will never be possible," he said coldly.

The valet pushed the earl down the corridor, through his bedroom door, and closed it behind him.

"What a terrible man, to speak to you in such an abhorrent manner!" her mother said.

"I know. He's old and sick. It will take him time to-to—"

"You are too kind, Victoria." Her mother searched her eyes. "That is an accomplishment I take pride in."

Victoria blinked back tears of gratitude. "Come, Mama, let's go see off Louisa and Meriel."

When David returned at mid-morning, he found Victoria waiting in the drawing room. She was alone, for which he was grateful. He thought that it might be easier to steer her wardrobe choices without her mother in attendance.

She stood up when she saw him, her expression polite but reserved. "I am ready, my lord."

She looked so prim and proper, garbed well but not looking indecently wealthy.

And she was his. For the first time he truly looked at her and realized that someone finally belonged to him. He felt rather bewildered at such emotions, and decided it was only because he was physically frustrated by the slow pace of their intimacy.

Or maybe he was still feeling guilty that he'd allowed his mistress in his home, something he'd never done before.

He sighed. "I hope you do not feel like I'm intruding on you."

She blinked her eyes. "Why . . . no, my lord. I promise I will not burst into noisy tears if you look at me crossly."

He held back a grin. He liked her spirit—but then again, hadn't he always?

At the dressmaker's shop on Bond Street, David descended first then helped Victoria down. Inside, several customers were being waited on by the dressmaker and her assistant. Glass cabinets displayed lace and ribbons and garters. Since he was the only gentleman present, he found himself being watched and giggled at by two young ladies, obviously sisters by their resemblance. Then their mother turned around at their behavior and saw him.

He knew the moment she recognized him.

"Lord Thurlow, how good to see you again," she said, curtsying, followed quickly by identical curtsies from her daughters. The three were as colorful as peacocks, done up in pink, blue, and yellow satin.

"Lady Augusta, it is a pleasure," he said, bowing. He turned to the daughters. "Lady Alice, Lady Athelina."

Their three identical gazes bore in on Victoria.

"And this must be your new bride," Lady Augusta said, oozing kindness and an underlying fascination.

"May I present my wife, Lady Thurlow. This is Lady Augusta Clifford, and her daughters Lady Alice and Lady Athelina."

They all curtsied together, and Victoria performed hers with simple grace.

"How clever of you to surprise us all with your . . . marriage," Lady Augusta said. "Never quite gave the other ladies a chance, you young rascal."

He understood that for the snide insult it was.

David smiled. "One's heart shall always lead in the right direction, Lady Augusta."

Victoria watched the scene unfold with a morbid fascination, even as she was trying hard to think of something to say. *One's heart?*

"The good of the family should also be a concern in marriage decisions," Lady Augusta said.

And Victoria knew that Her Ladyship was implying that *this* marriage was not good for the Banstead family. *It was good for my own family*, Victoria thought, but she was hardly going to say that. Everyone must already know that she brought nothing to the marriage. Even the earl himself was quick to point that out.

Her husband watched the lady and her daughters, saying nothing, leaving that rude statement just hanging there uncomfortably.

Lady Augusta was the first to back down, and she turned to Victoria with a sweet smile. "Lady Thurlow, how lucky you are to have a husband who takes an interest in your clothing. Or is it that you can't be separated so early in your marriage?"

"I am fortunate, my lady," she said. "I tried to tell Lord Thurlow that he did not have to accompany me today—"

She felt her husband's arm slide about her waist and she kept her smile frozen on her face, as if this happened all the time. But even Lady Augusta looked surprised at such an intimate gesture.

"And I told my wife," he interrupted smoothly, "that to be with her is the highlight of my day."

Oh, now he was *lying* to people, Victoria thought worriedly. Why? He was only reinforcing to Victoria that appearances mattered more than the truth. And if she didn't live up to the necessary "appearance," what would happen? "Appearances" would matter little if he discovered the truth about her father's death.

Lady Augusta looked her up and down, still smiling. "Then, Lady Thurlow, you should have your husband escort you to the milliner's just down the block. You may tell the proprietress that I sent you."

Lord Thurlow released her.

Victoria assumed that Lady Augusta was only insulting her choice of bonnet, but any mention of a milliner reminded her of Miss Lingard. Was Victoria actually jealous of something that had happened before she'd married Lord Thurlow? What did that say about her feelings for him?

"Thank you for taking such an interest in me, my lady," she said, wishing she could let her sarcasm show.

The older woman nodded. "A good day to you, Lord Thurlow. And do consider attending my breakfast on Saturday, Lady Thurlow. You would be the center of attention as the new bride. Come along, girls."

Victoria sighed as she watched them leave the shop, understanding exactly why she'd attract attention at such an event.

"And she wonders why I never attend," Lord Thurlow said.

Victoria looked at him, and knew this was something they would need to discuss in private.

Madame Dupuy approached them, obviously salivating at the thought of Lord Thurlow's money.

And Victoria's obvious lack of a sterling wardrobe.

They were ushered into the next room, where there were several chairs gathered around a table piled with sketches. For the next hour, Victoria sat beside her husband as the dressmaker showed her sketches of gowns and discussed the various fabrics. She had expected Lord Thurlow to be bored, but he was obviously following the discussion quite closely. Since he was the one being so generous, she could not refuse him one or two small requests, even when she thought the colors would be too flamboyant on so plain a woman as herself.

Madame Dupuy stood up, a stack of sketches in her hand. "Lady Thurlow, I do have several lovely gowns in your size already pieced together, if you would like these sooner."

"I have enough for now, madame," Victoria said, rising to her feet.

Lord Thurlow didn't move, and both women looked down at him. "You should try them on," he said.

Was that hesitation she heard in his voice?

Victoria stared at him in surprise. "Now?"

He shrugged. "Why not? You might like them."

But he seemed suddenly uncomfortable, as if he now regretted the idea. Why was that?

Lord Thurlow wasn't meeting her eyes. She found herself far too curious than could be good for her.

"Very well, Madame Dupuy," Victoria said slowly, studying her husband.

The dressmaker soon returned with an armful of gowns and shooed Victoria behind the changing screen. Victoria stood still as the woman helped unhook her gown and replaced it with one only basted together. It felt loose in some places, tight in others.

The dressmaker turned her toward the standing mirror and Victoria tried to look at herself objectively. She saw a blushing woman, but she realized that it was not out of embarrassment.

She was actually . . . excited to be seen in new garments by Lord Thurlow. He would be looking at her body—and she liked the thought.

Then she was being led out from behind the screen. She stood still as Lord Thurlow's gaze dwelled on every part of her. Under that pale blue stare, she'd once felt . . . frosted with cold, but instead a warmth started from her chest, where he stared the most, and spread outward at a slow languorous pace. She'd spent so much of her life feeling invisible around men. But now her husband wasn't looking past her, or thinking ahead with distraction to his next appointment. His attention was focused all on her.

And she liked it.

She felt attractive, even . . . sensual. Though she'd always been considered plump, it was definitely an asset to fill out the dress's bodice.

Someone bolder seemed to take over her tongue.

"Madame Dupuy, this is a ball gown," Victoria said. "Will the neckline do?"

Her husband's startled eyes met hers, then focused back where she wanted them.

And that's all she'd meant to accomplish, but Madame said, "Ah, I had forgotten. The necklines are lower this season."

Shocked, Victoria watched as the dressmaker stepped in front of her, folded down the bodice, and pinned it in place, looking amused as she stepped aside. The air that swirled from her movement felt cool against the tops of Victoria's breasts. She was more exposed that she'd ever been.

And her husband couldn't stop looking at her.

Maybe "plump" wasn't such a bad thing to be.

Lord Thurlow finally shifted in his chair and looked away.

Madame Dupuy began to chuckle. "Ah, newlyweds. And we yet have several gowns to try on. This one has your approval, *oui*, my lord?"

"*Oui*, madame," he said, glancing once more at Victoria with a gaze so hot she felt burned.

Victoria tried on four more gowns, all of which

met with Lord Thurlow's approval, though now he betrayed a polite impatience to leave. Victoria had to work hard to withhold a grin. She made arrangements to have these last gowns delivered within the week, and the rest would be sent when they were ready.

David barely listened to the dressmaker's last instructions, so consumed was he with the need to leave. He was feeling overly warm, almost smothered in the shop's confined quarters. To make matters worse, they had to thread through new customers as they headed for the street, and he stood out as the only man there.

Whatever had possessed him to come? Victoria probably would have spent much less of his money, and done fine without him. He couldn't fault her sense of style at all. But it was so hard to trust anyone, when everything concerned with his railway plans had to be perfect.

After he got into the carriage beside his wife, he tried not to study her so obviously, but he found that she wouldn't leave his thoughts. There was such a calmness about Victoria, a feeling of capability. He knew that she was the one who had kept her family together in the trying times of the last year.

Who had taken care of her?

He had plenty of money to spend on his wife. Had anyone ever done so? Hell, she'd obeyed him and gone to the dressmaker, but she had never even looked at the ribbons on display. He would talk to his steward about her pin money.

He inhaled a hint of perfume, a warmth of woman, and just like that he forgot the rest of the day's plans. He looked down at her hands loosely clasped together, and wondered what she would do if he took her hand by daylight instead of waiting for the night.

She tilted her head and looked up at him, giving him a glimpse of her magnificent eyes.

"So how do you know so much about the latest fashions, my lord?" she asked.

He found himself wanting to smile down at her. There was strand of hair across her forehead that needed brushing back. Yet he resisted. "I will admit that it has been a while since I studied them."

"You do have another chance. We could accept Lady Augusta's invitation to breakfast."

"You already know my answer to that," he said dryly.

"My lord, surely as a member of Parliament, you have to attend certain social functions."

"It is not even worth subjecting ourselves to people like her."

"So it is not just Lady Augusta?"

He frowned down at her. "What do you mean?"

"I saw the stack of invitations, and your father told me that you never attend any of the *ton*'s events."

"So my father decided to leave his room to harass you, did he?"

"It is his home. He can go anywhere he pleases. But you are attempting to distract me by using your father."

"If I was attempting to distract you," he said in a low voice, "you would notice."

They stared into each other's eyes. Hers were the deepest color of violets, reminding him of the scent of flowers about her. He glimpsed bravery and determination in her. He could tell that she wanted him to talk to her as he used to. But he didn't want someone knowing such details about him. Sharing personal feelings left one vulnerable, and he wasn't that trusting boy anymore.

"My lord, we were discussing your social engagements." Her voice was almost a whisper.

And he only wanted to think about kissing her again. Instead he turned away and flicked the reins. "I don't need worrying over, Victoria," he said mildly.

At luncheon with her husband and mother, Victoria watched Lord Thurlow eat, and wondered about their conversation that morning. She admitted to herself that she wanted to know him again, to understand him. She knew the taint on his family name bothered him, but he had withdrawn from society rather than confront it. And since she didn't know what the scandal was, she didn't know what to do to help.

And he needed her help.

"Mama, I am so thankful you joined us today," Victoria said. "I miss you when you take so many meals in your room."

"You are newly married, my dear," Mama said, not looking at the viscount. "You don't need your mother intruding."

To Victoria's surprise, Lord Thurlow looked up at them. "Mrs. Shelby, I am seldom able to be home for luncheon. I'm sure Victoria would appreciate your company."

Her mother leaned over her plate, but her soft words could be heard clearly. "If you want my daughter to be at ease, then perhaps you should speak to your father."

Victoria coughed and took a gulp of her wine, which only made her cough more. The two footmen retreated from the room and shut the door behind them.

Lord Thurlow carefully set down his fork and gave her mother all his attention. "What did he say to Victoria?"

"It was nothing," Victoria said quickly.

"He insulted my daughter," her mother went on with calm deliberation.

Victoria looked between them, then focused on Lord Thurlow, whose face briefly showed anger, before he trapped it beneath the polite mask he wore. That small blaze of emotion robbed her of speech, left her wondering what he hid from her. As a child he'd hid behind the fiction of Tom, and now she was beginning to think he had mastered too well the art of deception.

Lord Thurlow turned to Victoria. "What did my father do?"

"Truly, my lord, he doesn't yet know me."

"All the more reason for him to be civil."

Victoria could only bite her lip, uncertain if she should step between her husband and his father.

But her mother, once so bold, seemed to be trying to regain her former self. "My lord, he insulted my daughter, as if glancing through the day's mail was not her right as mistress of the household."

Oh heavens, Victoria thought, please let her not mention the earl's words about Lord Thurlow having an affair.

But her mother only finished with, "And he accused her of marrying to rise in social status, as if it were a sin, instead of something that most young girls should do for the good of their family."

"Mama, please stop this. We all know exactly why I married Lord Thurlow."

He sighed. "Ladies, allow me to apologize for my father. Illness cannot absolve his behavior."

Hadn't Victoria hoped to bring harmony between father and son? She would have to make clear to her mother that she didn't need defending.

Lord Thurlow carefully set down his napkin and rose to his feet. "Victoria, I have several things to take care of in my study. Have a good afternoon."

Victoria stared after him, then looked back at her mother, who calmly continued eating with an improved appetite.

"Mama, you know Lord Thurlow and his father are at odds. You did not need to tell him about our confrontation with the earl. You drove him away from his own dinner table."

"You need to be protected, my dear, and I am grateful to be able to do it."

Victoria felt a chill as she remembered the last several years. "But Mama—"

"I promise you it will be all right, Victoria. He'll learn to protect you, too. Just wait and see."

Chapter 9

David tried to concentrate on the letter he was writing to the secretary of foreign affairs, but he was interrupted by the door swinging open unannounced.

Nurse Carter, a tall, big-boned woman, pushed his father's wheelchair into the room, and couldn't meet David's gaze.

David sat back in his chair and tried to size up his father's mood. The earl wore an air of satisfaction that was confusing.

"Father, once again you didn't have luncheon with us. Rather rude of you, wasn't it?"

The earl glanced over his shoulder. "Nurse

Carter, you may leave us. Wait outside the door. I'll call for you."

When they were alone, the earl spent a moment studying David, as if he were waiting for something. David remained silent, much as he'd like to tell the earl what he thought of his treatment of Victoria. That would only make the old man's hostility worse.

Confronting Lady Augusta had made David realize that now Victoria would be paying for his father's sins, too, and that wasn't fair.

"I imagine the girl came running to tell you what transpired between us," the earl said.

David smiled without amusement. "Victoria is too good-natured for that. It was her mother who did the correct thing by telling me about your insulting behavior."

"So the old battle-ax has some spirit. I've seen her skulking about the house. Got exactly what she wanted, didn't she. A countess for a daughter."

"A viscountess," David said.

"Not for long, eh? Soon she'll have it all."

"Stop it." David went to the window and stared out at the gardens, his hands clenched behind his back, looking for a measure of peace he usually never found with his father. "Every time we have an argument, you bring up your eventual death to wield against me. It never works."

"Perhaps not, but it makes me feel better," the

earl said, his voice betraying an exhaustion he seldom showed anyone.

David turned to face him. "Why did you come to talk about this? I made apologies for you. Now you can do your part and leave Victoria alone."

"If I insulted her, then at least you now know how I felt whenever you insulted my Colette."

David stiffened, and his growing anger melted into the icy coldness that always lived within his heart. "I never insulted your mistress."

"Not directly, but she knew how you felt. She cried about it. And now she's dead, and you can't apologize. You couldn't even come to console me at her funeral."

Closing his eyes, David pinched the bridge of his nose between his fingers. He didn't want to relive the months after his mother's death, when his father had found a mistress and moved the crude woman right into the house, for all the *ton* to gawk at.

David kept his voice even. "If you can't be civil to Victoria, then don't leave your room when she's about."

His father stared at him, a bitter smile tilting the corner of his mouth. "Is she under your skin already? That was quick. Not wise to let a woman do that to you, boy. They just break your heart."

"As if you speak from experience," David scoffed.

He thought his father winced, but he didn't want to believe it.

"Just do your duty and get me a grandchild," the old man said.

"You're making damn sure Victoria won't ever let our child near you."

His father froze, his glance wintry. "Is that a threat, David?"

"No, just a prediction."

"The girl can't already be carrying a child, is she? Is that why you married such a plain thing?"

David thought of Victoria pregnant with his child, and something deep inside him went cold. He stalked to the door. With his hand on the knob, he said over his shoulder, "Unlike you, I controlled myself."

He didn't wait to hear the reply, just opened the door and asked for Nurse Carter.

When his father had gone, David paced his study. His father had hurt Victoria—but so had he.

He hadn't planned on hurting her. Yet he'd allowed his mistress into the house yesterday.

His father had brought home a mistress, too.

David felt disturbed to even consider that what had happened with Damaris and Victoria was in any way like his father bringing Colette to live with them.

Yet if anyone but Victoria had discovered Damaris in his home, it could easily have been a terrible scandal. How close had he come to being the center of controversy, instead of just the innocent son?

On the carriage ride to the Bannaster home, Victoria tried to quell her nervousness. She'd had luncheon with some of these people, but that didn't make her feel better. Lord Thurlow had told her there would be eleven other couples—twenty-two people! Victoria assumed that Miss Lingard wouldn't be there, because she wasn't a railway director.

Victoria was still so bothered by the fact that her husband might run into his former mistress for business reasons!

The Bannaster town house was larger than even Lord Thurlow's home, and Victoria knew that Mr. Bannaster must have very successful investments to be able to afford it. The drawing room they were shown to was large enough for them to dance in, but instead a dozen couples mingled between groupings of furniture scattered through the room beneath frescoed ceilings.

After meeting the Bannasters, they were greeted by the Huttons, their hosts from the luncheon, and soon Lord Thurlow went off with Mr. Hutton, leaving Victoria with his wife.

Mrs. Hutton introduced her to other wives, and Victoria found herself in the middle of a friendly group. Her fears that her old shy ways would surface came to naught, and she started to enjoy herself. When needlework became a topic, she even had a lot to say.

During a lull in the conversation, their hostess, Mrs. Bannaster, turned the attention to Victoria, speaking with the faintest accent of a poorer section of London.

"Lady Thurlow, I don't know if ye remember, but we met many years ago."

Victoria studied the older woman. "I'm sorry, I don't."

"You were much younger, closer to my daughters' ages than mine. But I wanted to tell ye how impressed I am with how ye've grown into a lovely young woman."

Victoria glanced across the room at her husband, knowing what they all must think about her marrying into the nobility.

"No, my lady, you misunderstand me," Mrs. Bannaster said. "I remember ye as a very shy girl who seemed frightened to converse with women, let alone men."

Victoria blushed.

Mrs. Bannaster put her hand on Victoria's arm. "Please do not be embarrassed. You are to be commended on how ye conquered your weaknesses. One of my daughters is very shy. I will hold ye up as an inspiration for her."

"Mrs. Bannaster, please, I don't feel like anyone's inspiration," Victoria said. "You're all being very kind to me, but as you all know, life is what matures us. And having to face situations we never thought we could."

They looked at her with such kindness. Of course they all knew that her father had died leaving the family nothing. But they didn't seem to judge her for it, and she was grateful. She knew that wouldn't happen with the *ton*.

"And how are your sisters?" Mrs. Wilton asked.

She was much closer to Victoria's age, and even looked a bit familiar.

"I knew Louisa well," Mrs. Wilton continued. "She is a sweet young woman."

"Thank you," Victoria said.

She explained about the positions her sisters had taken, expecting to experience everyone's pity, but once again these women surprised her, showing genuine interest in her sisters' lives. Why had it taken so long for Victoria to realize that these women had so many things in common with her? Some must have started under mean circumstances before their husbands rose to power with their successful investments. Perhaps Lord Thurlow liked being with the husbands for the same reasons. They were hardworking people who knew where they'd come from, and looked down on no one in the same position.

Thinking about her husband made her look through the crowd for him. He wasn't difficult to find, being the tallest man in the room. He'd spend several minutes with a group of men, then approach the next group. She'd never noticed how . . . graceful he was (if you could call a man that), how every muscle moved with precision and purpose. He should be awkward or clumsy, but instead . . . instead she watched him walk and felt all strange inside.

Her cheeks grew warm, as she remembered that she was the one he'd come home with tonight.

Mrs. Wilton drew closer to take Victoria's elbow. "You know, my lady, my husband, Mr. Wilton, enjoys working with Lord Thurlow. It's hard to believe your husband comes from such a loftier family than any of ours. It's such a shame."

Victoria frowned. "I don't understand."

"It's such a shame that his own people won't have anything to do with him."

Victoria felt chilled as she looked around at the circle of women. Mrs. Bannaster gave her a sympathetic look, but there were one or two women whom Victoria had not been introduced to yet, who exchanged satisfied expressions. Though the majority liked Lord Thurlow, there were always people who enjoyed seeing the mighty fall.

Victoria felt the need to defend him. "That's not true, Mrs. Wilton. My husband receives invitations every day. But he chooses the events he enjoys, like this lovely party of Mrs. Bannaster's."

Their hostess beamed. "That's sweet of ye, my dear, but we all know our husbands are meeting for business tonight as well. After dinner, we'll be without them for several hours at least. Things are coming to a head with the Southern Railway."

All the other women nodded their agreement, some showing excitement, others nervousness. And Victoria remembered once more how it felt to be on the outside—because her husband had confided nothing to her.

Mrs. Bannaster sighed. "The end is near, ladies—or should we say the beginning. Lady Thurlow, it was wonderful of your husband to offer the use of Banstead House for the last meeting. I'm sure ye'll make the celebration a memorable event."

Victoria smiled and nodded, and used every bit of her willpower to hold back the tears that stung her eyes. "Excuse me, ladies, I need to speak to Lord Thurlow."

"Ah, newlyweds," Mrs. Wilton said with a giggle.

Hadn't the dressmaker said the same thing? But it didn't mean anything in Victoria's marriage. She was denying her Lord Thurlow his legal rights as a husband—and he was denying her a real place in his life.

Victoria crossed the drawing room, nodding and smiling appropriately as she passed several people. Lord Thurlow was talking with two other men, so she waited where he could see her. When she finally got her husband's attention, he smiled at her with an excitement she'd never seen before. But she knew it wasn't about her—it was this Southern Railway business.

Was she actually jealous of an investment now?

"My lord, might I speak with you in private?"

"Of course."

He gave their apologies to the other men, and then he took her arm.

"Is something wrong?" he asked.

But he wasn't looking at her as he spoke. His gaze was for the railway directors, and the success of whatever event this actually was.

She sighed. "Is there a place we can be alone for a few minutes?"

Now she had his attention. He watched her with the beginnings of a concerned frown.

"Of course. I know where the library is."

He escorted her from the room, and soon the noise of two dozen people speaking at once faded away. The library was at the end of the corridor, and when they were inside, he closed the door and leaned back against it.

"What's wrong, Victoria?"

She looked about her at the thousands of books

lining the walls from floor to ceiling. She didn't know where to start, how to make him understand her position without angering him.

But she was already angry enough for both of them.

She decided to be direct. "I just learned we're to host a party for your railway directors."

He nodded. "It was planned long before our engagement. My steward has everything under control."

"But I will be your hostess. That was one of the reasons you married me. Am I correct?"

"That is true for any wife, Victoria. You're saying I should have remembered to tell you about the dinner party."

"Yes. Usually a wife does the planning, not the steward. I would have enjoyed helping you with something I actually know how to do."

He linked his hands behind his back. "That never happened in my household, since my mother was so ill."

Her anger slipped away. "I'm sorry. I didn't realize—"

"I don't mean to keep putting you in these positions," he said.

His eyes were sincere as they stared down at her. They made her want to believe everything he said. She would gladly melt into his embrace—

And then he'd get away with not explaining the

rest. She took a step back, and his eyes widened. Did he know how easily his face swayed a woman?

"I have more questions, my lord. All of these women know about the Southern Railway except me. I thought it was just an investment of yours, but that can't be true."

"It started that way, yes," he said, beginning to pace back and forth in front of her. "But I discovered that I enjoyed the railway business, for the reasons I gave you when I first took you to the office."

"It's England's future; I understand that. But why wasn't investing enough for you?"

"Because when I had the majority shares, I thought I could make more of it. There are dozens of railways throughout England, all of them running their own little line with a different gauge track, their own little kingdoms. You haven't ridden a train, so you don't understand. Often, when you reach a town, you have to leave one train, cross town by carriage, and board another train from a different railway company. The time lost is ridiculous."

"But surely the train saves so much time as it is."

"Yes, but it could be more efficient, especially when transporting goods. So I'm the unofficial chairman and my railway board has come up with a bold plan. We're going to buy three other railways in the south of England and consolidate them. All the same gauge track, and every line will be accessible without leaving the train."

"That's a sound plan," she said, although inside she grew more and more worried about the extent of a peer's involvement in a company. "But why the secrecy? I understand how you can't allow your peers to know that you're involved in commerce. It would be a scandal. Is that all it is?"

"Only partly," he said, coming to a stop in front of her. "There's another man, Mr. Norton, owner of Channel Railway. He's been talking to one of the companies I want to buy out. The directors and I already have some shares in each of our targets, but not yet enough. We don't want him to know what we're doing, or we'll risk him trying to buy the other companies before we can. If these railways know he's interested, the price could rise too high."

"It sounds risky," she said.

He shrugged. "I've invested a lot of capital, but nothing I can't do without. My estates are bringing in a sizable rent these days."

But that wasn't what she meant. He risked his future among the *ton* if all this got out. She'd thought his work in Parliament was important to him. But when his father died and he moved to the House of Lords, how could he deal with the other peers if they didn't consider him a gentleman because of his business dealings?

But she was only his wife; it wasn't her place to tell him what he must already know.

It was only her place to worry.

"Do you understand, Victoria?" he asked.

She nodded. What else could she do?

He smiled. "You're the perfect wife," he said, tucking her hand into his arm as he led her back to the drawing room.

The perfect wife?

As he left her to join his fellow directors, she thought about that phrase. Soon it came to her—she'd once written to him in their journal and described what she thought would be his Perfect Wife.

And at the time, she'd assumed it would never be she. She'd thought his perfect wife would be as brave and adventurous as he used to be—as he still was. He was moving into industrialization like an explorer, the first of his kind to try something new.

And all she could do was worry. What a perfect wife.

The coachman pulled up before Banstead House long after midnight. David had enjoyed the ride, because Victoria had fallen asleep against his shoulder. The warm weight of her made him think of more pleasant intimacies ahead of them. When he escorted her to her bedroom, she looked so drowsy that he wondered if he should not disturb her any more that night.

But he was selfish. Every time he'd caught a glimpse of her from across the room at the dinner party, he'd thought of being alone with her again. He'd thought of that dress he'd watched her try on, and the way it had made her breasts look like the most touchable, tasty—

David went to his own room before he swept her into his arms. His valet had turned down the bed and left candles lit. But the man had long since retired for the night, knowing that David preferred to bathe in the morning and to prepare for bed alone.

Especially when he might not be sleeping immediately.

He stared at the door connecting his room to Victoria's, yanking off his cravat and dropping his coat onto a chair. He was normally fastidious about his clothing, but tonight he felt . . . restless.

Off came his waistcoat, and he tossed it into a corner, feeling some satisfaction.

He stared at her closed door, knowing that due to his own wedding night suggestion, Victoria was just as closed off from him.

But he wanted to make her groan and know that it was all because of him. He wanted her as his real wife, so there would be no more uncertainty between them. Surely then she'd know she could trust him.

But he hadn't done a good job of proving that so far.

He meant well—he just kept forgetting to inform her of things. He knew he wasn't deliberately hurting her, but the look in her eyes tonight, when she'd realized that every other woman there but her knew the railway's plans . . .

Leaving on his trousers, he drew his dressing gown over his bare chest. He leaned against Victoria's door and heard the cascade of water. Unbidden came a vision of her sunk in her bath, her nude body glistening, her hair tumbling down around her wet, dimpled shoulders. He would offer to scrub her back, then slide his hands around the front of her and—

He pulled back from the door and shook his head to clear these foolish thoughts. What was he, a boy waiting for his first woman? At the washstand, he splashed cool water onto his face.

Eventually he knocked on her door. There was absolute silence for several seconds.

"Just a moment," she called in a breathless voice.

He wondered at his own impatience—it was not as if he was going to see even one bare limb. And maybe she was still angry with him. But he couldn't ignore her.

"Come in, my lord."

He entered her room, and immediately that peculiar scent wafted over him—the smell of jasmine soap from the hip bath cooling near the fire, the warmth from the grate, and finally the scent of Victoria herself, so unusual he couldn't place it.

Tonight she stood near the hearth, always as far away from the bed as she could get. She wore the same dressing gown, belted at her waist. It showed off her well-curved figure as it flowed in cream silken lines over her hips. Above the sash, the silk expanded over her breasts, meeting again at her throat. He could see her pulse fluttering just above the neckline. His gaze traveled up, to where she moistened her lips. The dart of her tongue made him harder, and he hadn't thought that possible. Her lashes were lowered demurely, but she sneaked a glance at him with eyes that glowed violet in the low light. For a moment he froze, entranced by their shine.

How would she look at him if he pressed for more tonight, if he laid her down on that big bed and—

But then he'd be disappointing her again, breaking their agreement.

She frowned at him, her blond brows losing that delicate arch. Since when had this fascination with her appearance crept over him?

"My lord?" she murmured uncertainly. "Shall I send for a glass of wine? Or brandy?"

He shook his head as he touched the end of the

sash falling from her waist. She bit her lip, a familiar gesture that always riveted his attention on her full mouth. He tugged harder than he meant to, not realizing the sash was knotted. She stumbled toward him and put a hand on his chest to catch herself. Without thinking, he lowered his head until he could inhale the damp, fragrant scent of her hair. He put his hand over hers and held it to his chest—until he realized what he betrayed by his pounding heart.

He let her go and she stepped back, her face awash in its usual pink glow.

"Forgive me, my lord, I wasn't expecting—"

He guided her hands away from her waist and plucked at the knot himself. The backs of his fingers brushed her stomach, and he felt the catch in her breathing, saw the way she kept her face averted. Then the sash dropped away, and the folds of the dressing gown fell straight from the curves of her breasts. If only she weren't wearing anything underneath, but he knew better.

He reached up to undo the single clasp at her throat, and she finally met his gaze. She was as still as a deer, those eyes shining at him—but not with trust.

The clasp came free and he spread the dressing gown wide, letting it fall back from her shoulders. It slid off her arms to pool on the floor. Of course, she was wearing long sleeves, and she was covered from her toes to her neck, but the fabric was so sheer that he could see her nipples, and watch them pucker from just his look. She was breathing so quickly that everything trembled.

Chapter 10

Victoria stood trapped beneath her husband's stare, feeling naked though she wore her nightdress. He was staring at her as if he could see through it, and she wished for the protection of a corset. She didn't know her own body tonight, the way it ached when he was near her.

She'd felt his heart beneath her palm, and its racing speed had matched her own. He wore no shirt under the dressing gown, and the triangle of bare skin at his throat drew her gaze constantly. So she stood still and waited. When he said nothing, she finally raised her eyes to his. Would he touch her? Would he kiss her again?

But then from somewhere in the depths of the house, they heard a door slam and a woman's harsh sob.

Lord Thurlow stepped away from her and cursed aloud. "Go to bed. I'll take care of this."

"But what is it?" she asked, trailing him as he strode to the door.

"My father."

And then he went out into the dark corridor without even a candle to guide him. Victoria hesitated. Would the earl want to see her when he was in distress? Could it make everything worse? Or could she help? For a long moment she wanted to remain there, to avoid the confrontation she knew might happen. But she had spent a lifetime doing that, and it had only made her an easier person to lie to.

She chose to disobey her husband. She donned her dressing gown, grabbed a candleholder, and followed him.

The house was coming back to life. Victoria should have felt foolish in her nightclothes, but everyone else was dressed similarly as they came down from the servants' quarters at the top of the house. She saw the head cook, the butler, two footmen, and several maids. They milled about in the entrance hall, as if awaiting orders. Victoria began to push her way through them, but as they realized who she was, they all fell back, leaving her alone in the center of the room.

Smith the butler gave her a proper bow, as if he were clothed in his livery instead of a robe. He had hastily donned his white wig, which was slightly askew. "My lady, do forgive this commotion."

"Is this something that happens often?" she asked, setting down the candleholder.

"Occasionally, my lady."

"And does my husband usually handle it?"

This time he hesitated. "No, my lady. The earl's valet or nurse do."

"Then who was crying?"

"The nurse."

"Oh." She straightened her shoulders. "Perhaps they need my assistance."

Smith's eyes widened. "But my lady—"

She walked past him and down the corridor to the earl's chambers. The nurse was standing alone outside the door, sobbing piteously. This was someone she could help, Victoria thought with relief.

"Nurse Carter," she said, putting a hand on the woman's trembling arm, "do tell me what's wrong. Surely it can't be this bad."

The tall woman hugged herself, tears running unchecked down her face. "I tried to help him, mi-lady, I did. But when his legs start painin' him, nothin' helps, and his temper strains somethin' fierce. Please, milady, I'm doin' me best. I don't want to lose me position!"

"I'm certain your position is not in jeopardy. Lord Thurlow will handle everything."

But the woman burst into fresh tears. "Milady, it's me fault it got this far. Lord Thurlow is *never* to handle things. It only makes the earl worse!"

Victoria frowned as she patted the nurse one last time, then walked to the doorway. There was a tray and its contents scattered on the ground between the earl and his son. A servant knelt between them, cleaning up the mess, his shoulders hunched as if he could make himself disappear.

Lord Thurlow stood in profile to her, staring at his father. Frustration and anger warred in his expression, obliterating his usually pleasant mask.

"Father, you must cease tormenting the servants." His voice was very controlled.

"They're mine to do with as I wish," said Lord Banstead loudly. "You're not the earl yet."

Victoria saw pain and sleeplessness etched across the old man's haggard face. For the first time she pitied him. She could not know what it was like to face one's imminent death, to lose control of everything one had worked for, everything that gave one pleasure.

Lord Thurlow gripped his hands together behind his back. "I never said I was the earl, but someone has to manage the household, and you refuse to do it."

"Are you saying I don't know how to rule what's mine?"

"Do you hear yourself? You are not some king whose every wish has to be granted."

"But I deserve the respect of my title. What's going on around here?"

Lord Thurlow sighed. "I don't know what you mean."

"You never attend parties. Yet tonight you take your wife to a dinner. Something's different."

"Father, I didn't know you needed to approve my schedule."

Unnoticed, Victoria stared wide-eyed between them. Lord Thurlow had asked her not to confide his railway plans to his father. She imagined that would lead to many more arguments.

She stepped away from the doorway when she heard Mrs. Wayneflete in the entrance hall, consulting with Smith and then sending everyone off to bed. The housekeeper bustled up the corridor, gave Victoria a brief smile, then put an arm around Nurse Carter.

"Go to the kitchen, dear, I've put on a pot of tea. I'll be in to speak with you soon."

After the nurse walked away hugging herself, the housekeeper glanced into the earl's room, then gave Victoria a sympathetic smile.

"Right on schedule," Mrs. Wayneflete said.

Victoria could only blink at her before saying, "This has happened before?"

"Every night since I've been here. The earl's in a lot of pain, and wants more of his medicine, which the nurse can't give him for fear of killing him. He sets up a fuss and attempts to bribe the servants, threatening them with the loss of their positions if they don't do as he says. Why do you think so many housekeepers quit?"

"I am so sorry to involve you in all this," Victoria whispered. Would Mrs. Wayneflete finally leave her after all these years?

"Now don't you worry, my lady. I feel sorry for the old gent. Menfolk always do like to feel above the ruin of time. But your husband, he seems to be making things worse, now doesn't he?"

Victoria winced. "He doesn't know what to say to his father."

"Why don't you take him on back to your room and let me deal with this?"

Mrs. Wayneflete sailed into the earl's bedroom, wearing her uniform as if she never took it off, bringing with her surety and common sense.

"Now my lords, we all need to be going to bed here. You can talk in the morning."

"Thinks he knows better than everybody," the earl grumbled.

But Victoria could see him rubbing his legs where they were covered by the blanket.

"If you haven't scared off Nurse Carter, I'm sure she'll come give your legs a good kneading. And then in the morning, we're sending for your doctor."

"It's about time," Lord Thurlow said.

Mrs. Wayneflete sent him an arch look. "Then why haven't you done it before now, my lord?"

The earl shook his finger at the housekeeper. "I won't be ordered about like a child. That old quack can't help me anymore, said so himself!"

The housekeeper straightened the crumpled blanket over the earl's lap. "Nurse Carter tells me it's been months since you saw the doctor, my lord. Maybe he can provide new medicine."

"Nothing will help but to die, and I'm just trapped in this body waiting."

"Father—"

"Get out of here." The earl pointed at the door, and then saw Victoria.

She saw the wash of red stain his pale face, and she realized her mistake.

"Do you like what you're seeing, girl? Do you feel closer to my fortune?"

Blood drained from her face. "My lord, I never—"

Lord Thurlow stepped between her and the earl. "I told you to leave her alone."

Victoria turned and ran down the now-deserted corridor and up the stairs. The candle in her hand flickered wildly and then went out all together when she reached the top. In the darkness, she kept her hand on the wall and almost knocked a vase from its perch on a table. Tears clogged her throat, but she would not weep. How was she ever to help Lord Thurlow and his father? It seemed like such an impossible task.

When she was finally inside her room, she had almost closed the door when it hit a solid object.

"Victoria?"

It was her husband. He'd been so quiet that she hadn't heard him following her. Taking a deep breath, she swept the door wide. "Come in, my lord."

"No, you've had enough of us for one day, I think," he said gruffly.

His eyes showed a brief embarrassment that made her feel better.

"Again, allow me to apologize for my father's behavior—and my own."

She sighed. "It is difficult to deal with seeing one's parent in constant pain."

He frowned and shook his head. "That does not excuse my own inability to hold my temper."

"Our parents can sometimes bring out the worst in us, can't they?"

She smiled at him, and his stiff shoulders

seemed to relax. Why did she find him so compelling, when in so many other ways he disappointed her?

"I envy your relationship with your mother," he said.

She knew that he must be remembering his own mother. But all she could think about were the lies her parents had told, and the desperation it had led to.

"Every day I work diligently to keep my mother close to me," she said.

He arched a brow. "And you're suggesting I do the same? Believe me, there is nothing left to repair in the Banstead family."

She didn't believe it, but saw no use in telling him that tonight.

They stood there awkwardly, the threshold a barrier between them. Victoria clutched her dressing gown to her throat against a draft, and she was reminded of what they'd been doing before the interruption. Her movement seemed to remind her husband, too, because his gaze dropped down her body. She stilled, and her anticipation slowly grew. A shudder swept through her, leaving her stunned. She felt weak with the need to be held in his strong arms.

"It's been a long evening, Victoria," he said, his voice unusually husky. "Sleep well."

She watched him walk down the dark corridor

and disappear inside his room. Shutting her door, she leaned against it in thought.

She found herself wondering what it would be like to be comforted by him. Sometimes he actually seemed sensitive. Would his strong arms around her make everything all right? But maybe only she could do that for herself.

She took out her private journal to record the day's events, especially her frustration with her husband. And that eventually led to her problems with the earl. As always, writing calmed her, forced her to think and plan. She had to make the earl tolerate her, and he would only do that by getting to know her. If he wouldn't come out of his room, then she would just have to walk into the lion's den.

In the morning, Victoria awoke early enough to hear her husband speaking with his valet in the next room. She was finally going to have breakfast with him. As she dressed, she tried to pay attention to when he left his room. Instead, she actually heard him *bathing*. That seemed far too personal, but of course, all she really heard was the splash of water.

He was probably using the same hip bath she used, and the thought made her feel warm. Her bare skin touched the same places his did. She should go to the far side of her room to ignore the sounds. But she remained frozen where she was, letting scandalous images of him play in her mind. She'd seen his throat—what did his naked chest look like?

She'd forgotten to inform Anna that she was awakening extra early, so she chose a gown that buttoned up the front allowing her to dress alone. It was a simple morning gown with tiny brown and yellow stripes, and she reminded herself that her husband liked looking at her. It was a good feeling.

She soon heard him walking briskly down the hall, then let him get to the stairs before she followed him. When she reached the dining room, he was already seated at the table, his newspaper held up before his face, a cup of coffee and biscuits on the table before him.

The footmen wished her a good morning, and her husband looked up with a sharp rattle of paper.

"Good morning, Lord Thurlow." She set her notebook on the table, then took a plate to the sideboard to choose her breakfast.

"Good morning, Victoria."

When she turned around, he was glancing at his paper again, but this time he'd lowered it so that she could see him.

"Don't let me disturb your reading," she said, sitting down to his right. "I imagine one needs to know what's going on in the world when one is a member of Parliament."

He nodded and sipped his coffee. "Do you read the paper, Victoria?"

"Not often enough. We had stopped receiving it, of course, after my father died. And before that, it seemed so . . . depressing." She did not mention that education had not come easily to her.

"Young women do not discuss the news with each other?"

"No, my lord. From what I remember, it used to be gossip and fashion. My sisters were better at keeping up on that than I was. Although Meriel could converse with any man on the news of the day. Maybe I should read the paper, because that would be something you and I could talk about."

"There are even papers devoted to the railway, if you'd be interested." He smiled. "So do we need planned conversation topics? I could come up with a few, if you wish."

Ah, she liked this relaxed side of him and hoped to see it more. It made his eyes sparkle like blue diamonds. She leaned her chin on her palm and regarded him. "Then what should we talk about?"

"Not the railway?"

She smiled. "Perhaps something different."

"Did you know the Ojibwa Indians were coming from our Canadian colonies this summer?

They're going to demonstrate their archery skills in Regent's Park."

"Really? Maybe they'll have a contest. That was one skill I almost excelled at."

"Almost?"

He was watching her lips as she spoke, and it was distracting in a very pleasurable way.

"Well, it didn't compare to needlework, of course." Was she actually flirting with him? "But both were things I could do alone."

"You did not have any girlhood friends besides your sisters?"

She met his gaze with deliberation. "Don't you remember?"

There was a very revealing pause.

"I meant after we stopped writing," he said.

"Ah, I see." She gave him a small smile. "There were daughters among my parents' friends, but Louisa and Meriel blended in far better than I did. In fact, I met a few of them last night. But when I was young I preferred the companionship of my sisters."

"I envied you, you know."

She leaned toward him, glad to be the focus of his attention. "What do you mean?"

"I would have given anything for siblings."

He spoke quietly, and her heart broke for him. It was one of those moments that she wished could go on forever, a moment that made her feel as if they might someday have a marriage to treasure. But how to make that happen?

He briskly folded the newspaper and set it beside her. "I'll leave this in case you're interested," he said, getting to his feet. "I've instructed my steward about your pin money, so see him when you wish."

"Thank you, my lord."

"I'm not sure when I'll return, so have a pleasant day, Victoria. I'm off for a ride through Hyde Park."

"May I consult with your steward about the dinner party you've begun planning?"

"Of course."

He hesitated, and their eyes met. She wondered if he was truly sorry he'd withheld things from her. Or did apologizing just make things easier for him?

He left the room, and several minutes later she heard the front door close. With a sigh, she slumped back in her chair. She had to do something to attract his interest, to give them more than newspaper articles to discuss.

She thought about him riding alone through the park, exercising his horse. Did he remember why she'd never learned to ride?

Chapter 11

Victoria knocked on the earl's door. A kitchen maid stood beside her, holding a tray with tea and biscuits and a vase of flowers. Victoria was tempted to steady the tray because the maid was shaking so badly. When they heard nothing, Victoria knocked again.

"My lord?" she called. "It is I, Victoria."

She knew he was in there, since the doctor had just left. He'd said that the earl's condition was deteriorating at a steady pace, and had agreed to increase the dosage of medication.

She couldn't let the earl wallow in the despair of his prognosis. So she opened the door. The maid gasped and took a step back. The earl's wheelchair was pushed against a table with a sheaf of papers spread across it. He glanced at them and scowled. She thought he looked paler this morning, the lines on his face deeper. She knew he wouldn't want her pity, but he had it anyway.

She gave him a bright smile and motioned for the maid to set the tray on a side table. Then the girl fled, closing the door behind her.

"I picked flowers this morning to brighten your room, my lord. Where shall I put them?"

"Away from me. The smell annoys me."

Her smile faltered just a little. "Well, the colors are cheerful. I'll put them in this corner."

With his spectacles on his nose, he looked down at his papers.

"Am I disturbing you, my lord?"

"Yes."

She knew he was trying to frighten her away, just as he did to everyone. "I won't take long. Shall I pour you some tea?"

"No."

"Then I'll help myself."

She was proud that her hand didn't shake as she poured her cup. After setting a plate of biscuits at the earl's table, she pulled up a chair nearby.

"Would you care for a biscuit, my lord?" she asked.

When he ignored her, she helped herself to one.

"You've had enough of those, haven't you?"

She choked, then sipped tea until she could swallow, remembering that he was a man in pain.

"I do enjoy biscuits," she said ruefully. "I'll have to stay away from them to fit into all the beautiful gowns your son was generous enough to give me."

"He obviously didn't want to be embarrassed by you." The earl calmly turned over a paper to continue reading.

"And I don't blame him," she said softly. "I'm the first to admit that I'm uncomfortable in your world."

He looked at her coldly. "Then why are you here?"

Did he truly not know the real reason for the wedding? She didn't know what she was supposed to keep hidden.

"Because Lord Thurlow asked me to marry him."

"Why?"

"You'll have to discuss his reasons with him, my lord."

"I think he married you out of pity."

She remained silent, knowing he was partly right.

"He felt sorry for you. Father dead, money gone. Shelby was my banker—I know what state he left you in. Contemptuous. Yet you accepted the proposal. Can you live with the fact that now he'll never be able to marry a woman of his own class?"

Her throat was tight, but she found she didn't want to cry. "My lord, I have no choice but to live with that. I will do my best as his wife."

"Even if it means putting up with me."

"I don't see you as someone to put up with, my lord. You are my husband's father and deserve my respect."

"Are you asking to befriend me?" he scoffed.

"I cannot aspire to that. But I would like your acceptance."

"You fulfill your function and bear my grandchild. That's all I want from you."

She stiffened at his crudity, but she couldn't be surprised by what he expected from her. "Perhaps your son needs something more from the both of us."

He put his hands flat on the table. "Are you, a mere slip of a girl, trying to tell me how to be a father?"

"I wouldn't dream of that, my lord. I'm trying to figure out how to be a wife."

"Then go figure it out somewhere else."

"Of course. Shall I leave the tea?"

He raised his voice and pointed at the door. "Take it and get out!"

Only when Victoria was in the corridor did she

remember to breathe. Strangely, she didn't feel like crying. She felt a resolve to the depths of her soul. These two men needed her help. But how?

Victoria spent an hour with her music late in the afternoon, using it to soothe herself before facing her husband at dinner. She was surprised when Smith interrupted her.

"My lady, your dinner guest has arrived."

Victoria froze at the piano. "Dinner guest? Is Lord Thurlow at home?"

"No, my lady, but I'm certain he'll be home momentarily. Lord Wade is down in the drawing room."

Once again, her husband had made plans without informing her. She sighed.

"Oh goodness." She looked down at her gown. "Am I dressed well enough for a dinner?"

Smith cleared his throat. "My lady, I'm not the one to judge such a thing."

"Of course. Is Lord Banstead going to be joining us?"

"No, my lady."

She nodded, ashamed to feel relieved. "Do tell Lord Wade that I shall be down momentarily."

Victoria walked up to her room at an unladylike pace and examined her hair. There was no time to change into a more formal gown for dinner. She felt frazzled at the thought of entertaining Lord

Wade alone, even though she'd already spent an afternoon in his company. Thank goodness Lord Wade was the talkative sort. Didn't she have a list of conversation topics with men in one of her journals? It had been so long since she'd had to use that particular list, and she didn't have time to go searching for it now. She hastened to her mother's room, thinking she'd have to force her mother to join them.

But her mother only studied her briefly before saying, "Of course I'll have dinner with you and Lord Wade, Victoria. Just help me change."

Victoria's relief only lasted until she looked at the mantel clock. "Oh dear, the gentleman has already been waiting for half an hour. Do hurry!"

Soon they were walking arm in arm into the drawing room, her mother in her customary black, and Victoria in pale green. Lord Wade was standing near the piano, looking through sheet music. He glanced up when they entered, giving them a wide grin.

"Lady Thurlow, you look lovely this evening." Lord Wade came forward, bowing low so that a tumble of blond hair fell across his forehead. "Mrs. Shelby, your beauty continues to shine through your daughter."

Her mother gave a little curtsy and a half smile, but said nothing. Victoria hoped it was not going to be another of her mother's silent spells.

"Lord Wade," Victoria began, "I must apologize for my husband's absence. I have no idea what is keeping him."

Lord Wade studied her, his dimples deepening. "Thurlow forgot to mention my invitation, eh?"

She smiled and gave a little shrug.

"He does get caught up in whatever he's working on. Must be the railway, as Parliament isn't meeting today."

Victoria had never asked Lord Thurlow what she was supposed to keep secret. But Lord Wade already seemed to know.

"The railway?" her mother asked in confusion. "Is Lord Thurlow going on a journey without his wife?"

Lord Wade gave Victoria an apologetic look.

"No, Mama, he invests in a railway company."

Her mother shuddered. "I would never ride on a machine. I hear they cause milk cows to stop producing!"

"Only a rumor, Mrs. Shelby," Lord Wade said.

"Do sit down, Lord Wade," Victoria said. "We'll delay dinner a bit in hopes that my husband will soon join us."

Lord Wade rubbed his hands together and grinned. "Then I'll have time to relate to you how Thurlow became so fascinated by trains. Wouldn't want him to overhear, of course."

Victoria smiled. "I'm quite interested in anything you have to say."

"Because it's about your husband," he said with a sigh. "Usually the ladies like listening to me because of my way with words."

"I'm certain I'll be very impressed."

"Remember to let me know," he said with a serious expression and a twinkle in his eye. "Let's see, it was four years ago, I think, and we were on holiday from Oxford. The Southwestern Railway had just opened the line to Southampton, which happened to run very near one of the Banstead estates." He glanced at her mother. "No cattle were terrorized, Mrs. Shelby."

"That's good to hear," she said primly.

Victoria smiled with pleasure.

"We received word at the house that a train had come to an unscheduled stop nearby, so Thurlow went racing to it, tiring a very good horse in the process." He glanced at her mother. "The horse seemed unperturbed by the train."

"I'm glad," Mama said, obviously trying not to smile.

"Come to find out," he continued, "they'd run out of coal. Thurlow couldn't wait to be of help— all he asked was that they let him see how they run the engine. So he had the servants loading coal on every cart and wagon they had. I couldn't even recognize him because he got so filthy himself. I, naturally, made myself useful by calming the ladies left stranded on the train."

"How good of you," Victoria said.

"Yes, they would have quite run wild. But Thurlow had his engine demonstration, and an obsession was born."

"And did you make many new acquaintances?" Victoria asked, smiling.

"Several. Some of them were even unmarried."

"Lord Wade!" her mother scolded.

But to Victoria's delight, her mother seemed more amused than anything else.

They eventually went in to dinner, and Lord Wade changed the subject as a dish of turbot and lobster sauce was brought in. "Did you receive the invitation to the Duke of Sutterly's ball?"

Victoria shrugged and smiled. "I'm not sure, Lord Wade, but doubtless we won't be attending."

He studied her, his smile fading. When he looked so serious, she knew an intellectual man hid behind those green eyes.

"I had thought for sure once Thurlow married . . ." he began in a soft voice. "Forgive me for being blunt, my lady, but Thurlow can be an ass."

She gave a shocked gasp, glancing at her mother in hopes that the woman wouldn't leave the room in protest.

But her mother smiled and nodded. "Like father, like son."

Lord Wade laughed aloud.

"Mama, please!"

"No, no, the fault is mine," Lord Wade said, waving his fork. "Thurlow is like a brother to me, but at times—"

"At times what?" Lord Thurlow asked as he came through the doorway.

He seemed to actually be hurrying.

Victoria rose to her feet. "Good evening, my lord."

Lord Thurlow walked to her, his frock coat spattered with rain across his broad shoulders. For the first time, she saw embarrassment in his eyes, as if he remembered his vow to treat her better. She felt . . . respected. And it made him so much more appealing.

"Victoria, forgive my tardiness. A meeting was delayed."

"Of course, my lord."

She knew she was looking at him with hope in her eyes, as a woman being courted instead of only as a wife.

His gaze lingered on her before he finally turned to his friend. "Now Wade, what were you saying?"

"I was saying, you're an ass," Lord Wade repeated cheerfully.

Lord Thurlow sighed. "Ladies, you must forgive him his crudity."

"He doesn't need my forgiveness," Victoria's mother said, continuing to eat.

Lord Thurlow shot her a surprised look, but his amused attention went back to Lord Wade.

"And why would you use such a vulgarity, Wade?" he asked.

"Because you haven't informed your lovely wife about Sutterly's ball."

"I didn't know about it myself."

"Still throwing away all the invitations unread?" Lord Thurlow took his place at the table and motioned to one of the footmen, who brought him a steaming plate. "I may not read the post immediately, but I do get to it all eventually."

"Then you should also get around to accepting an occasional invitation once in a while."

As Victoria ate, she wondered about Lord Thurlow and his preference for socializing with businessmen instead of the *ton*. She liked the serenity of home—even her new home—but wouldn't going out into society again be good for her husband? People forget every scandal eventually.

"When an event is of importance," Lord Thurlow said, "I'll attend. Are you planning on hosting a party?"

"In my bachelor's flat?" Lord Wade said with a snort. "You know that's not likely."

"What about at your grandmother's estate? It's near enough to London. You could host a house party."

Lord Wade actually paled. "For an entire weekend?"

"I—*we* would attend, just to help keep you respectable," Lord Thurlow said, glancing at Victoria. "Wouldn't we?"

"Of course, my lord."

If he was going to say something else, he seemed to forget. Instead his gaze roamed down her body in a lingering fashion, so intent she could almost feel it as a touch along her skin. A blush rose to overtake her face, and she prayed no one noticed.

After dinner, Lord Thurlow escorted Victoria and her mother up to the drawing room, assuring her that he and Lord Wade would be joining them momentarily. And then he went back down to the dining room and firmly shut the door.

Victoria put her hands on her hips and frowned.

"Why are you upset, my dear?" her mother asked, taking a seat on an overstuffed chair near the bare hearth.

Why *was* she upset? Gentlemen usually wanted time away from the ladies after dinner. But listening to the men talk revealed so much about her husband. She didn't want to miss any of it.

"It's nothing, Mama." She found her needlework where she'd left it. She liked to lose herself in the colors and textures, to examine the possibilities of the designs only she could create. But tonight it did not soothe her mind.

Then she realized with shock that her mother had also begun her own.

Her mother took a few stitches, then without lifting her head, said, "Frowning will give your forehead wrinkles, my dear."

Victoria tried to smile, but her pleasure at her mother's progress slowly faded as she imagined what her husband and his friend were discussing. Would Lord Wade try to talk Lord Thurlow into attending the ball?

Chapter 12

David poured Simon a drink and then helped himself. "Did you enjoy teasing my wife?"

"I never teased her," he said solemnly, almost successful at hiding the twinkle in his eyes.

"Then did you enjoy teasing me?"

Simon's amusement faded, and he actually looked tired. "You need to get out more."

"I'm out every day."

"Let me be more specific. You need to take your wife out and about."

David studied his glass very deliberately. "She's already attended a luncheon and a dinner party with me."

"Whose?" Simon asked with disbelief. "I attend every luncheon and dinner party."

"The Huttons and the Bannasters."

He frowned. "I've never heard of them. Could they be—railway directors?"

David smiled. "How did you ever guess?"

"Oh, that's right—you were using your wife as a social partner to further your business interests. Hope she didn't mind that."

"She didn't. She's even planning our own dinner party as we speak."

"With the railway directors."

"Yes."

"Well, *that* you'll have to invite me to. I can't imagine you as a host. But after that you need to try exposing her to the society you were born into. They're your birthright, and your future children's birthright."

"Simon—"

"I think it's a little too easy for you to just keep things the way you've always done them, because Victoria gives you no trouble. Yet she obviously means a bit more to you than you thought she would, so perhaps you're even worried about society's reaction to her."

"I already know how society reacts to her, because she told me." David drained his glass. "She doesn't need that kind of humiliation again."

"Was whatever you're referencing a recent event?"

He frowned. "She wrote it in our journal, so no."

"This girl who can confront your father—and yes, your servants told me she visited with him today—is not a girl any longer, but a woman. She could handle herself, if given the opportunity. But I think you also have memories you don't wish to confront, and going out into society will make things uncomfortable for *you*."

David rose to his feet, ostensibly to refill their glasses, but a lurking part of him wanted Simon to leave. His friend was as inquisitive as a physician. "More brandy?"

"Of course." When David was leaning over him to pour, Simon said, "No one will remember Colette."

David stiffened, then turned his back to set down the decanter. "I don't wish to discuss her."

"Or your father, obviously. She was his mistress, David, not his wife. No one will even remember that she lived here."

David remembered well enough for everyone. "Simon, don't be naive. It was only a few years ago. Hell, two families refused me their daughters in marriage because of my father's scandalous conduct."

Simon stared at him. "You never told me that."

"It was hardly something to brag about," he said dryly.

"Good God, you're a future earl! That alone should guarantee you the ability to marry whomever you wanted."

"But it didn't. Victoria is not the only one to benefit from this marriage."

"David, we both know any number of women who would have married you. You can't be telling yourself that Victoria was the only one."

"Of course not." David frowned and considered his glass, knowing that what Simon said was true. He'd been dwelling on his frustration at being refused, when he damn well knew there might be other ladies of the *ton*, perhaps of a lower nobility, who wouldn't care about his father's indiscretions. David hadn't gone any further in his search for a wife, only continued to nurse his anger. Then he'd focused on Victoria, and marrying her had seemed the perfect solution.

"I will consider your advice about my wife's daily schedule," David said.

Simon shook his head. "Only consider?"

When they rejoined the ladies in the drawing room, David silently watched Simon attempting to persuade Victoria to sing for them. She looked embarrassed to perform in front of an audience, and no one pushed the idea further. Couldn't Simon see how difficult society women would be on Victoria?

And she had visited his father today? Why would anyone willingly do that?

For once he found himself impatient for Simon to leave, something he'd never felt before. He couldn't place his motivations until he realized he was watching Victoria more than talking to his friend. Good God, was he anxious to be upstairs with his wife? This was another night he would not have a husband's satisfaction, yet it strangely did not affect his desire to be alone with her.

Simon eventually took the unspoken hint and left, not bothering to hide his smile. Victoria escorted her mother into the hall, leaving David alone. He stepped out of the drawing room and watched them ascend the stairs. Victoria's bottom swayed enticingly beneath her skirt. She glanced over her shoulder at him, and David didn't bother to pretend he wasn't watching her. She quickly looked away.

When Lord Thurlow eventually arrived in Victoria's room, dressed in his usual trousers and dressing gown, she noticed that this time, besides lacking a shirt, he also lacked shoes. His bare feet seemed strangely intimate. Or was it that she was remembering how he'd looked at her last night, when he'd removed her dressing gown? He'd been so quiet, so intent—until they'd been disturbed.

What would he do to her tonight? And what

would her own expression reveal? She had already sensed that emotions were not something he wanted to deal with. He was a businessman at heart, after all. Some people's eyes revealed things about them, but Lord Thurlow's were like frosted windows in the winter, hiding what was inside. She had written her feelings down, hoping that would help, but for once her journal wasn't a comfort. She stood before him, wanting to speak but not knowing what to say.

Her husband inclined his head. "I hear that you visited my father today."

"Yes, my lord. Since we live in the same house, it would feel awkward not to know him better."

"And how did you find him?"

"Very sad."

" 'Sad' is not a word my father would want associated with him," he said.

To her surprise, he began to walk slowly around the room, looking at the little things she'd brought from home—the fan her father had brought her from France, the sheet music she'd left on her desk. Thank goodness she'd put her journals in the desk drawer! Although she could not imagine him to be the kind of man who would insist on reading her private thoughts.

But of course, she'd once let him read everything she'd written.

"Well, the earl must be sad, my lord, because he did not want flowers, and *everyone* likes flowers."

He smiled. "They do?"

"Yes. One usually prefers to be cheerful—but not your father. Of course," she hastily added, "he has every reason to be depressed."

"You sound like you plan to visit him again."

"Of course! He is such a sad man, after all."

One corner of his lips quirked up, but it was not a smile. "To me, he only shows his anger."

"Maybe that's what he wants you to see. Sadness seems to be an emotion no man wants to reveal." She thought of her own father, who'd never revealed anything, until his suicide had spoken for him.

He smiled. "Do you know so much about men?"

Victoria felt her blush start at her chest and race upward. "Of course not, my lord."

He walked toward her. The closer he got, the more she had to tilt her head to see his face. He touched her chin lightly, and she froze.

"I was merely teasing you," he said.

"Oh." Her voice sounded breathless, but she couldn't help it. Just a simple touch from him, and her breathing was impaired.

He put his hands on her shoulders, then lightly ran them all the way down her arms. He linked his fingers with hers.

"Your hands are cold," he murmured.

He rubbed them gently and she felt each touch deep in her body. No wonder ladies wore gloves. And then he began removing her dressing gown again. As she stood waiting, she had a thought of doing the same thing to him, as if she'd *ever* be that adventurous! But hadn't she said that the Perfect Wife should be adventurous? Was such a thing within her grasp?

He seemed to be struggling with the knot in her sash. His knuckles brushed the lower curve of her right breast, and she betrayed herself with a soft gasp.

When he said nothing, she peeked up into his face again. He caught her gaze and held it as the dressing gown came free. He undid the clasp at her throat, and then the fabric slid from her shoulders. Tonight the nightdress she'd chosen only reached her collarbones, instead of her throat, and he stared at the extra three inches of skin revealed. Her gaze dropped to the floor as she waited.

"Look at me."

He took her face in his large hands, and her eyes lifted to his. His skin was so very warm on her cool cheeks. She didn't understand him or what his expression revealed, but she let herself enjoy the gentle way he caressed her cheeks with his thumbs. The stroking continued across her lips and lingered there, brushing the full lower lip.

Her breath touched his skin, her body felt flush and full and far too hot than could be good for her. But she couldn't look away from the intent way he stared at her, the way he watched his own fingers caress her.

Like a blind man, he used his fingers to slide up the bridge of her nose and across her forehead, but again he returned to her lips as if he had to memorize them. Strangely enough, it felt so very right to be touched by him, so right that her embarrassment faded away. His thumbs brushed along the crease of her lips, then gently parted them until the faintest moisture from her mouth glistened on the tip of his finger.

She found herself watching his mouth, leaning toward him, waiting . . .

"Can I kiss you?"

This time he asked, rather than commanded, and she whispered, "Oh, yes."

He placed gentle kisses on her lips, then across both her cheeks. Her forehead benefited from his touch, then even her throat. She dropped her head back and moaned. She would have staggered if he hadn't caught her arms.

And then he stepped away from her, and her skin went cold.

"Good night, Victoria."

It was their usual parting, but she found she had to swallow twice to repeat the farewell back to him. When he had gone, she touched her own face softly, but it wasn't the same.

He was capable of great gentleness, and she wanted to experience more of it. She was trying to make the best of this marriage after all.

Her marriage would only thrive if she could help Lord Thurlow and his father achieve peace. If she knew her husband better, surely life would be easier. Not only would she meet him for breakfast, she would follow him out to the stables and see what happened. She wanted to be more than a dinner companion to him.

As David walked down the gravel path toward the stables, he heard a sound from behind and found Victoria following him. She waved, and he waited until she caught up with him.

"Did you need me for something, Victoria?"

She shook her head. "I just had other things I wanted to talk to you about. And also . . . I thought it would be good to see what you enjoy doing. Would you show me the stables?"

She seemed to square her shoulders as if in preparation for an argument. How could he refuse her?

"Come along then," he said, noticing her relief as she fell into step beside him. The day was warm, and he found himself watching Victoria as she strolled through the garden, smiling at the flowers, with the sun glinting from her hair.

"Have you ridden since you moved in?" he asked.

She shook her head. "I've only ridden twice in my life," she confessed, a reluctant smile forming.

David glanced at her in surprise. "Twice?"

She shielded her eyes from the sun and stared up at him. "Do you remember why?"

For a moment there was something between them, a ghost of words from long ago. He tried to remember the boy he'd been, the eager way he'd looked forward to reading everything—anything she'd written. That boy was so innocent, so un-comprehending of the realities of life. David couldn't remember what it felt like to *be* that boy, when the world was still fresh.

"No, I don't remember," he said.

He could see her brief disappointment. Her every thought was always laid out for him to read on her face. She never held anything back, as far as he could tell. That showed a kind of trust he wasn't used to.

She gave a dramatic sigh. "I guess it wasn't very memorable, then, though you teased me about it for months afterward."

"Now you *have* to remind me," he said with a smile.

"My father's head groom was in charge of my training. I was ten, and my sisters eight and six, so it was up to me to set a good example. Naturally, they wanted to be there for my first lesson, which made me very nervous."

"I can't imagine how difficult it must be to learn to ride sidesaddle."

"Now you see my predicament. I constantly felt like I was going to fall off. And that's what I did."

"I don't remember you being seriously hurt," he said with a frown.

She tilted her head, eyebrows raised. "I thought you didn't remember much at all."

"Sometimes things come back to me," he said gruffly.

"Well, I fell off, all right, but my fall was cushioned." She grimaced. "By a pile of manure."

His laugh was sudden and spontaneous, and soon he was bent over with a stitch in his side. Victoria put her hands on her hips and gave him an arch look, but there was definitely a smile flirting with the corners of her mouth.

"I seem to recall you having this same reaction," she said dryly, "although you spelled your laughter out for many lines."

"And that made you quit riding?" he asked, trying to catch his breath. "Surely we've all fallen into horse shi—manure."

"I did not quit. My sisters hounded me so terribly about how foolish I looked covered in . . . manure that I was determined to try again."

"More manure?" he asked with amused sympathy.

"This time I slid right into a water trough. Louisa swore that several horses had just spit into it, so I promptly relieved myself of lunch right into the water."

He groaned.

"So I was covered in horse spit and vomit. Meriel teased me for weeks, saying that the horses wouldn't use that trough anymore."

He grinned. "I'm sure they would have rather gone thirsty."

"That's exactly what you wrote to me!" She laughed until she wiped tears from the corners of her eyes.

He watched her, enjoying her mirth. It made him feel peaceful. Slowly his smile died.

When they reached the stables, some strange emotion passed over her face as she looked up at the wooden building, wiping out all the laughter. Worry? Sadness?

David went into the dim stables to saddle his horse Apollo, knowing that Victoria followed him. Several horses leaned out their stalls to look at her.

He opened the gate to Apollo's stall, and the large horse tried to push past him.

"He wants you to pet him," David said over his shoulder.

She reached and ran her fingers down the white strip that bisected Apollo's face.

"He's beautiful," she breathed, smiling.

"Do you want me to teach you to ride?"

It was like the sun bursting through the dawn, the way her face lit up. He felt almost embarrassed to be seeing such emotion—unworthy of it. He turned back to his horse.

"I've always wanted to try again," she said. "Thank you so much—David."

Outwardly, he ignored the way she'd used his Christian name, as if he expected no less. But inside he couldn't hide from his feeling of relief. If she could use his name, maybe she was on her way to forgiving him the mistakes of his childhood.

Chapter 13

*D*avid.

Victoria had said his name quite deliberately, listening to the sound of it on her tongue. It was a good name, solid and steady as he seemed to be.

Now if only she could overcome the wave of sadness that had swept over her when she entered the stables, which so closely resembled her own. Though she tried to forget the image, she still thought she could see a dark body in the shadows, swinging overhead. Her stomach roiled with a twist of nausea, and she put her hand there as if she could press it all back inside her. She would learn to ride for her husband, and banish from this place the memory of her secret.

She countered that terrible memory with the thought of her husband's laughter. She'd never heard so wonderful a sound. Had he ever been so relaxed with her, without the railways or their families between them?

"Can we begin the riding lessons today?" she asked. "I know I don't have a riding habit but there is no one here to see me."

"I have some time before I must be at the Members' Lobby. I'll saddle a gentler horse for you."

Somehow she had equated "gentle" with "small," and that wasn't true. She remained outside the stall while David saddled a mare who kept nudging his shoulder as he did so. She saw him smile and nudge the animal back.

He was a good man, to relate to a horse so. Then he led the mare past her, and she stepped back as that great head turned to look at her.

David was a patient teacher, discussing a horse's temperament and the way to approach a strange animal. She did her best to concentrate on everything he said, because she wanted to prove worthy of his time. And because it made her forget her sorrows. Soon it was so difficult to look at his hands and not remember how he'd touched her face last night, gentling her as if she were a wild animal who might flee. And sometimes she felt like that. Did he know it?

He showed her to the mounting block and how to get into a lady's sidesaddle, once used by his mother. He ended up helping her because she was too short. His hands at her waist made her feel delicate, light as he lifted her easily into the saddle. The ground looked very far away, and she held his hands for a moment, keeping them at her waist.

"Are you all right?" he asked.

She certainly didn't want to inspire his impatience, so she nodded and let go, and tried to remember climbing into the willow tree in her father's garden, and how high she'd once gone. She'd been a child then, and she was an adult now. A horse's back was not so very far above the earth.

He took the horse's reins and began to lead her about the yard, while she held the pommel and tried to get used to the rhythm.

She was finally beginning to relax, to look about her and feel a bit more confident, when she noticed that David was leading her dangerously near to a water trough.

Her grip tightened on the pommel.

He glanced up at her and smiled. "I won't let you fall, Victoria. I'll catch you."

"Oh no, I'm far too heavy. If you could just lead us over that way—"

"Heavy?" he said, his tone full of disbelief.

And then he scooped her right off the horse, as if she weighed nothing at all. His arms were behind her back and beneath her knees, and it felt wonderful to be held so close to him.

"My, you're very strong."

"Thank you."

She stared up into his face, so very near to hers. "But you should be careful. I'm cursed where horses are concerned."

His foot seemed to slip out from beneath him, and she cried out and flung her arms around his neck. That left their cheeks pressed together, and she could smell the scent of his hair, feel its soft texture.

"I did that deliberately," he murmured.

She felt the vibration of his voice in his chest.

"I guess that wasn't very nice of me," he continued.

"I didn't mind," she whispered.

She wanted him to turn his face, to kiss her. But he suddenly seemed uncomfortable with their playful behavior, because he set her on her feet and stepped back.

"I should be going," he said. "We'll get you on a horse again soon."

"Thank you, David."

The moment ended awkwardly, but Victoria was buoyed on a feeling of hope.

That afternoon, Mrs. Wayneflete informed Victoria in a hushed voice that the earl had had a spell of breathing problems, but was now resting comfortably in bed. Victoria went to his suite, and Nurse Carter let her in.

Lord Banstead lay in his enormous bed, looking thin and even small. His chest rose and fell reassuringly.

"How is he?" Victoria asked in a soft voice.

Before the nurse could answer, the earl said, "The hearing hasn't gone yet."

Victoria gave a little jump, and Nurse Carter shrugged apologetically.

"Speak to me and not the servants," the earl continued.

"Of course, my lord." Victoria walked to the bed. "And how are you feeling?"

"None of your business." He turned his head away from her and kept his eyes closed. "You can leave now. Go back to that piano—you never seem to tire of it."

"You can hear me play, my lord?"

"The music room is right over my head, you silly girl."

She never had been good at understanding the layout of a house. "Forgive me, my lord. I won't bother you like that again."

He opened one eye and looked at her. "Never said it was a bother. Tried for years to get my son to play."

She subdued her eagerness as she took the chair beside his bed. "I saw all those instruments in the music room. Lord Thurlow didn't enjoy it?"

"He was terrible. At every instrument. Never much for giving it a decent try. Did far too much writing than was good for a boy."

Writing? she thought, feeling gooseflesh prickle across her arms. Writing to her?

"But you play quite naturally," the earl said.

Victoria could only stare at him in shock. He was positively chatty today, and after suffering a dangerous attack.

"Thank you, my lord."

He gave a heavy sigh as he turned his body stiffly. She bit her lip and waited, knowing he would hate an offer of help.

She spotted a book on his bed table. "Shall I read to you, my lord? When I can't sleep, it passes the time."

He ignored her, so she took that as reluctant approval. She read a chapter of Dickens's latest novel, until the nurse assured her that he was finally sleeping.

Just as Victoria was opening the door to leave, the earl surprised her again.

He cleared his throat. "Tell your mother to stay on our grounds."

"Pardon me?"

"I saw her walk into your old gardens. My steward informs me that your cousin is quite bothered that you live next door—worried you'll want to visit him too much, the fool. He might not take kindly to your mother's intrusions."

"Thank you for the warning, my lord. I'll speak to my mother. And if I'd known you were still awake, I'd have kept reading."

"The book won't go anywhere," he mumbled, then rolled away from her and pulled the blanket up to his neck.

It was midnight when David returned to the town house. Wilfred the footman was asleep in the foyer propped on a chair, but he stumbled to his feet to take David's hat and cloak. David sent him off to bed and walked up through the silent house alone. There was still a lamp burning in the drawing room, and before turning it out, he looked about in confusion. It took him a moment to realize what was wrong—someone had filled the room with things he remembered from his childhood, items that had been packed away after his mother died. A small framed portrait of him as a child was propped on a table. He stood looking at it, caught in a memory of his mother telling him that it was her favorite portrait, because he looked about to do mischief.

The familiar stab of pain had dulled over the years to a spark of distant sadness, full of useless what-ifs. His father had rid the house of memories of David's mother when his mistress had moved in. David had almost been glad to forget as well, because the waste of her life had hurt too much.

But Victoria must have gone exploring and discovered these long-ago relics as she prepared the house for their coming dinner party. He touched the ceramic bird his mother had once brought home from a shopping trip; it had reminded her of their estate in Lincolnshire, where they seldom visited anymore. David couldn't remember the last time he'd been there. Only his steward made occasional trips there now. Would Victoria like it?

He blew out the lamp and walked up to the next floor in the dark. His wife was never far from his thoughts. In just a few days, she seemed to have brought life back into the old house. Draperies were always thrown open to the sun, when he knew his father preferred to sulk in the gloom. And now she'd resurrected memories of his mother, though perhaps she didn't know it.

He stopped outside her door, listening. Except for the creak of an ancient floorboard, he heard nothing. During the evening spent at his club, he had forgotten to send word home that he'd be late until the dinner hour. He told himself that Victoria would understand, because at least he'd remembered to let her know.

But had she? Once again she'd been alone with his father and her mother. He knew he himself would go crazy dealing with his father alone all day, yet Victoria never complained. He felt a stab of guilt. The emotion was fresh and unexpected. He was doing the best he could; he was in the middle of delicate negotiations that took all his concentration. He couldn't fail now—and he couldn't let thoughts of his wife distract him.

Yet when he went into his own bedroom and began to disrobe, he kept looking at the door that connected their rooms. If he didn't go to Victoria, it would be the first evening since their marriage that he hadn't.

When he had disrobed down to his trousers, he hesitated, then knocked softly on her door. There was no answer.

He should just go to sleep. Instead, he opened the door and peered inside, unable to stay away. There was still a candle glowing beside her bed. Victoria lay curled sideways upon the bedspread, still clothed in her dressing gown, looking as if she'd fallen asleep waiting for him.

He walked to the bed and leaned over his wife.

Her long blond hair partially covered her face. With a finger, he eased a curl back from her cheek, and she stirred with a small moan. Something deep in his gut twisted, and he recognized the desire she drew out of him. She was warm and soft and smelled of jasmine from her bath. He continued to comb his fingers through her hair, releasing her scent, making her move restlessly. She rolled onto her back and he leaned over her, bracing himself on one arm and one knee, as if he'd crawl into bed with her.

He wanted to.

Her eyelashes fluttered, and she gave a soft, secret smile. "David?"

She murmured his name in a husky voice that made him hard.

He continued to stroke her hair, feeling the warmth of her scalp out to the ends of her soft curls. He brought a lock up to his face and inhaled, torturing himself over his wedding night promises.

"You're here," she murmured. "I waited for you."

He traced her hair down her neck and across her shoulder where it curled provocatively beneath her breast. She opened her eyes slightly. Holding his breath, he followed the curl down her side, then across her ribs.

She did that little moan and squirm again that

was almost his undoing. He was consumed by the line of her throat disappearing behind her neckline. He sat on the edge of the bed and slid both hands into her hair, cupping her head.

She sighed and almost closed her eyes again, like a cat rubbing against him, but suddenly she looked at his chest. In her eyes, was that the fear he thought he'd conquered?

In Victoria's mind, the warm, drowsy remnants of a pleasant dream sank away as she saw that her husband wasn't wearing a shirt. He was leaning over her, the dim light from the lamp casting half his face in shadows. Her gaze slipped downward, and she saw the sleek, sculpted muscles of his chest, like a rare piece of art come to life. The hollows were darkness along his skin, highlighting the clean lines of him. His nipples were brown points on the bulge of muscles beneath them. His arms were on either side of her, his large hands buried in her hair.

He sat back, pulling away from her, and she wanted to call him back, but was unsure of his reaction.

She came up on her elbows, wanting to see as much as she could. Her gaze traveled from the width of his shoulders, down the flat planes of his stomach, to his narrow waist. In the front of his trousers, there was a prominence she was sure she hadn't noticed before.

He gave a half smile that made him look so handsome.

"Go to sleep, Victoria. I'll see you in the morning."

The urge to call him back was strong. But was she ready for everything marriage entailed? She thought of his patience that morning, and knew he would be gentle with her. Yet she could not place her trust in him, not when there seemed to be secrets in this house—secrets between the two of them.

"You've been practicing," David said.

Secure on her mare in the yard next to the stables, Victoria felt very pleased with herself. "I practiced for several hours yesterday."

"Then you don't need me to give you another lesson," he said, guiding his horse ahead of her.

His words dealt a blow she hadn't anticipated. But then he looked over his shoulder at her and smiled, and she realized he'd been teasing her.

"So you're ready to take your first ride away from the grounds?" he asked.

Something deep inside her eased, and she smiled at him. "I would enjoy that."

Though the hour was still early, there were many men, and a few women, exercising their horses along Rotten Row. He guided her through the paths beneath the trees, giving her occasional instructions. It was a peaceful moment she cherished.

Someone called his name from behind, and he wheeled his horse about. Victoria concentrated on steadying her mount, and it was a moment before she felt confident enough to look up. A couple had ridden up to them, and Victoria admired the woman's grace and ease in the saddle.

"Thurlow, how good to see you about," the man said, tipping his hat. "Lately I only see you in the chambers. Are you defending the factory bill today?"

David nodded. "I'm certain my speech would bore you, Your Grace."

Victoria looked between them with interest. The other woman—his duchess?—watched the men, but sent Victoria an occasional curious glance. Victoria kept waiting for David to introduce her, but once again he seemed to have forgotten.

"Thurlow, you never bore me. I keep telling my wife that you would make an interesting dinner guest."

The woman smiled. "And I keep inviting him, Your Grace, but he continues to refuse to attend."

Victoria knew that it wasn't good for David, who would one day be in the House of Lords, to ignore socializing with a duke.

David pulled back on Apollo's reins to bring him in line with her. "Forgive me, Your Grace, for not introducing my wife, Victoria, Lady Thurlow.

My lady, this is the Duke and Duchess of Sutterly."

The duchess smiled. "Lady Thurlow, perhaps you can convince your husband to attend our ball."

Victoria didn't know what to say. How could she explain that her husband didn't consult her on his social engagements?

"We have a previous engagement, Your Grace," David said.

The men spoke for several minutes on the bill before Parliament, leaving Victoria to feel concerned rather than angry. She'd tried to talk to her husband about his evasion of the *ton*, but he'd made it clear he wasn't going to discuss it. Was he holding his peers at bay out of guilt over his railway business? Or was he angry that he'd been included under the umbrella of his father's scandals? She was ignorant of so much that had happened to him. He should want to prove that his father's sins weren't his own. Surely there was a way to make him see that he couldn't make a problem go away by ignoring it.

She was finished hoping he'd confide in her. It was obvious he'd been ignoring his emotions for a long time. She would take matters into her own hands.

She would be the kind of wife he needed, and create the marriage they both deserved, giving him back the eagerness with which he'd once approached life. She would help him be at ease in *any* society and find the boy inside the man.

As they approached the Banstead stables, David looked over his shoulder at her. "Victoria, I've been thinking about our dinner party."

"You don't need to worry, David. I've discussed everything with your steward. It's only a day away and the preparations are almost finished."

He helped her down from the horse. "I wasn't worried about that. Things are going so smoothly in our talks with the railway companies we want to buy. This last meeting at our house is almost a formality, a celebration. So perhaps we should have dancing after dinner."

He was consulting her just as she had wanted. So why did her stomach tighten? "Dancing?"

"Yes. Do you think that would be a good idea?"

"Of course. I'm certain the women would appreciate it." She waited until the groom had led their horses away. "Do you like to dance?"

"It's not my favorite activity, but I was trained from a young age." He frowned at her. "If I remember correctly . . ."

She sighed. "I can't dance."

"That's not a worry," he said, putting out his hand.

She stared at it. "I don't understand."

"I'll teach you to dance."

Excitement rose up inside her as she stared up

at him. He looked amused, interested in such a simple thing as dancing.

"If I remember correctly," he said dryly, "you used to write that you stepped on men's toes."

She smiled with pleasure. "Oh yes. My mother despaired of me, and finally gave up."

"I'll wear my riding boots for protection."

He tucked her hand in the crook of his arm and led her back through the garden and into the house. "We'll go up to the blue drawing room. That's where we used to dance."

"But there's no music," she said.

"We don't need music."

No, surely she didn't, for there was a whole orchestra playing in her heart. As they walked up through the house, arm in arm, Victoria told herself that she mustn't make so much of this. David did not want her to embarrass him, so he would teach her to dance.

But when they swept into the large drawing room, beneath the multitude of chandeliers, her heart was beating so fast, she could swear her chest vibrated.

"We'll start with a waltz," he said, positioning her in his arms.

She felt his hand high on her back, the other hand warm in hers.

"You know the basic steps?" he asked.

She nodded. "But I was never very good."

Then he started to count and whirled her away, and she forgot everything as she stared up into his face. It was the stuff of dreams, of magic, of moments that come only once in a lifetime, dancing alone with her handsome husband staring so intently down at her. The room might have been lit by the sun streaming through the tall windows, rather than bathed in candlelight, but that did not take away the romance of the moment, the way her heart swelled with hope that everything could work out between them.

David smiled. "I thought you said you couldn't dance."

As if the spell was broken by speech, she stumbled and stepped on his toe. He laughed, a deep rich sound, and caught her in his arms. The air was suddenly full of a crackling tension that had nothing to do with dance, and everything to do with a man and woman locked close together.

"Let's try it again," he said, stepping back. "This time don't think about it. Trust me to lead you."

He wanted her trust, but she despaired whether he would ever give it in return.

Chapter 14

At luncheon Victoria told Mrs. Wayneflete and her mother about David speaking before the House of Commons that afternoon.

Her mother sighed. "You've married a very important man, Victoria."

"I know, Mama. I want to help him in every way I can, but it's hard when he has such a separate life from mine."

"You can always show an interest, my lady," Mrs. Wayneflete said. "You can watch him speak. The ladies have their own gallery above the main floor of the Commons. It's not too late since the speeches never begin until four in the afternoon."

Victoria smiled. "Your knowledge always continues to amaze me, Mrs. Wayneflete."

The housekeeper shrugged, obviously pleased
with herself. "The steward keeps me informed. So
will you go to Parliament, then?"

"Are you sure everything is ready for the dinner party? Perhaps you need me here."

"We can go over our final plans right now, my
lady, and then you'll be free this afternoon."

Victoria thought of her new resolve where
David was concerned. She wanted to understand
everything that was important to him. "Then I'll
go to Parliament."

That afternoon, Victoria set off with Anna, her
lady's maid, in the Banstead carriage. When they
arrived at the palace yard, Victoria discovered that
they needed passes to enter the ladies' gallery. She
was not giving up so easily.

She looked up at the policeman with wide eyes.
"But, Officer, my name is Lady Thurlow, and I just
found out that my husband, Lord Thurlow, was
speaking today. We are newly married, and it
would mean so much to me if you'd let us in."

Lines of people backed up behind them, and
Victoria found herself jostled. She gave the officer
a helpless, pleading look, and to her relief he let
them pass. She found the long staircase that led
up to the ladies' gallery, and soon she and Anna
were seated in the front row, looking down at the

long, tall room with green benches crowded on steep angles on both sides. Hundreds of men congregated to talk. She couldn't see David until after the factory bill had been read, and the debate began. From his seat he was recognized, and he began to speak in a calm, forceful manner, without all the arm waving and shouting so many of the other men seemed to employ. His voice rang through the room, interrupted by occasional cheers or boos, as he spoke about the plight of women and children in the cotton mills. Victoria stared at him in shock, never having heard about sixteen-hour workdays and young children who were drugged to make their care easier.

She leaned on the balustrade, enraptured by her husband's conviction, shocked that anyone would argue, even in the name of too much government interference. As David responded to the opposition with keen intelligence, he glanced about the room, and she knew when he saw her. He did not lose his train of thought; he didn't look angry with her. His gaze returned to her occasionally, and she could not look away.

Here was something else he was passionate about, something he believed in. He wanted to do good for people in worse conditions than their own, and she felt humbled that she'd narrowly escaped such a state with his help. In some ways, she had been another project he took on.

Now *he* would be *her* project.

She and Anna left hours later, but long before the debates were finished. She knew not to expect him for dinner.

After her bath, David knocked on her door. She didn't jump with nervousness, but with anticipation.

Since she was trying to find the boy she remembered, she deliberately left their tattered childhood journal out where he could see it. Would he ever write in it again, maybe sharing things he couldn't speak?

"Come in," she called.

When she saw David, she was disappointed that he was wearing a dressing gown again over his bare chest. He didn't see the journal where she'd left it. But that was all right, there was time.

He walked across the room toward her, and she held her ground, her heart pumping quickly, her breathing much too fast. If she let him touch her, they'd never have a conversation. And she so wanted to understand him again.

"I saw you at the Commons," he said. "You should have told me you wanted to come. I would have arranged everything."

The deep voice that had held hundreds of men under its spell this afternoon could also work its magic on her.

"I didn't know about the gallery until Mrs. Wayneflete told me." She smiled up at him. "I *thought* you saw me. When I heard the duke mention your speech, I wanted to hear it."

"I'm sorry it was so dull. Were you trapped there for very long?"

"Dull? I found it fascinating. You were very good defending the bill."

"It has a long way to go before it's acceptable to a majority."

She softened her voice and chose her words carefully. "There must be many meetings outside the Commons, to learn about such things."

"There are."

He frowned, and she knew he didn't understand where she was leading.

"Do the members discuss such things at social events, like you do with the railway directors?" she asked.

"I'm sure discussion goes on anywhere men congregate," he said. "That's why I occasionally attend my club."

Oh well, she'd tried to be subtle and it hadn't worked. "We received an invitation to a dinner today being given by Mr. Dalton, the man who read your factory bill. I thought you might like to attend, since you enjoy politics so much."

He smiled. "It's not necessary, Victoria. I'm having luncheon with him tomorrow."

Darn.

She accepted his response—for tonight. She would try again the next day—and the next—until he understood how important it was for him not to ignore part of his life.

"Is there anything else?" he asked softly, taking a step nearer.

Her breathing quickened at the smoldering look in his eyes.

"Anything else?" she echoed, rather dazed.

"If you have any questions—"

"No, no questions."

And then his hands were loosening her sash and undoing the clasp and pushing her dressing gown off her shoulders. The languid feeling of passion was sweeping over her again, making everything else fade away but the need to be touched by him. How would it feel to touch in return? Every evening it seemed more difficult to let him go.

When he spoke, she was startled, and her gaze lifted to his.

"When we were dancing today, I noticed what a delicate waist you have."

She gave a breathless laugh. "Surely it was because of my corset."

"I'll have to find out for myself."

He put his hands on the front of her stomach, then oh so slowly slid them around her waist. His

thumbs feathered along her ribs, light touches repeated over and over just beneath her breasts.
They were heavy with an ache she'd only begun to
be aware of the last several days.

He leaned over her, the width of him blocking
out the dim candlelight. His chin stirred the hair
above her ear.

He whispered, "Your nightdress is so sheer that
I can almost see through it."

She held her breath, her focus concentrated on
the nearness of him, the need inside her to lean
against him.

"Do you want to know what I can see?" he
asked.

She hesitated so long, but he waited. "Yes."

His head lowered; his breath was hot against her
neck, and she knew he was looking down her body.

"Your nipples are hard against the silk."

She couldn't control the shudder that swept
through her. His hands continued to play at her
waist, teasing higher, but never touching what he
was looking at. She felt an urgent need to touch
him as well, to take part in this strange dance they
did every night.

She lifted her hand, and he stilled. Was he holding his breath as she had? Hadn't he touched and
been touched by women before? Or was it different because she was his wife?

She put her hand on his left wrist and felt his bare skin, and the scattering of hair. Trembling, she let her fingers slide up his arm slowly over his dressing gown. There was a hardness to him that she lacked, a curve of muscle that she had seen for herself just the night before. With her gaze she followed her hand up his arm until she reached his shoulder. She was looking up at him, and he was still leaning over her, their heads so close. She couldn't read his expression, only knew that he was intent upon her.

To David's surprise, tonight had proved that the touch of a virgin could be more intoxicating than that of an experienced woman. Or was it only because it was Victoria who touched him, Victoria who was proving that she wanted this marriage.

Maybe as much as he did. But his were purely practical reasons.

He said, "A few weeks ago, you wouldn't have wanted to touch me."

She tilted her head to look up at him, and her hair tumbled freely past her shoulder. "I felt that you should not be the only one to make . . . an effort."

He smiled. "'An effort' sounds like a difficult thing to do. Was it such an effort, then, to touch my arm?"

"No," she whispered. Her eyes grew determined. "I can be bold sometimes. Did you see the journal I left on the table there?"

He frowned.

"Don't you recognize it?" she asked.

"Yes." She was watching him carefully now, and it made him uneasy. Why did the sight of that journal disturb him?

"I kept it all this time."

"I'm not surprised."

"You once offered to marry me."

"I did?"

"You said you wanted to marry me because I was the least like a girl of any girl you knew."

He kept his voice light. "I was full of compliments, even then."

She smiled. "It *was* a compliment—from a twelve-year-old boy. I wrote back that my father would choose my husband, but in truth, I didn't want to hurt you. I knew my father would not choose a cook's son. How things have changed—*your* father wouldn't have chosen me."

He felt . . . uncertain, something he hadn't experienced in a long time. "Is that why you never married—you were waiting for me?"

"Of course not. I'd rather spend a quiet evening with my music than socialize. You surely know by now that I have never been comfortable with men. I never can think of the right things to say."

"You don't seem to have trouble speaking to me."

With a rueful smile, she said, "Trust me, it comes with much practice. I don't have your gift for easy speech. You have a natural confidence that makes being with people effortless."

He spoke without thinking. "That's not true. Sometimes I can put on a performance when necessary."

She narrowed her eyes in concentration. "When are you putting on a performance?"

She looked at him with far too much perception. It made him feel . . . vulnerable, as if she could see things inside him that he didn't want known. She was still watching him solemnly when he turned away.

He saw the journal and, unbidden, memories he wanted to forget welled up, memories of a boy who made up another life because he was tired of being afraid and sad all the time. He'd concentrated on his adventures, told her about catching frogs and planning great journeys by the globe in the library. He'd wanted to escape back then, and it had taken him years to realize he never could. Over time, he *had* become very good at acting.

"Good night, Victoria."

This time she silently let him go.

Chapter 15

After their morning ride, David left for the day, promising to return well before their guests that evening. Victoria felt nervous about hosting her own party, but Mrs. Wayneflete had the whole household organized. Victoria wandered from the kitchen to the dining room to the drawing rooms, overseeing the placement of the flower arrangements, because everything else was ready.

As she stood alone in the drawing room, admiring how everything looked, she saw the little bird statue that had belonged to the countess. It made her think of David and his inability to talk about the past. The countess's death had started the earl on his descent into scandal, but things had always been strange next door. Banstead House had seemed to be draped in mourning through some part of every year when she was a child. She had often wondered how many elderly relatives the earl must have, for there to be so many deaths.

This was a mystery she had to solve. In the library, she found the family Bible, and the year of the countess's death—the exact same year David had stopped writing in the journal.

After Lady Banstead's death, the parties had started. The house had seemed to come alive, ablaze with lights several times a week, with carriages lined along on the road to disembark their passengers. Her father had complained about the loud voices in the garden so late at night and the music that had gone on until the early hours of the morning.

And what about David? How had such disrespect for the year of mourning affected him? He hadn't even been able to write to her anymore.

Absently, she looked farther down the page, and what she saw made her blood chill in her veins. After David, there were five other babies born—and all had died on the day of their birth.

"What are you doing?"

Victoria gave a jump and almost dropped the huge Bible. She turned to find Lord Banstead in his wheelchair with his regular frown in evidence. Nurse Carter stood behind him, her gaze lowered awkwardly.

"Good morning, my lord," Victoria said. "I was just on my way in to visit you."

"Don't think you're reading the Bible to me. Had enough of that as a child."

"Of course not, my lord." The poor man. He'd had so many children die. No wonder the house had been under the blackness of mourning. And the last baby's birth had also killed David's mother.

Could tonight's party help David and his father?

"My lord, you've seen all the preparations for the dinner this evening. Won't you do us the honor of attending?"

"Those days are long past me," he said gruffly. "Good of you to ask."

She sighed. Even her mother had refused to attend, claiming a headache.

"You can always change your mind, my lord. As for our reading, shall I follow you to your room? Or perhaps you'd prefer I read to you in the conservatory today. The flowers are lovely."

To her surprise, he agreed to the conservatory. The sun was shining through the glass, ferns and plants rose high all around them, and Victoria experienced a feeling of peaceful resolve. At least her relationship with the earl was improving, which was a step in the right direction in her very deliberate meddling between father and son.

As couples made their way up to the drawing room, Victoria stood near her husband and greeted their guests. To her surprise, she found that having to coordinate the evening actually gave her less time to worry. Mr. and Mrs. Perry, an older couple, came through the door. Mr. Perry immediately drew David aside, and Victoria found his wife looking very apologetic.

"Good evening, Mrs. Perry," Victoria said.

"Good evening, my lady. I hope you don't mind, but we brought our daughter this evening."

An extra guest at the table. Victoria's mind was busily rearranging chairs, even as she said, "It is no problem at all, Mrs. Perry."

The woman turned to bring her daughter forward, and Victoria froze.

"Lady Thurlow, this is my daughter, Miss Perry."

Prudence Perry. Victoria had known the last name was familiar, but she had never thought beyond that, until she was confronted by her childhood tormentor.

Prudence had matured into a stunning young woman.

"Good evening, Lady Thurlow," Prudence said. "My mother tells me you are the former Miss Shelby?"

Victoria cleared her throat and wanted to wince when that captured David's attention.

"Yes, Miss Perry, I'm the eldest of the Shelby daughters." She hesitated. "Do you not remember me?"

"I think so," she said uncertainly. "But I remember your sisters more."

Mrs. Perry laughed a bit shrilly. "Yes, hard to believe shy Victoria Shelby has matured into such an accomplished lady."

Accomplished? Victoria stared between mother and daughter, not knowing what to say. Mr. Perry hustled them into the crowd, and Victoria turned to stare after them.

David stepped up beside her. "Is something wrong?"

"I don't think so," she said slowly. "I used to know her, but it seems she doesn't remember me."

"That's a shame."

"No, that's good. She used to tease me unmercifully about my lack of dancing skills, and the stuttering way I spoke when I was overwhelmed."

He smiled at her. "Then Mrs. Perry was right— you've become an accomplished woman."

"Because I no longer stutter?" she countered dryly.

He laughed. "Didn't you write about this girl in the journal?"

More and more he was bringing up the journal

himself, the man who wanted to forget the past. "Yes, I told you all about her. I'm sure I whined terribly, but that's what a girl of fifteen does. You offered to avenge me."

"I would have done anything to figure out how to meet you." He winked.

Oh, how she liked this amusing side to him. She wouldn't have believed it possible just weeks ago.

"Your idea of revenge was gratefully accepted in the spirit in which it was offered."

"What did I offer to do?"

"You wanted her address, so you could dump mud in her bed."

"Ah, yes, I knew how to win a young girl's heart."

She felt tears sting her eyes. He really had. Maybe that had never gone away.

"Well, I didn't take you up on it, and it's a good thing, because here is Miss Prudence Perry in person."

"Did you invite her?" David asked.

"No, and they seemed quite embarrassed to bring her. I wonder why."

They were distracted by the Staplehills, the next guests to arrive, but Victoria found her gaze wandering often to the Perrys.

Before dinner, Victoria moved through the crowd in the drawing room, never stopping to converse for long, feeling the need to make sure everything was running smoothly.

As she passed a gathering of younger wives, she heard a voice call, "Victoria—I mean Lady Thurlow! Could I have a moment of your time?"

Victoria pasted a smile on her face for Prudence, and allowed herself to be pulled near the windows, away from everyone else.

Prudence smiled nervously. "I just wanted to apologize for my parents' behavior. I have no idea why they insisted I come tonight. They even made me cancel my own plans to accompany them."

"Miss Perry, as I told your mother, it is no inconvenience. And I'm glad we have the chance to become reacquainted."

Prudence nodded. "Maybe that's the reason they wanted me to come. I confess I have little memory of you, but then again in those days, I was mostly concerned with my wardrobe."

Her manner seemed embarrassed, and Victoria found herself relaxing. Maybe what she'd built up into this terrible, humiliating assault was really the antics of a spoiled girl, as young as she herself had been. Perhaps Victoria wasn't the only one who'd matured.

The women were waiting for the men to emerge from the library after dinner, when they heard the sound of raised voices echoing from the entrance hall. Victoria tried to stem the tide, but everyone rushed to the corridor to look over the balustrade.

Mr. Staplehill was trailing Mr. Perry, who was striding away from him toward the stairs.

"I don't know why you've taken such offense," Mr. Staplehill said in his very young, pleading voice. His face went pale.

"When you have a daughter, you'll understand," Mr. Perry said. He started up the stairs, then came to a halt when he saw all the women staring down at him speechless. His face reddened. "Mrs. Perry, Prudence, we need to leave now."

Prudence gasped. "But Papa, the dancing hasn't even begun yet!"

But her mother took her arm, and both headed downstairs. Victoria followed them, sending the butler for their wraps.

David met them at the door. "Perry, don't leave. Staplehill is a young pup, and doesn't think before he speaks."

"It's all right, Thurlow," Mr. Perry said. "I'll be at the meeting when the announcement of the consolidation will be made. Nothing will keep me from that, I swear."

He left with his wife and daughter. Victoria gave her husband a worried look, but then she swept back up to the drawing room to tell the orchestra to begin.

*   *   *

255

Hours later, when everyone had finally gone home after the dancing was finished, Victoria spoke briefly to the servants about their duties cleaning up, then she went to look for David in his study. She leaned her head inside and saw him sitting behind a massive desk, account books spread out in front of him. The light of a single oil lamp sent his shadow monstrously large against one wall of the study. He sat back and motioned her in.

"I didn't see you leave the party," she said, sitting down across from him.

"I was walking people to the door." He smiled at her. "You were quite the success. Thank you."

She smiled back. "I'm happy to help you." When he remained silent, she knew she could not. "So what happened between Mr. Staplehill and Mr. Perry?"

He stretched back in his chair and ran a hand through his hair. "Something very foolish, from what I could see. Staplehill is like a puppy. He needs to be the center of attention. In a dull moment, he brought up something about a girl who'd allowed herself to be compromised. It happened a year or two ago; it all ended well. I have no idea what set Perry off. But he was offended for the girl and her family, and he let Staplehill know about it."

"Could this cause problems for your railway?"

"I don't think so. But Perry is our biggest investor besides me, and he's the one with the controlling interest in one of the railways we've targeted. I'll meet with him and make sure everything's all right."

Silence settled between them, and it felt comfortable, as if she could ask anything and he'd talk to her.

"David, why are you doing this? I mean being so involved in Southern Railway, when it is not something a gentleman does."

He considered her. "I've already told you that the railroad is important for England's future. If my money can make it happen, then I want to help."

She thought he wouldn't say any more, but then he spoke in a soft, contemplative voice.

"Though it's not true right now, someday any man can help shape the country, and not be looked down on for it. It's more than just setting policy in Parliament. If I help start it at the beginning, I can show people that a name can have power without a noble title behind it. It's something to be proud of—that our children can be proud of."

"So that they'll forget the things their grandfather did?"

He looked out the darkened window. "Yes. Go on to bed, Victoria. I'll join you soon."

* * *

257

David stripped down for bed, forgetting that he usually wore clothes to his wife's room. He was distracted by how easy it was to talk to her, by the things he'd almost revealed. He didn't want her knowing every detail of his father's scandals. He didn't want those rumors to hurt her. She'd been hurt enough in her life.

He donned his robe, shrugging at his bare legs. She'd have to see them eventually.

When he knocked, she answered, and he went in. She was sitting at her desk, writing in her notebook—but not the same notebook, he realized. There on the small table was their old journal, and he'd seen her carry a different color notebook down to breakfast in the morning. How many did she have? And why so many?

"Am I interrupting?" he asked.

"Of course not, David."

He remained silent as he watched her gaze sweep down his body. Her eyes widened at his bare legs, but she said nothing.

"Victoria, I—" And then he stopped. What did he want to say?

She closed the notebook and rose gracefully to her feet. Walking toward him, she asked, "Should I remove my dressing gown, David?"

He let all his doubts go and just concentrated on her. He traced his fingers down her soft cheeks, then pushed her hair back over her shoulders. "No, I like removing it."

Ah, that virginal blush was far too provocative. Maybe his near nakedness was a mistake, for surely his robe was already pushing away out front.

Chapter 16

Victoria saw her husband through a haze of want that must be desire. She wanted to be near him, wanted to feel him touch her. It swept through her, burning, and she gave herself up to it. As he unclasped her robe and pushed it away she swayed toward him, barely able to keep from rubbing her chin against his hands at her throat.

When the dressing gown was gone, his hands didn't move away. She was wearing the nightdress with the lower neckline, which still didn't even betray the tops of her breasts. David's fingers caressed her throat, down into the hollow at the base. She watched the intent expression on his face, the way his eyes looked heated instead of distant. His hands followed the sweep of her collarbones, light touches that crossed between pleasure and a kind of pain she couldn't resist. When he reached her shoulders, he started inward again, but this time his fingers slid beneath her neckline and traced along it from the inside.

Her breathing was ragged, her skin so sensitive to everything he did. At first she wanted to look away, but she found herself trapped in his gaze. He watched her every response, and she couldn't even think about embarrassment or awkwardness. His fingers slid lower as they neared the center and touched the slopes of her breasts and dipped into the valley between. Somehow her hands were on his waist, holding on as if she would sink to the floor if she let go.

When he pulled his fingers away, she wanted to call him back, but choked on the words as he flattened his hands at the front of her shoulders, and slid down her sides, just brushing her breasts. To her relief, he circled her ribs and moved up again. His large hands cupped her breasts from below, gently lifting their weight in his palms. A low moan escaped her as her nipples brushed lightly against his palms. The most wondrous sensation shot through her body, catching her by surprise.

"I've wanted to do this for so long," he whispered.

That melted her, and she clutched his waist tighter. His voice sounded husky, as if even he had trouble speaking. The ache she'd felt in her breasts whenever he touched her now bloomed into a need so fierce, she didn't know how to react, what to think. She just stood there as he gently kneaded her breasts until she could feel every caress tugging deep into her stomach, even between her thighs.

It was she who pulled away this time, stumbling backward as she crossed her arms over her chest. It couldn't be right to need him this badly, to surrender herself so completely. There were so many things unsaid between them.

"Did I push too fast?" he asked softly.

She shook her head. "No. I just never expected—never imagined—"

She wanted to ask if it always felt like this, but she didn't want to hear how other women had once made her husband feel.

"In the end, I'll touch you even more intimately, Victoria," he said, and there was a rawness to his gaze that made her feel needed.

"I know," she whispered.

"Good night."

He turned and walked away, and she let him go.

When David entered the dining room for breakfast, Victoria was already there, reading the newspaper with a look of concentration that he found endearing. He didn't see a notebook in sight. Didn't she always study it to begin her day?

She looked up at him, and instead of a smile, she watched him solemnly, her eyes half lidded, a woman contemplating passion.

She wet her lips, and he watched her mouth. He wished fiercely that this half marriage could be over and a real one begun. The moment lasted long between them, and it was finally Victoria who glanced at the footman and took a deep breath.

"I keep looking, but I don't see anything more about the factory bill."

David was in a daze as he filled his plate at the sideboard. "We're still debating it. It might take weeks before it even goes back to committee for revision."

Now she was studying him in a way that no longer had anything to do with passion. He inwardly braced himself.

"I'm still thinking about Mr. Dalton's dinner party," she said. "He is a member of Parliament, and perhaps it would help your career to attend."

"Victoria, he and I speak every day."

"But you don't speak to all the other people he would be inviting."

"I probably do. You have said yourself that you have no fond memories of dinner parties. Last

night was the last you'll have to attend—or host—
for a while. I'm sure that will give you plenty of
time for your music."

They ate in silence for several very long minutes. But his wife was not a woman to dwell in
petulance. Before long, she was speaking again as
if they hadn't had a disagreement.

"I received letters from my sisters today," she
said.

"And how are Meriel and Louisa?" he asked.

"Very well, but of course you already know
that."

"What do you mean?"

She laid her hand on his, and he stilled at her
touch.

"You've begun to send them each an allowance." Her voice was soft, mild, with traces of
an emotion he couldn't name.

"They are my dependents now, too."

"You're not fooling me, David." Her eyes glistened as they stared into his. "You don't owe them
anything. You just want to help out of the goodness of your heart."

"Perhaps I just don't want them underfoot
someday." He slid his hand out from under hers
and continued eating. "That is a rational motive,
after all."

"Yes, you're a rational man" was all she said.

"I'm sorry that I don't have time to ride this

morning," he said, standing up. "I'm going to calm Perry down. Have a pleasant day."

Victoria watched David leave, feeling an aching sweetness toward him that had nothing to do with physical intimacy. She wanted to be his confidante; she wanted to unburden him of his painful secrets. He was trying to be such a good man.

And he needed friends among his political acquaintances—even friends among the *ton*, though he didn't believe it now. The longer he held a grudge against the more mean-spirited people, the harder it would be on him.

David seemed to respect her wishes in every other way. Perhaps he felt he was sparing her ridicule. If she made it obvious she really wanted to go to this dinner party, he would escort her, wouldn't he? If she accepted, he couldn't refuse without making her look foolish.

She sent out a footman with her acceptance before she could change her mind.

That afternoon, Victoria took her next step in being the wife David needed. If he planned on having a future in the House of Lords someday, he had to be at ease with them, and put the past behind him. She would start by introducing herself to as many women as she could, in hopes that she'd begin a new reputation for the name of Banstead. She'd begin with the women who'd sent them wedding gifts. Even if those ladies were only being polite, perhaps they'd be open-minded as well.

That afternoon at precisely three o'clock, Victoria and Anna set off in the Banstead carriage with a footman clinging to the back. It took six stops before Wilfred the footman returned to inform her that the lady was at home.

The small neat town house near Hyde Park was the home of Sir James Fogge, a member of Parliament. Victoria was shown up to a lovely gold and cream drawing room, which was occupied by two ladies, obviously mother and daughter.

The older woman came forward and curtsied. Victoria curtsied in return.

"Lady Thurlow, I am Lady Fogge. May I present my daughter Miss Fogge."

More curtsying followed, and Victoria studied their pleasant, round faces with relief as they invited her to sit. Maybe this wouldn't be so difficult. "Thank you so much for receiving me—and for sending a wedding gift."

Lady Fogge waved a bejeweled hand. "Sir James speaks so highly of your husband, my lady. They sit on committee together. We were thrilled that Lord Thurlow found a suitable match. Having a lady at home always makes a man happier."

Victoria smiled and imagined their reaction if they only knew the truth. As they discussed the weather, she noticed that Miss Fogge often glanced at a piano in the corner of the room.

In a moment's silence, Victoria asked, "Do you play, Miss Fogge?"

The girl, not more than eighteen, gave a guilty start. "I do, Lady Thurlow."

"So do I. I would love to hear you play sometime."

Miss Fogge studied her, then after glancing guiltily at her mother, began to speak quickly. "Lady Thurlow, do you play at the piano in the Banstead drawing room?"

Victoria smiled at the girl. "I have. But I usually use the one in the music room. Are you familiar with the house, Miss Fogge?"

Lady Fogge frowned at her daughter and shook her head. "No, Lady Thurlow, we have never been to Banstead House. Please forgive my daughter for being so forward."

"But, Mama," Miss Fogge said plaintively, "that piano has such a titillating history! And I heard about the parties that used to be held there—"

"That is enough, my girl. We do not repeat unsubstantiated rumors." Lady Fogge turned back to Victoria. "Have you been to the new dressmaker on Regent Street?"

The final few minutes passed uneventfully, with Lady Fogge always finding something new to say. She was obviously giving her daughter no chance to speak, and no chance for Victoria to ask questions.

When Victoria finally took her leave, she tried five more residences, and no one was at home to her. She refused to be disheartened. It would take time to overcome her former state as a business-man's daughter. Victoria was a liability to David's social position in the world of the *ton*, so she had to do everything possible to overcome that.

Chapter 17

Instead of thinking about how to tell David about the dinner invitation, the arrival of night made Victoria remember what had happened between them the previous time they were alone together.

When he arrived, obviously nude beneath the robe, she was so flustered, she could barely think. His eyes lingered on her in a smoldering way, silently saying that he wanted to show her the next stage in their intimate journey.

His hands were sliding up her arms, then his fingers tugged at the dressing gown clasp at her throat. She felt hot and needy, and already her breasts tingled as she remembered what he'd done to them last night.

Her dressing gown slid to the floor and he pressed his mouth behind her ear. His robe brushed against her delicate nightdress, and the sensation against her breasts was consuming her every thought.

His hands slid up her back, then down to cup her behind. She gave a little gasp as he pulled her hips against his, and she felt the long bulge she'd noticed before. Only thin garments separated her from discovering everything about it. Was this what Mrs. Wayneflete had meant when she said he put part of himself inside her?

And then she couldn't think anymore, because he'd pulled her totally against him, his arms holding her close, his mouth spreading kisses down the side of her neck. But she could smell his hair, feel its silky texture against her skin. The buttons at the back of her neck came free, and her nightdress slid loose at one shoulder. He followed its descent with his lips, the moist softness of them making her shudder. She held him close, his shoulders so impossibly wide. He made her feel wanted, needed, and no longer worried about her nudity. He was not a man to judge her.

He dropped to his knees before her, holding her about her waist. The neckline of her nightdress hovered at the upper curve of her right breast, in front of his face. She could even see her own flesh tremble. With a slight tug, he pulled the material, and one breast was revealed.

She felt the air on her brief nudity as if she'd never undressed before. But David was staring at what he'd revealed with a heat that seemed to jump between them. She wanted him to touch her there again, and her nipple hardened into a point at just the thought. He gave a slow grin that was very male, very possessive, and she thrilled at the sight of it. And then he did something she never expected.

He leaned forward, opened his mouth, and licked her nipple, a slow, wet, hot, rough sensation that would have sent her swooning to the floor if he hadn't held her so tightly. Darts of pleasure shot low into her belly, and she wanted to press that part of her against him, as if just touching him could somehow make everything better.

Her moan seemed loud as he continued to taste her. When his mouth closed over her and suckled, she cried out, shuddering. She found herself on her back on the carpet before the hearth, not even remembering how he'd laid her there.

This was going too far—and she hadn't told him what she'd done.

"Wait, wait, David, I have to tell you something. I should have said it before we even started."

David sat back on his heels and looked at his

wife, all flushed and soft and aroused just for him. He had thought of this all day, to the point of distraction. How was he supposed to get any work done, when he was contemplating new ways to seduce his wife?

In the candlelight, her plump, pink breast glistened with moisture, and he wanted to taste it again, to tear the garment from her body and taste everything.

He was surprised by how difficult it was to stop, how hard it was to think when he was touching her. He'd once thought himself in love, yet he'd never felt *this* way before.

But Victoria needed to talk to him, and he found he could refuse her nothing. He reached a hand down to her, and although she took it, she fumbled to cover herself. Her breast, so plump and delicious, disappeared from his sight as she rose to her feet.

"I'm sorry," she said softly.

"Don't be, Victoria. Go ahead and say what you need to."

"I accepted Mr. Dalton's dinner invitation for both of us."

He frowned. "I thought you understood that I didn't need to go."

She pressed her lips together and continued to hold her nightdress against her throat. "I think we should attend, for the sake of your career and your place in society."

"But this doesn't matter to me."

"I think it should. I'm trying to be a good wife to you, David. I thought a good wife should help you socially, not be a hindrance like I am, with my common background."

He rubbed his hand across his face. "You don't need to put yourself through this. People of the *ton* are not nice, and in the end they'll hurt you."

"Have they hurt you, David?" she asked softly. "Is that why you don't wish to be among them? What went on in this house after your mother died?"

He stiffened, and silently cursed that he'd so revealed himself to her. "She has nothing to do with this, Victoria. Good night."

"You could try writing your thoughts in the journal," she called. "That helps me think what I can't say aloud."

And there was that old journal, on the table where she'd left it for him to see. He wanted to fling it across the room with an anger he thought he'd put behind him. Instead, he went into his own room and very carefully shut the door.

In the morning, Victoria was shocked when David took her horseback riding, as if they hadn't had an argument the night before. It was as if he'd shut her behavior from his mind, because he didn't want to deal with it. He certainly had not been lying when he said he knew how to play a part.

Was that how he wanted to spend his life, hiding behind the facade of the man he *thought* he should be? It made her angry all over again that he'd decided the course of their marriage, and he wanted nothing changed.

She wanted change; she wanted to change for him. Didn't he realize how hard she was trying? She needed him to meet her even part of the way.

She had accepted a dinner invitation; she was not going to give society another reason to ridicule her by changing her mind. David would be gone in the evening, as usual. She would attend without him.

Her decision put her in a nervous flutter all day. When she went upstairs to dress, her mother followed her and sent the maid away. Victoria stared at her with suspicion.

"I'll help you" was all Mama said.

Victoria was down to her corset and chemise before Mama spoke again.

"Your husband doesn't know you're going, does he?" she asked.

Victoria bit her lip. "It's important to go. He'll never get over his past until he confronts it. If my meeting people helps, then that's what I have to do."

"I'm worried about you, Victoria, but I'm not sure I have any advice to give—none that you'd take anyway."

Tears sprang to Victoria's eyes as she realized that her mother was right. Since her father's death, and the revelation of their financial problems, Victoria had lost faith in her mother. She didn't know how to get it back. She was arrogantly trying to heal the rift between a father and son, but had never seen that she had to work on her own relationship with her mother.

"I have to do this, Mama," she whispered.

"I know. But I worry for you. I remember every party you hated, how miserable you were. Now you're going all by yourself."

"I've grown up, Mama. I handled David's business colleagues; I can handle his political colleagues. It's a first step to facing all of the *ton*."

Her mother said nothing else, just silently helped her to dress.

Just before leaving Banstead House, Victoria looked at herself in the reflection of the entrance hall mirrors that surrounded her. Her bodice was cut straight across beneath her shoulders, and the very tops of her breasts were daringly evident. The bodice sloped to a point deep below her waist, making her appear somehow slimmer. Lace gathered beneath her breasts and flowed down the front of her green silk gown, parting to show her underskirt. She looked . . . like a woman, and not a naive girl.

Could she do this? Could she really face a roomful of strangers without David? She clutched her reticule, where she'd hidden her journal with its many lists, suddenly impatient to be leaving.

"Victoria?"

She turned to find Lord Banstead laboriously trying to wheel himself down the hall from his suite. She rushed to him and he stopped, sitting back, breathing heavily as he looked her up and down.

He cleared his throat. "You look . . . well tonight."

She beamed at him, so relieved. "Thank you, my lord. I'm attending my first dinner party with members of Parliament."

"Is David to meet you there?"

Her happiness faded. "I don't think so. He does not like this sort of thing."

There was an uncomfortable silence between them. Would he forbid her from going? She would feel the need to obey him.

"Go on, go on," he said gruffly. "I'll get Nurse Carter to read to me, though she doesn't have your voice."

"You could ask my mother. She had a gift for making characters come to life when I was a child."

He shuddered. "Stupid idea. Get on with you."

Victoria went out to the carriage, where Wilfred the footman grinned as he helped her inside, where Anna was already waiting.

David sat in his office at Southern Railway, looking through paperwork, although everything was as ready as he could make it. They owned enough shares in the three smaller railways; the final buyout should be easy, as long as no one interfered. They'd kept their secrecy intact.

He just couldn't stop thinking about Perry's behavior at the dinner party, even though the man had assured him he was over Staplehill's remarks.

Was David missing something crucial? He was so distracted by Victoria lately, something that he'd never imagined. He'd once wanted her for so many reasons that had nothing to do with the person she was. And now all he could do when he was with her was be swept up in her emotions, in her needs.

But still he was hurting her.

There was a knock on the door. David called for the person to enter, and was surprised to see one of the Banstead footmen.

"Yes, Henry?" he asked, realizing that the servant seemed different without his wig and livery. A person, instead of just someone to meet David's needs.

More of Victoria's influence.

"I was to bring ye this letter, my lord," Henry said, holding up a piece of parchment spotted with rain.

"Who is it from? And why the urgency?"

"It's from Your Ladyship's mother, my lord. And she told me it was important."

David nodded, even though his insides clenched. "Is something wrong with my wife?"

"No, my lord."

David tried to relax. "Very well. Did she need a response?"

"No, my lord."

"Then you may go. Have something hot to drink when you get home. It's the devil of a night."

Looking confused, Henry left. David broke the wax seal on the letter and spread it open beneath the desk lamp.

The letter seemed to wander as if Mrs. Shelby needed an explanation of her point. She wrote that her daughter was trying to be a good wife to him, and had even gone on morning calls the other day. Out of eleven people, only Lady Fogge would see her.

David imagined sweet Victoria waiting outside

house after house, trying to make friends with people who didn't know how to *be* friends. Did she understand that the rejections were because of *his* family, and not her?

And then finally Mrs. Shelby explained the real reason that she'd written. Victoria had to do what she felt was best, so she'd gone to Dalton's dinner party—without him.

David slowly crumpled the paper in his fist but felt no satisfaction. His wife had gone—*alone*? Didn't she understand what might be said about her, showing up without her husband? Why was she letting herself be hurt like this?

It had started to rain, but he wouldn't find a hack in this part of town at night. So he rode his horse and hoped his overcoat absorbed most of the rain.

When he arrived at Dalton's, he handed his wet top hat and coat to the butler and managed to greet Mrs. Dalton with civility, even as she told him she was glad he was feeling better.

Feeling better? Victoria had told them he was *ill*?

He was shown to the drawing room, where various people acted surprised and pleased to see him. But he didn't have time to exchange inanities; he had to find his wife.

He almost didn't recognize her, though surely he'd watched her try on that gown last week. Back then he'd only noticed how attracted he was to her. But tonight he saw the confidence that had been blossoming within her.

It was the gown with the neckline Madame Dupuy had altered. Victoria filled it out so well that he was uncomfortable with other men staring at what was his. But he was proud, too. She looked . . . beautiful, her blond hair in ringlets about her ears, tiny diamonds glittering from the mass of her hair at the back of her head every time she moved. And she moved often, because she was freely laughing.

And it was Simon who was making her laugh. David felt a flare of jealousy that was positively . . . primitive.

Chapter 18

Lord Wade could always make Victoria laugh. He was the only person she'd known at the party, but he'd made her feel at ease, introducing her to several women who had shown her curiosity, but no disdain.

Lord Wade's smile turned rather thoughtful.

"Well, look who's here," he murmured with satisfaction. "It's about time."

Victoria followed his gaze, and to her shock, David was walking toward them, rain speckling his face and evening coat. He was easily the tallest, most powerful-looking man there. And he was . . . hers. She felt foolishly satisfied by that. Did that mean she was falling in love with him?

For a moment, she thought he was angry. How had he discovered her plan?

And then that display of his emotion was just . . . gone, wiped off his face as if it had never been there. He nodded to Lord Wade, took her gloved hand and brushed a kiss on the back of it. Lord Wade was showing the open curiosity she was feeling, but David didn't respond to it.

"Lady Thurlow, forgive me for being late," he said smoothly.

"Nice to finally see you here, my good fellow." Lord Wade betrayed a wicked gleam in his eye.

"Thank you for amusing my wife."

David spoke blandly, but Victoria noticed that Lord Wade's eyebrows shot up, and his grin became wider.

"Any time," Lord Wade said.

Then finally David met her questioning gaze, but he said nothing. She knew he would never say anything in public, but she didn't know what to expect when they returned home. And she welcomed their coming discussion. He had to see the logic of her position. Somehow she would explain it to him.

Two by two, people began to press forward to speak to them. David remembered to introduce her each time.

Soon a man pulled David away, and Victoria

was left with one of the wives, Lady Walcot. The woman rattled on about the lovely evening, and the beautiful painting on the wall above them. Victoria nodded at the appropriate points, but her gaze followed David as she admired the easy way he spoke with people. She was so proud of him—proud to be with him. Was this love?

The switch in topic came so suddenly that Victoria almost missed it. Lady Walcot was forced to repeat herself.

"Lady Thurlow, is Banstead House still as grand as it used to be?"

"It is a wonderful home, my lady, but I never visited it before my marriage, so I cannot truthfully answer."

"I, of course, never attended one of those . . . *parties*," she hastened to say.

She emphasized "parties" as if they were a forbidden pleasure.

"My young cousin Humphrey attended. Such stories he brought home—" She leaned forward, blinking eagerly through her eyepiece. "The women—so scantily clad!"

More scantily clad than tonight's ladies—like Victoria herself—with necklines that displayed so much? Perhaps Lord Banstead's guests had not been *proper* women? Her eyes sought out her husband again. She could only imagine how he felt having such things occur in his own house.

He was speaking to a tall young woman, with very dark hair and very pale skin, who was staring up at him intently with a look that Victoria found . . . confusing.

Lady Walcot was still talking, but Victoria only caught the end.

"And the piano! Surely it was burned afterward."

"The piano in the drawing room?" Victoria said, remembering Miss Fogge's similar conversation. "I cannot be certain, but surely it is old enough to be the original. Burned, you say?"

To Victoria's regret, Lady Walcot reddened and excused herself. As Victoria turned to watch the older woman leave, she realized why—another woman was approaching.

The woman David had just been speaking to.

Victoria smiled up at her, suddenly feeling very short and very plump. But very intrigued.

"Good evening, Lady Thurlow," the woman said. "I know I should have waited to be introduced, but David—Lord Thurlow—would surely want us to meet. I am Lady Sarah Palmer."

"How pleasant to meet you," Victoria said, hoping that it would be.

They curtsied to each other.

"It's good to see that Lord Thurlow has finally married," Lady Sarah said in the sweetest voice. "I did worry about him after . . . well, you understand."

Victoria smiled. "I'm afraid I don't."

Lady Sarah tilted her well-coifed head, and feathers fluttered. "You did not know that my father adamantly refused when Lord Thurlow asked permission to wed me?"

"No, I did not," Victoria said, wondering how David felt that this woman even dared to speak to him again. Or were they both still heartbroken over her father's decision? There were so many ways that she could act on such news. "It must have been dreadful for you."

"It was far worse for Lord Thurlow," the woman said.

She oozed a compassion so sugary that it set Victoria's teeth on edge.

"For I was the second woman to have to refuse him."

Victoria must be falling in love, because her heart hurt for poor, proud David. What would make any family refuse a future earl, especially someone as wonderful as he was?

But Lady Sarah was no lady, to discuss such things with David's new wife. The woman was waiting patiently like a spider for Victoria's reaction.

"Lady Sarah, though it was such a dreadful

thing to happen to you, do tell me you have found a husband at last."

The woman's smile grew faintly pinched. "I have. I'm engaged to the Marquess of Cheltenham."

"Then I hope you are as happy as I am with my dear husband. No man could be as sweet. Do thank your father for saving David for me."

"Did I hear that someone saved me?"

Victoria gave a start as David took her elbow. He looked between her and Lady Sarah with interest.

Lady Sarah only curtsied and moved away at a pace that tried for languor but only showed speed.

David looked down at Victoria, one brow raised in question.

Victoria smiled. "I told her to thank her father for saving you for me."

He only had time to betray surprise because dinner was loudly announced.

"I have to escort someone else to the table," he said in a low voice, bowing over her hand.

"That's all right, David. I understand how important rank is. I'll join you after dinner."

Victoria was relieved when David rode inside the carriage with her, leaving his horse to be tied up behind. She'd hoped they could speak about the evening, but instead the strained silence between them was dreadful. Throughout dinner, although they had sat almost a table length apart, she had an unimpeded view of him. And he had a much closer, unimpeded view of Lady Sarah.

No wonder he didn't like to attend these events, when he had to meet up with women who'd rejected him.

"David." She said his name softly, her voice stark in the dark carriage. Did she dare put her hand on his arm?

But it was as if he was just waiting for her to speak, for he stiffened and said in a low voice, "When I first arrived, I noticed that Wade was ogling your breasts."

Stunned, she stared at him. "*This* is what you want to talk about first?"

"Might as well begin at the beginning of the evening," he said.

"David, I am short. All men look down at me when we speak. Besides, Lord Wade is your friend after all. And I did not ask the dressmaker to lower this neckline!"

He roughly turned her toward him and parted her cloak, baring her upper bosom to his angry gaze.

"I let it go because I thought I could view you in private," he said.

She remained still, letting him look his fill. "Then did you expect to keep us both locked away, where no one would ever see me dressed for the evening?"

After a frozen moment, when his hot gaze remained on her chest and she wondered with a thrill of excitement what he meant to do with her, he looked up at her face.

"All right, I'm not making sense. You know I haven't kept you locked in the house. I've even purchased an opera box because I know how you like music."

"Oh, David," she whispered helplessly.

"But tonight I had to chase you down. I felt like a fool."

"You didn't look like a fool," she murmured, her face hot. "You looked like a man who'd . . . recovered. And if you want to be upset about such silly things, maybe I should be upset that I had to find out in such a public manner that you'd asked two other women to marry you."

"You can see now why I thought I'd spare you such evenings."

"You mean spare yourself from having to tell the truth." Victoria couldn't believe she was talking like this, after she'd begun the evening on a lie in the first place! "Were you worried I would meet people who would reveal Banstead secrets?"

"As you have already seen, there are no secrets among the *ton*. But I'll tell you another one. Lady

Sarah was not only congratulating me on my marriage, but she was offering herself on the side."

Victoria frowned at him and pulled her cloak closed. "Offering . . . herself?"

"As my mistress, or however else she would want to amuse herself." He suddenly looked tired. "My, what a pleasant evening, wasn't it?"

"She would do such a thing in public?" Victoria asked, aghast.

David touched her hand where it rested on the bench, smoothing her fingers through the gloves. "You are such an innocent, Victoria."

"You didn't have much innocence growing up," she whispered, not wanting him to stop touching her, but afraid to lose this chance for honest conversation.

"No." He looked out the darkened window as if he could see something. "After my mother died, my father found a mistress rather quickly, and moved her right into the house."

She tried to withhold a gasp, but in the lamplight she saw David's bitter smile.

"An understandable reaction," he said. "You can see why a duke would not wish his daughter to marry me."

"But that was your father's doing!"

He looked at her intently, and she couldn't say anything over her heart's terrible pounding. She wanted to take him into her arms, to comfort him the way only a wife could.

"Of course it was my father's doing," he continued quietly. "We'd never had much of a relationship, and the mistress killed it completely. She would throw parties, invite the most unsavory of guests. My father indulged her, trusted her. Hell, he must have loved her, because she had the run of the house, even when he was away from London. He didn't know about the worst of these events, but I did. And the *ton* knew, and never let me forget."

She wanted to shield him from what she'd heard, but she knew he wouldn't like it.

"Lady Walcot mentioned the parties, and the 'scantily clad women.' It's not the first time I've heard something like this."

He sighed. "It's been five years since his mistress died. You'd think such speculation would eventually end, but it never will. I'm sorry you had to be subjected to it. I wanted to protect you."

"I know." She touched his arm, and he didn't pull away.

"Now you know why Southern Railway has been so enjoyable for me. Those directors only care about my money, and the power I can wield. It's refreshing."

She sighed. "Can I ask one more thing?"

"Of course."

"Lady Walcot also asked if the piano had been burned."

He gave a bitter laugh. "Thoroughly cleaned, yes, but not burned."

"What happened, David? I'd rather be prepared when people speak of it."

"One of Colette's friends—Colette was my father's mistress—became so inebriated that she removed her clothes while dancing upon it. Then she sat and accompanied herself while she sang opera. She was quite talented," he added mildly.

Victoria could not imagine baring herself before dozens of people. She would surely die from the shame. When that woman had awakened the next day, had she been overcome with remorse? Or hadn't she cared?

He sighed. "You're scandalized, as I knew you would be."

"No," she said firmly, knowing her own secrets were much worse. "I'm trying to imagine how that woman felt the next day."

A sad smile tilted one corner of his mouth. "Always worried about everyone, aren't you? Then worry about my character, because I hid behind the ferns and watched her whole performance."

"How old were you?" she whispered.

"Sixteen."

"Oh, David, you were still but a child, traumatized by your mother's death—"

"I wasn't a child, Victoria. Not by then."

He removed his hand from under hers and went back to staring out into the blackness. An occasional gas lamp illuminated shadows beyond his profile. With aching eyes she refused to let find relief in tears, Victoria could only watch him and worry.

For the first time, he didn't come to her bedroom that night. Only then did she cry.

Chapter 19

Victoria came down to breakfast alone. She knew David had not left the town house yet, but he didn't join her, either. To her surprise, his father did.

Nurse Carter positioned his wheelchair at the table, then curtsied as she took her leave.

Victoria smiled at the old man. "Good morning, my lord."

He only harrumphed, then had a footman bring him ham and eggs. Surely that was more than he'd eaten in a while, and she held her breath as he dug in. By the time he'd eaten a few bites, it was obvious he still did not have a healthy appetite, but it was a start. If he took better care of himself perhaps he could hold off the consequences of his illness for a while longer.

He looked up and caught her watching. "The dinner party a success?"

She wasn't sure how he meant the question, so she just answered truthfully. "Not really." She hesitated. "Lady Sarah Palmer made certain to introduce herself to me." She glanced at both footmen, and they wisely bowed and left the room.

Though the earl scowled, she thought she saw a flash of pain and guilt in his eyes. "Never much to say for the girl. Somehow landed herself a marquess."

"But not your son."

"No." He swallowed and sat back. "The boy was devastated. I wouldn't see that it was my fault until—until recently."

She held her breath, hoping he wouldn't stop.

"I found a woman to keep me company in my old age. I had to pay her, but that didn't matter. Every man pays the woman in his life in some manner."

He looked away, and the gesture reminded her of his son.

"David didn't understand," he continued. "I don't blame him. I thought the *ton* wouldn't care what I did, that an earl was above any petty gossip. Even after he married you, I still didn't realize what I'd done."

She stiffened. "You were angry at him—at me."

He gave a grudging smile, something she'd never seen on his face. "For a while."

"Why don't you talk to him about these things?" she asked gently.

"It's too late. He'll be rid of me soon enough. Things will be better between you."

"You are not standing between us," she insisted.

He shrugged. "Get me more eggs, girl. I find myself hungry today."

Later, after the earl had been wheeled away, Victoria debated her strategy for her marriage. She was not deterred by David's stubbornness. She deliberately left her household journal at his place at the table, knowing he hadn't eaten yet. Then she went off to visit her mother, who expected a report on the dinner party.

As David walked down to breakfast, he was still berating himself on how late he'd risen. It had been difficult to sleep, knowing Victoria was just next door, waiting for him. But too much had happened last night, and he didn't know what to think about it all. He hated that she knew some of his secrets, and couldn't decide if this strange sensation was relief or just further confusion. And who was he punishing by staying away from her room—her or himself?

She was already gone from the dining room when he arrived, and it seemed very empty without her. But at the head of the table, one of her notebooks had been deliberately placed. Victoria *had* been trying to get him to read their old journal, though this wasn't it. Maybe this was a new tactic.

He filled a plate, then pushed the notebook aside to begin eating. But his gaze kept darting back to it, and finally he opened it and flipped through several pages. The first date was the day he'd proposed to her, and so began list after list of everything she felt she had to do to prepare for the wedding. He sensed fear and relief and . . . something else, something hidden.

He forgot that thought as she related her attempts to soothe her troubled mother. Soon his father was thrown into the narrative, and with Victoria's frustration came a stubbornness he admired. He could see her thrill at her first success, when the old man didn't force her to leave his room.

How decent of him, David thought bitterly.

But as he got close to the last written page, going past menus and scribbled music notes and lists of wedding presents, he saw that she'd somehow reached his father.

David could feel it within the house. The tension had eased, and being at home wasn't fraught with waiting anxiety. He'd hoped for this when he'd married her, and he'd succeeded. She'd succeeded. He didn't feel good about using her.

Then he realized that there was nothing in her notebook about him. Wasn't their marriage worth writing about? He remembered the different notebooks he'd seen spread on her desk. She was giving him a glimpse of her life with this one book, but wasn't letting him see her truly personal thoughts.

She was trying so hard to be a wife to him, and he was selfishly trying to keep everything just the way he wanted it. She was attempting to cross a line to reach a compromise, and he was holding back like a coward.

It was his turn to give something back. If it meant so much to her, he'd take her to the duke's ball tonight, and anywhere else she damn well wanted to go. She'd heard some of the worst about his past—at least the public scandals. And she didn't despise him or his family. She didn't seem hurt by it all, except . . . on his behalf.

But there were other ways he could hurt her, if he wasn't careful.

Victoria was giving her mare a carrot when she felt someone watching her. She turned around and knew it was David, silhouetted against the brightness outside the stable door. She felt a thrill at his very presence, followed quickly by trepidation. Had he read her journal? Did he understand that it was time for him to try to reach his father before it was too late?

He walked toward her, and gradually his features sharpened. He was watching her, his pale eyes full of—mischief?

"Do you have another evening gown?"

She was confused. "The bulk of my new wardrobe won't arrive for several more weeks, but you did purchase me several gowns. Don't you remember?"

"I remember."

His voice went intimately deeper, and she caught her breath.

"Then you know the next one will have an equally revealing neckline," she warned him. "Madame Dupuy took liberties."

"I'll put up with it."

"You will? Why? Are we attending the opera?" she asked with rising excitement.

"We're attending the duke's ball tonight."

She knew she gaped at him, and he actually seemed to enjoy her reaction.

"We are?"

"We are." He tilted his head. "Is this not what you wanted?"

"Yes, but . . . why did you change your mind?"

He looked embarrassed. "Because it was the right thing to do."

That was the only reason?

She couldn't expect declarations of undying love—not yet, anyway. But a girl could hope.

Victoria had several quiet minutes to spare before Anna returned to help her into her ball gown. She went to her desk, and to her surprise, she noticed that the household journal had been returned to her. Cautiously, she opened it to the last page, and found a man's straight, heavy handwriting.

She gave a little sigh of pleasure and read:

I enjoyed our dance the other night. I'll claim a waltz tonight.

She traced the words with her fingertip, and then opened their childhood journal to compare how his penmanship had changed. He had a bolder hand now, full of confidence. Hers had changed as well, becoming more precise, more careful, rather than hurried and exuberant. They could never go back to the children they were, but she considered this marriage a fresh beginning, and it finally seemed to be that for him as well.

He'd written to her! She put the household journal on the table near his room, hesitated, and then laid out the childhood journal as well. Maybe now he'd want to read and remember.

In her personal journal, she began to write about wanting to make him proud at the ball. With a frown, she sat back and looked at her words. She was so dependent on recording her every thought, as if something might disappear if she didn't write it.

She couldn't take a journal to the ball. She would make no lists of conversation topics, write down no one's name.

Her palms began to perspire, and she wiped them on her dressing gown. She could do this. He needed her to be with him, not to be dependent on a book she couldn't look at.

Very carefully, she opened the drawer and put the personal journal away. Anna soon arrived, and they were busy dressing her hair and stitching her into her gown, but Victoria found herself glancing often at the drawer, as if the journal called to her.

It was a book, not a crutch.

When she finally descended to the last staircase above the entrance hall, David and her mother were waiting below. He was dressed in black coat and tails, with white cravat and gloves. He was so very elegant, the Perfect Husband, who looked at her with admiration, who'd compromised when he hadn't wanted to. Was she really the Perfect Wife of her childhood imagination?

He stared up at her, and in his eyes she saw her future. And she could make it become everything she ever wanted, everything she ever dreamed. On her wedding day she had not dared to hope for so much. She had only thought to be content with a place to live, with the possibility of children.

But now she wanted all of it—she wanted his love. She would make sure he never doubted for the rest of his life that she loved him.

Slowly Victoria walked down each stair, reveling in his smoldering gaze. She felt as if she came out of a trance as she remembered they were not alone.

Her mother stared between them with a look of pride and wonder on her face that Victoria had not seen in a long time. She kissed her mother's soft cheek, then noticed the earl down in the shadows at the far end of the corridor, watching. Victoria waved to him, and he nodded his head.

When she turned, David was looking at his father with an unreadable expression. Victoria quickly took his arm.

"Is the carriage ready?" she asked.

He nodded, and Smith opened the front door for them. She smiled at him, and the butler gave her the most serene, small smile in return.

When their carriage eventually pulled into line behind dozens of others, Victoria peered out the glass window. Down the streets, she saw a palace, not simply a town house. She stared wide-eyed at her husband.

He smiled. "You can see Sutterly Court?"

She nodded solemnly.

"He is a duke," David said with a shrug.

When she allowed David to help her from the carriage, several other couples were disembarking before and behind them. Then the greetings started, names called out back and forth, some she'd heard, some she hadn't.

David smoothly answered any greetings sent their way, then led her up the stairs to the ground floor. Inside, a massive hall rose four floors through the center of the building, ending in a immense dome at the ceiling. A marble staircase split and wound its way up through the town house, and dozens of couples followed it up.

Victoria's nerves were manageable, though still present. She was a viscountess now; she had to act the part.

No wonder David had said he could act. So much of his life seemed about doing that very thing, and now it was her turn.

At the entrance to the ballroom, there was a receiving line with the duke and his duchess. Victoria and David waited for their turn behind several couples.

David leaned down to her. "Are you well?"

Only weeks ago, she would have wanted to retreat to her house and be the kind of wife David had wanted.

The kind of wife he'd *thought* he wanted.

"I'll be fine," she said serenely. "What about you?"

He cocked his head. "Do I look nervous?"

"No, but you're a born performer."

He laughed. "You *are* a wonder, Victoria."

As she smiled up at him, a booming voice said, "Ah, newlyweds. You've managed to leave Banstead House, I see, Thurlow."

It was the duke, and he was smiling at them.

She swept into a deep curtsy, knowing so many people were watching. "It is good to see you again, Your Grace," she said, before rising.

After several pleasantries that David handled, they entered a crush of people. It was hot and loud, and she felt a drip of wax land on her shoulder from an elaborate chandelier overhead.

David smiled and brushed it off. "Let me know when you want to leave."

"We just arrived," she said, as someone bumped into her from behind. "And besides, I haven't yet begun to make you proud of me."

Chapter 20

David stared down at Victoria, her determined eyes reflecting the light of thousands of candles. He knew that there had been a time in her life when this would have frightened her to death.

Not anymore. Now she intended to make him proud of her. For a moment he felt a lump in his throat, a feeling of tenderness for her that startled him with its intensity.

Regardless of who was watching, he trailed his gloved fingers down the side of her face, imagined the softness of her skin.

"I'm already proud of you," he whispered. "Can you be proud of me?"

"Oh, David, maybe we each have to be proud of ourselves first."

She looked at him as if anything was possible. He gave her a brisk smile and stepped back.

"Are you ready?"

He pulled her hand around his elbow and led her through the room, stopping at occasional clusters of people to introduce his wife.

Victoria was serene and elegant and charmed every person she met. David began to think that it was because of her that he noticed so few undercurrents in every conversation. But he kept waiting for someone to be openly rude, and it could have ruined the evening for him.

But he wasn't going to let it.

Then Lady Augusta Clifford, whom they'd last encountered at the dressmaker's, cornered them between a potted fern and the piano.

"Lord and Lady Thurlow, how good to see you again." She glanced down at Victoria's gown, and her smile faltered. "How wonderful you look in the garment Madame Dupuy pieced together for you."

David took an angry breath, but Victoria squeezed his elbow and said, "Thank you so much, Lady Augusta. And I feel wonderful tonight, which is even more important, don't you think?"

"Hmmm," the woman said, then fixed her gaze on David. "I have a question that only you can answer, Lord Thurlow. Have you heard of Southern Railway?"

He called on every acting skill he possessed to look at her blankly. "Yes. Why?"

"I'm traveling to Dover in several months, and I was going to use their trains. My husband suggested that since you invested in it, perhaps we should do the same."

She only wanted to talk about investments, but David's worst fear about the ruination of all his plans hit him hard. "It is a good investment." He took Victoria's elbow. "Excuse us, but we're both quite thirsty."

Lady Augusta blinked. "Why—of course."

David used his height to his advantage, and spotted the quickest way to the terrace. After threading his way through dozens of couples, he reached the tall glass doors and pushed them open. The gust of cool air refreshed him.

"Breathe, David."

He frowned down at Victoria as she drew him to the balustrade, then slipped behind a tall column, shielding them from any curious people near the door.

She tried to fan him with her hand, her laughter swelling her breasts rather dangerously in that gown. Under the moonlight, her skin glowed, her eyes flashed.

"I think I'm breathing well enough," he said.

"Good."

And then she kissed him. The shock of her softly parted lips against his inflamed a desire for her that had become so much a part of him that he didn't question it any longer. He pulled her against him, groaning at the pressure of her full breasts against his chest.

Victoria's senses floundered. She was pressed up against her husband, who held her as if he might never let her go. His mouth was so gentle at first, as always, light kisses against her lips. She felt the prickly brush of his chin, heard his groan that echoed her own. She didn't care where she was, or who might be watching her.

All she cared about was that David was kissing her back—an unplanned, spontaneous burst of passion practically in public. It satisfied her right down to her toenails.

And then he nipped at her lips, and when she parted them in surprise, his tongue swept into her mouth, and she could taste him in a way that made every intimate act they'd shared before seem incomplete. The way he licked deep inside her made her shudder with an urgent need for more. His mouth clashed with hers, opening, parting, almost drinking from her. After sweeping his hands down her body, he pulled her hips against his. There were too many garments between them to feel much, but she reveled in this rare sensation of being wanted.

"Thurlow!" a voice called from far away. "I saw you come out here."

David ended the kiss, lifting his head but not releasing her. She swayed into him, and he smiled with a look of satisfaction and promise.

"This isn't over," he said in a low, rumbling tone that set off an answering vibration deep inside her.

How she loved what his voice could do to her.

She clutched his sleeves before he could release her. "David, can I face somebody like this?"

He cupped her face in his gloved hands, and she wished for the feeling of his skin against hers.

"You look like a wife, *my* wife. And besides, it's only Simon." He guided her away from the balustrade.

Lord Wade was walking toward them, his stride as jaunty as his manner. She couldn't read his eyes in the moonlight, but his grin was wicked.

"Lady Thurlow," he said, "your husband dragged you from the room before I could say hello."

She smiled. "Hello, Lord Wade. And I wasn't dragged. I came quite willingly."

"Yes, married ladies have all the fun," Lord Wade answered.

"You know that as well," David said dryly.

Victoria stared in shock at Lord Wade, who only laughed.

"Ah, David, any married ladies sneaking off with me do so quite willingly."

"Just remember the 'willing' part."

Lord Wade put a hand dramatically on his chest. "Why, Lord Thurlow, is that a threat? You've somewhere acquired a married man's jealousy." He glanced at Victoria. "Not that I blame you."

"Lord Thurlow has no need for jealousy," Victoria said. "And this conversation is silly. Shall we go inside?"

She took David's arm, and was satisfied when Lord Wade fell into place at her side.

As they entered the ballroom, no one seemed to be watching them. The orchestra was playing, and couples were jostling for position on the dance floor.

"Do you have a dance card?" Lord Wade asked.

David answered, "No" before she could even open her mouth. And then her husband swept her into a waltz that had almost the same intimacy as their kiss. She was floating through the air, as if her feet didn't need to touch the floor. David looked at her with smoldering eyes, full of promise that the night was nowhere near over.

They spent only an hour at the ball, but that was long enough for Victoria. In the carriage on the way home, she didn't want to break the delicious spell of anticipation that pulled between them.

Inside their town house, he took her hand and led a fast pace up the stairs. When she nearly tripped on the final steps, he swung her up into his arms and carried her the rest of the way, as if she weighed nothing.

She felt smugly happy when David ordered a grinning Anna out of the room and shut the door on her.

They were alone. Her arms were about her husband's neck; his arms held her close—as close as possible with skirts and petticoats puffing up her gown where it draped from her legs.

He let her down very slowly, so that her body rubbed against his. Then he pressed her up against the door and kissed her again, quick and deep and full of hot pleasure. She had felt certain David was hiding a passionate nature; every night's gentleness and intimacy had only proved it. But now she felt giddy with the knowledge that he *had* to touch and kiss her, *had* to have her.

His hands kneaded her shoulders as they kissed. With a sudden tug, her breasts were suddenly overflowing the gown.

He looked down at what he'd revealed, then murmured her name as he dropped to his knees. His mouth on her breasts made her melt inside, made every passionate feeling roar to unfulfilled heights. He licked her and nipped her and drew her nipple into his mouth, then worked his magic on the other breast. If he hadn't been holding her up with the press of his body, she knew she would have collapsed in a boneless heap.

David let his fingers caress her breasts as he spoke. "How do we get you out of this gown?"

She licked her lips. "Anna . . . sewed me in where the bodice meets the skirt."

He groaned and dropped his head to her chest. She let herself hold him then, circle her arms about his head, feel the texture of his hair.

He suddenly turned her around and began to unhook each clasp in the bodice.

"I'm ripping the stitches," he said.

As each thread popped, she gave a delicious little shudder. Soon her bodice slid to her waist, then the heavy mass of the gown fell around her feet. But there were still so many clothes between them.

David dispatched them quite professionally, layer after layer of petticoat, then her corset, all while she still faced the door. She took a deep, satisfying breath, expanding her lungs for the first time that evening. She wore only her chemise over her drawers, and even that had fallen to her waist. Then there was only stillness behind her.

"Turn around," he said.

She did so, leaning back against the door, hands pressed to the wood. David was sitting back on his heels, watching her with so much expectation.

Then as he looked into her eyes, he reached for

311

her chemise and pulled it off. He tugged on the string of her drawers, then guided the loose fabric slowly down her hips until she was naked.

Trembling, she let him look, knowing that the passion in his eyes was all for her. His hands settled on her hips and then skimmed down her thighs.

"Stand with your legs apart."

She obeyed, stepping out of her drawers, then held her breath as his fingers trailed up her thighs, then brushed across her curls. She gasped, but he didn't linger, just continued to caress a path up her stomach to her breasts, which he touched and teased until she was a quivering wreck.

"Please, David," she whispered, not knowing what she wanted. Could he give it to her?

He smiled as his hands began a downward journey. She watched the concentration on his face, experienced the knowledgeable gentleness of his hands. When he reached her thighs, this time he trailed his fingers up the insides, taking his time until she thought she'd whimper with the sensations he wrung from her. Was he really supposed to touch her *there*?

And then he did, caressing deeper and deeper with each sweet stroke. His fingers glistened with wetness.

"David," she whispered, "why am I the only one who's nude?"

Still kneeling at her feet, he looked up into her face. "Because I can't bear to stop touching you. Trust me."

She nodded. He leaned forward to kiss her stomach, and then his fingers resumed their questing. She felt a sudden surge of passion and groaned.

Then he was pressing soft kisses lower and lower, and she stopped breathing in shock as he put his mouth where his fingers had just been.

"David!"

He met her gaze, and licked her.

Her head slammed back against the door as she experienced the beginning of a pleasure that seemed too powerful to exist. She really did collapse this time, and he caught her, then swung to his feet and strode to the bed. He set her on the edge, spread her thighs even farther this time, and looked at her.

She tried to close her legs, and for the first time, David looked impatient.

Then his expression softened. "I have long forgotten what being a virgin is like, Victoria. I'm pushing you to things that you aren't ready for."

"You're not going to stop, are you?"

He chuckled. "Oh, I'm not going to stop, believe me." He shrugged out of his coat and let it drop wherever it landed. "But there are some things I'll save for another time."

Her questions died unanswered as she realized he was taking off his clothes. She watched fascinated as the absence of his cravat and stock left his neck bare. He removed his waistcoat, unbuttoned the top buttons of his shirt, and pulled it off over his head. His chest was as she remembered it, so broad and mesmerizing with muscle. He had to sit down to remove his boots and stockings, but he came back to stand before her. Then he unbuttoned the flaps of his trousers, and they dropped to the floor to reveal his loose drawers, and the bulge she'd seen before. He loosened the drawers, and as they fell, his penis dropped heavily as if it pointed at her.

She stared at it in shock, then raised her gaze to his.

He grinned.

Thank goodness he had not shown her this on their wedding night, or she might have run screaming from the room.

"Trust me," he whispered, leaning over her.

"I do," she said.

He climbed onto the bed, crawling over her, all smooth, flowing muscle. He kissed his way up her stomach and breasts, then devoured her mouth in a way that made her forget their nudity, forget what was to come, and just live in the moment.

For the moment had every pleasure she'd never imagined possible. He eased beside her and continued to kiss her breasts, while his hand moved between her thighs, parting them, stroking between them. She groaned and turned her face into his shoulder.

"Still shy?" he whispered into her ear. "That's part of your charm, sweetheart."

He'd used that word again, and she sighed her pleasure.

His mouth closed over her breast, suckling so gently, as his fingers began to move against her most private womanhood. She had had no idea that places on her body were so sensitive, but he treated her as if she were his own instrument, tuned by his hands, played to perfection as only he knew how. Her breath came in gasps; she burned with a desire so rousing she didn't know how her skin contained it. Every time she came close to the edge, he retreated, frustrating her so much that she finally cried out his name.

He renewed his efforts then, sending her flying up to a pinnacle as sweet and powerful as any musical note, held purely as she shuddered and fell into an abyss of deepest pleasure.

When she opened her eyes, David was watching her, a smile playing at the corners of his mouth.

He kissed her gently. "Did you enjoy that?"

She nodded. "It was . . . wondrous."

"There can be so much more."

Then he rolled over on top of her, parting her

315

thighs and settling between them. The hard length of him rode against her newly tender flesh, and it felt good. He propped himself up on his arms above her.

"Sweetheart, I've tried to prepare you, but the first time a woman will often feel a small amount of pain. It's just once, then never again."

"I understand."

"Then bend your knees."

She did, and he settled even more intimately against her. His smiles were gone, and his face bore an intensity she'd never seen in him before. She felt the hardness of him probing her, and even as she stiffened he leaned down to kiss her. His mouth was captivating, distracting, but still she felt him inch inside her bit by bit, stretching her to fullness, not quite pain.

"Easy," he murmured against her lips, "easy."

Then with a single thrust he settled deep inside her. There was only a momentary pain, then the most wonderful feeling of satisfaction. She was his wife in every way.

And then he started moving, and her body seemed to know just what to do. It came to life again, bliss rising in ever increasing waves. She clasped him with her arms, with her thighs, holding as if she need never let him go. This was the intimacy hinted at in poetry, two people moving as if one. It was beautiful, and she felt tears slide down her cheeks that she could experience these wonderful feelings.

He rounded his back to reach her with a kiss, then used one hand to pull her knee higher. The shift made her quiver, made the wild feelings climax within her again. And as he groaned, she knew that he joined her, for he shuddered and seemed to pour himself inside her.

She thought it was his seed.

As she held him hard against her, felt his breathing settle back to normal, she prayed to have his baby, so that their love would go on.

Chapter 21

David came up on his elbows and stared down at Victoria, all pink with passion, her eyes sleepy and satisfied.

"Am I too heavy for you?" he asked.

"Never," she whispered.

He lowered himself fully, and she gave a strangled gasp before he rose up again.

"I can be too heavy," he insisted.

She smiled. "Maybe."

He slid off her and watched as her eyes blinked slowly, so slowly.

"Thank you for taking your time with me," she whispered.

She nuzzled her head against his arm, getting comfortable.

"You're welcome."

She was asleep almost immediately, naked on top of the bed. He pulled down the blankets on his half, then slid her within and covered her right to her chin—as if not looking at her would somehow stop this obsession for her that seemed uncomfortably large.

He didn't want to recognize the feelings that fought within him—he didn't want to consider them, to think how his marriage had changed.

Then why did it feel as if everything in his life now revolved around Victoria, instead of his own meticulous plans?

He quietly picked up her garments and laid them over the chaise, then gathered his own clothes and took them to his room. His bed was cold and lonely, but . . . safe.

Victoria felt the sun before she even opened her eyes. She stretched with blissful contentment, then turned her head to say good morning to her husband.

But David wasn't there.

He had his own bedroom, of course. Her parents had slept in separate rooms. But somehow she'd hoped her marriage might be different.

It truly was, she reminded herself. David had

shown her everything she could hope for in a husband. He would confide in her now, tell her things that—

But would she confide in him?

A cold feeling weighted her heart. What would he say if she revealed her father's suicide? That she had lied to him, lured him into marriage with a falsehood, when he'd told her during his proposal how he felt about scandal? What would he think about her lies *now*, after they'd shared this ultimate intimacy?

She would not consider it. She knew now how bothered he'd been by the scandals of his household, how prideful he was. She could keep this secret. What did a commoner's death matter to anyone? No one knew, except her mother and sisters, and they wouldn't tell.

This decision had been made a year ago; she would not betray her family now—or her father's memory.

Not even for her husband.

Covered in a warm dressing gown, she sat down at her desk and opened the drawer where she kept her journals. What could she write? How could she describe what she'd experienced in David's arms? She closed the drawer.

After bathing and dressing, she went down for a late breakfast. To her surprise, David was just leaving his study. He looked up as she came down the stairs, and she gave him a radiant smile, feeling self-conscious but happy. Just seeing him made her want to shiver as she remembered what his hands had done to her, how he'd made her feel.

He nodded and returned her smile, but it seemed . . . too normal, almost distant.

"Good morning, Victoria."

His voice still moved her. "Good morning, David. Did you sleep well?"

Oh goodness. She might just as well have asked him why he left her bed.

"I did, thank you. And yourself?" He looked down at a sheaf of papers he was putting into a satchel.

A clutch of sadness hit her heart. It was as if he didn't care.

"I slept just fine." She wanted to say something funny, like he'd exhausted her, but his remote expression kept the words locked in her throat.

"I can't ride with you this morning," he said. "I have a meeting scheduled with my steward about our Scotland properties."

"Of course," she murmured.

"What time would you like to leave this evening?"

"Leave?"

"The masquerade begins at ten o'clock."

"Masquerade?"

He raised an eyebrow. "I assumed you now wished to attend every important event of the *ton*."

"Of course," she said quickly. "I'll be ready before ten."

"Perhaps you should be ready at seven. We have a dinner with the prime minister at eight."

"Oh." Her head was whirling. But this was what she'd wanted.

Yet—why suddenly did it feel as if he was keeping her busy, keeping a wall between them?

After he'd gone, she stared at the front door, considering what might have happened between last night and today. Did he sense her deceit? Or had she foolishly thought lovemaking would solve everything? He knew her body, but after all, he didn't know the secrets in her mind. How could she think to know everything about him?

After his meeting with the steward, David took a carriage to Southern Railway, and tried to think of the business ahead instead of his wife.

His radiant wife, whose face had lit like the sun when she'd seen him that morning.

Part of him had wanted to sweep her into his arms, to greet her as if the hours apart had been too long. And they had been. He had had a difficult time sleeping, knowing he could have been warm at her side instead of alone.

What was wrong with him? He had every night from now on to be alone with Victoria—hell, he could take her during the day if he wanted. And the moment he'd seen her, he'd wanted to.

As if he didn't have any control.

He was already making a spectacle of himself.

That afternoon, when Victoria arrived home and went to her bedroom to prepare for the evening, she noticed that the household journal was lying on her desk, not where she'd left it. She opened it and found that David had penned the words, *Until tonight.*

She closed her eyes as memories of their mutual desire awoke within her. How could she honestly worry about their marriage if they shared this?

She was still staring at the notebook when her mother knocked and peered around the door.

"Victoria?"

"Come in, Mama."

Her mother seemed strangely restless, moving about the room, distractedly touching furniture and rearranging pillows. Victoria watched her silently, waiting. When her mother stared out the window, Victoria knew she was seeing none of it.

"Mama? Is something wrong?"

Her mother sighed. "Anna mentioned that she . . . saw you arrive home last night."

Victoria felt a blush coming on. She understood her mother's implication.

"And I was in the library this morning," Mama continued, "and overheard you and your husband."

Even as Victoria told herself that this was nothing, she stiffened. "Yes?"

Her mother turned from the window and stared at her with plaintive eyes. "Oh, Victoria, do not be offended. You'll soon have children, and understand that we mothers only want what is best for them."

"You do?" She heard the cruel sarcasm in her own voice, and she was horrified.

Her mother flinched as if she'd been slapped.

"Oh, Mama, please, I'm sorry. I meant—"

"No—no, Victoria, you owe me no apology. I have tried to do my best, but I have not always been a good mother. I knew your happiness lay with marriage, and I pushed you toward it."

"You shouldn't have pushed so hard," Victoria said quietly.

"Perhaps. But now you have a marriage worth fighting for."

"You don't think I know that?"

Her mother hung her head. "I just don't want you to make the same mistakes I did."

Victoria held her breath, waiting.

"I thought your father and I were happy at the

beginning. I let his silences go, believing that he would turn to me when he needed me." She sighed. "And all that did was gradually make him think he didn't need to tell me everything."

"Just like you didn't tell my sisters and me." Victoria was shocked at her own words, but wouldn't take them back, not anymore. Had she always had this anger locked away inside her?

Mama sank onto the edge of the bed and huddled there. "I didn't know at first that your father's finances were going badly. We'd spent so much of our marriage avoiding conflict that I was used to avoiding . . . everything unpleasant. And then when it became difficult to pay the staff, he couldn't hide our desperate situation from me any longer."

"But you kept hiding it from us." Victoria's throat choked with emotion. "We trusted you!"

Mama buried her face in her hands, shaking, and Victoria just continued to watch until her mother reestablished her control.

"I wanted to protect you," her mother whispered. "That's all I ever wanted. Until the end, I thought I could help you girls find husbands, save you before you had to bear this terrible knowledge of our disgrace. Why do you think I have been so lost? I failed you!"

"Father didn't want to protect us," Victoria said bitterly. "He took the easy way out."

Her mother gave a quiet sob and covered her mouth with one hand. Then she looked up with red eyes. "Yes, yes, I know that now. He was . . . a coward. Somehow he became a man I didn't know. And I let it happen . . . gradually, quietly, one loss at a time. I don't want that for you."

Victoria bit her lip as she felt a rush of tears. She sat down next to her mother, and suddenly the words she wanted to share poured out of her. "I love him, Mama. But this morning, he seemed . . . distant, like a stranger again. I don't know what to do."

"Don't let him keep his silences, Victoria. You both need to talk."

"How can I expect him to talk to me when I can't really talk to him?"

"What do you mean?"

"I can't tell him about—about Father. David has experienced enough heartache that was not of his own doing."

Her mother softly snorted. "And we know where that scandal came from. But Victoria, your secret will poison your marriage."

"You want me to tell him?" she said in astonishment. "Meriel, Louisa, and I swore to you that we would keep this silent forever."

"I did not say tell the world—just your husband. Do you trust him to share your secret?"

Tears stung Victoria's eyes. "I—I don't know. I

would have thought . . . after last night . . . but this morning—" She broke off, knowing she was making no sense.

"I saw your smile this morning, Victoria," she said gently. "You are a woman in love."

"But is he in love, Mama? He looked at me today like—like—"

"Like a man who doesn't know what to do with his emotions, like a man taking the safe way out. And that won't make a successful marriage, not in the end. Trust me, passion itself is not enough."

"But what should I do? Do you think he senses that I'm not telling him everything?"

"I don't know, my dear, but if the secret is bothering you, can you live the rest of your life with it between you and your husband?"

Victoria slumped, and felt grateful when her mother gently slid her arm about her shoulders. "Oh, Mama, this is all so complicated."

"Yes, it is. But you can make it work, Victoria. Look at all you've accomplished already. I'm so proud of you."

Victoria hugged her mother, finally letting her tears ago. "Thank you, Mama."

Victoria approached the evening with a new determination. She wasn't sure what she was going to do about her terrible family secret, but she knew she couldn't take David's empty politeness for the rest of her life. She would force him to acknowledge her with other emotions. She would be a part of his life, and not live separately, as her parents had done in the end. She would prove to David that she was worth trusting—worth loving.

In the carriage on the way from the prime minister's dinner to the masquerade, she watched David, looking so serene and inscrutable. Then she leaned over, her hand on his knee, and kissed him.

There was no hesitation as he kissed her back with passion and heat and promise. Physically, they had no problems staying connected.

"Maybe we don't have to attend this one," David murmured as he kissed his way down to her neckline.

She groaned as he licked down her cleavage. "We accepted, so we're attending. Now help me put my costume on."

"Is that what was in the bag?"

From a satchel Victoria pulled out a fan of tall multicolored feathers. "Anna made it for me. Here, attach this to the little buttons she sewed on the back of my bodice."

She turned until her back was to the lantern, then waited patiently while David struggled.

"She could have made the buttons larger," he grumbled.

"And then they would have been seen by

everyone at dinner. Such a scandal," she added teasingly.

He pinched her waist, and she squirmed and giggled.

"So what are you?" he asked.

"Can't you tell?" She turned back to face him, holding an elaborate mask up to her face. Feathers curled everywhere.

"A bird?" he said.

"A peacock! Really David, you didn't try very hard."

"Sorry."

His smile could surely cause winter to become spring, and she basked for a moment in its warmth.

"What are *you* going to be?" she asked.

His hand began a slow slide over her hip and up her torso.

"What a man always is. Mysterious."

Her laugh turned into a moan as he cupped her breast. "Oh, David. Be serious."

"I am. I'll be wearing a mask. Very mysterious."

He started to lean over her, and she held him back. "Now, David, you mustn't crush my feathers. And we're slowing down."

She could see his disappointment, and it gave her a warm feeling of satisfaction.

After they came to a stop, the door was opened

by their footman. David stepped down, and Victoria suddenly heard someone calling his name.

"Lord Thurlow, don't go in. Ye must wait!"

Victoria slid to the edge of the bench so she could lean her head out the door. The boy who worked at Southern Railway was breathing heavily, even though he clutched the reins of a drooping old horse.

"It's a 'mergency meeting, milord," he said. "Mr. Bannaster said for you to come to the office."

David cursed aloud. "Very well. Do you want to ride with us? We can tie your horse up behind."

"Ye'd never go fast enough, milord. I'll meet ye there."

David swung back inside and shut the door.

Victoria watched him solemnly. "What do you think is wrong?"

"I don't know. We're all set to announce the merger tomorrow and sign the paperwork. There's no reason to think the worst."

"You're obviously better at remaining calm than I am," she said with a sigh.

They silently turned to look out their respective windows. She reached for his hand, and he held hers.

When they reached Southern Railway, she said, "I can wait in the carriage if it would be awkward to have me inside."

He took her hand. "I made that mistake once—I won't do it again. Come on."

Southern Railway had an outer office full of paper-strewn desks off a long corridor, and doors leading to several inner offices. The directors were milling about, talking excitedly, but they went silent when they saw David. Victoria thought they looked worried, not panicked, which made her feel a little better. Some of them gave her puzzled looks, and it took her a moment to remember that she was wearing feathers at her back.

"We were going to a masquerade," she said with a shrug.

"Were you a partridge?" Mr. Staplehill asked.

Was her costume *that* bad? "I'm a peacock!"

Mr. Bannaster opened the door to an inner office. "We're worried Norton might know about the merger."

Everyone filed into the other office and closed the door. Victoria found a chair in the corner near the main door and sat down to wait.

It wasn't long before she heard voices out in the corridor. Bored, she leaned her head against the wall, and the words became clearer.

"How dare you follow me to the office!"

She would recognize that indignant voice anywhere—Mr. Perry, who'd sounded just like that when he'd stormed out of her dinner party.

The other man was a stranger. "Ye're takin' his threats too lightly, mate. He doesn't want ye throwin' in your shares with Southern. He'll offer ye more."

"I would never do business with such an underhanded scoundrel. Imagine threatening a man's daughter!"

Did he mean Prudence? Victoria sat up straighter. She wanted to alert David, but she was afraid to miss something important.

"It's not a threat, mate. She's a pretty piece, your daughter. I can make sure no good man'll have her."

"She's well guarded—you won't get near her. Now take your cowardly threats and leave!"

The door slammed open, narrowly missing Victoria in the corner. Mr. Perry marched across the room and disappeared into the office. She held her breath. Had the criminal gone?

"Well guarded, is she?" said a low voice just outside the door. "What a nice challenge."

Victoria remained unmoving until she heard the front door slam at the end of the corridor. Then she ran across the room and threw open the door to the inner office.

"Mr. Perry!" she cried.

They all turned to look at her.

"I overheard that man after you left. He said it

was a nice challenge that you'd left your daughter well guarded."

David said, "Victoria, what are you talking about?"

But Mr. Perry clutched the back of a chair and swayed. "I've got to go, my lord. I didn't want to tell you—I thought I could handle it myself, but—Norton has threatened to compromise my daughter if I don't sell to him."

And then he was running past Victoria, breathing heavily.

"Wait, we'll take my carriage!" David followed him.

Victoria and the rest of the directors trailed behind. As she came outside, by gas lamp she watched Mr. Perry mount his horse.

"Your carriage will take too long, Thurlow. I can't wait!"

Men scattered looking for their horses and carriages. Victoria lifted her skirts and ran after David, who lifted her by the waist into the carriage.

"To Perry's!" he shouted up at his coachman. He got in beside her and slammed the door shut. "You know I would have left you there if I thought it was safe."

"I know, but I must come. Prudence might need me."

By the time the caravan arrived at Mr. Perry's

town house, there was already a brawl outside the gates, and a steady rain had begun to fall. Underneath a gas lamp, two hulking guards—obviously hired by Mr. Perry—watched in bemusement, and Victoria realized it was Mr. Perry fighting the henchman himself. Why had he not allowed the guards to help him?

He was far too old for such an endeavor, and it was obvious he would soon lose by the way he staggered back from a particularly nasty blow.

David jumped down from the carriage. "That's enough!"

Leaning even farther out the door, Victoria winced as David caught the henchman around the neck. The henchman struggled violently, until David spun him around and punched him hard in the stomach. With a groan, he collapsed to his knees.

"Let's go find Norton," David said, dragging the henchman back to his feet. "Who's got a horse we can tie him to?"

While the railway directors put forth various horses, the henchman kept saying, "I don't know any Norton."

When he was slung facefirst over the horse and tied down, David lifted his head by the hair. "So you want us to take you to the police? How noble of you to accept the blame for everything. I'm sure Norton will send you food in jail."

"All right, all right!" the henchman said. "He paid me. I was just goin' to kiss the girl, maybe scare her a bit."

Mr. Hutton held back Mr. Perry.

"That's my daughter you're talking about!" Mr. Perry yelled.

"Let's go see Norton," David said.

Everyone scrambled for their horses and carriages, and Mr. Bannaster led the henchman's horse. David looked up at Victoria.

"I'm not staying here," she said.

"But I thought Prudence needed you."

"I'm sure she's sound asleep in her bed. You need me more."

"I do?"

"Yes. Or at least I need to be with you. Now do you want everyone to reach Mr. Norton before we do?"

"To Norton's!" David yelled to his coachman before climbing up inside.

"The coachman knows where he lives?"

"I swear that man knows where *everyone* lives."

She leaned against him in relief.

"I'm wet, Victoria."

"I am, too."

The caravan descended on Mr. Norton's, and Victoria watched worriedly from the carriage as David dragged the henchman up the short length of the front pavement. The other directors followed behind in a group. David pounded loudly on the door over and over again, until finally a light appeared inside.

A butler in a nightcap tried to appear dignified. "Please return in the morning."

"Tell Norton that Viscount Thurlow is here," David said. "We have business to discuss. He'd better hurry unless he wants me to make sure he has not a business left to run."

Norton finally appeared at the door in his shirt-sleeves and trousers. He was a balding man, with his stomach hanging over his waistband. He was obviously incapable of mounting a credible threat to a woman all by himself, so he'd had to hire someone.

Not that he would admit it, as he stood just inside his door, out of the rain.

"I don't know what you're talking about, Thur-low," Norton said, smiling. "You woke me up for this nonsense?"

"You weren't sleeping," David said, dragging the henchman into the light. "You were anxiously awaiting a report from this cretin. Well, here he is to make his report, but he doesn't have much to say for himself. I'll say it for him. He failed. South-ern Railway will not fall apart at your hands. When we sign in the morning, we'll become the largest railway in the south."

Even from the carriage, Victoria could see Norton's teeth grind.

"As for you," David continued, "I'm prepared to forget this indiscretion."

Norton finally spoke. "But I won't. I'll make sure everyone knows that a *peer* is involved, Thurlow. You've been trying to keep it a secret, to protect the last shred of dignity the name Banstead might carry. But when I'm done—"

"Go ahead," David said.

Victoria gasped.

"I'm proud of what these men and I have accomplished," David continued. "We'll run a successful railway, which will give you more than your fair share of competition."

"I mean it!" Norton cried, then seemed to remember where he was as he looked around.

"You don't want your neighbors to hear the truth about you?" David said. He spoke louder. "I have no problem letting everyone know what I think of you. You don't want to go against a viscount, who's also a member of Parliament—especially one who has nothing to lose, where scandal is concerned, as you've pointed out. If I feel Miss Perry is in any danger from you, I'll make sure you lose every last investment you've ever made. Now where is a patrolling officer when you need one?" he asked, his voice carrying even louder.

Victoria stared at her husband as if he were a stranger. He'd just proclaimed that he didn't care about a new scandal, that he didn't care what people thought. Could it be true?

Chapter 22

David felt free, as if a chain around his neck had come loose. He really didn't care whom Norton told. No notoriety could be worse than what he'd already experienced.

"Be quiet!" Norton hissed.

"Is your wife inside?" David asked politely. "Perhaps we should awaken her."

"All right, you've won," Norton said between gritted teeth.

"You'll leave the Perrys alone?"

"Yes."

"If I hear you've threatened any of them—"

"What's the point? He'll have already turned over his shares to your company."

"You're a smart man, Norton." David tossed the henchman through the door, and he groaned as he landed on the floor. "Do something about this, won't you?"

The directors gathered around David, talking and laughing as they escorted him the few steps to the street. They clapped his back, they offered to take him out for a drink, but in the end, Victoria was waiting for him. He could just see her head through the open door of the carriage. The dispersal of the caravan took a few more minutes, and then he was finally able to climb up beside her, after telling the coachman to take them home. The door closed, the carriage pulled away from the curb, and they were alone.

"That was wonderful," she said.

"So you like to see me bullying people?" He arched a brow.

"Only for a good cause. Do you think he'll really leave the Perrys alone?"

"What else can he do? He wants to keep doing business in this city. He tried blackmail; it didn't work. I think he'll go onto his next little project."

Victoria hesitated.

"Go ahead, ask," he said.

"Did you mean what you said, that you'd go

public with your part in the railway if Norton didn't cease his pressure?"

"Yes. I'm not going to let innocent people get hurt because of my pride." He softened his voice. "And it really wouldn't have mattered. It only matters what you think, Victoria."

He looked down at her with a very thorough gaze.

"You can't stay in those wet clothes," he said.

She stared at him. "Well, of course I can. The journey home won't take long."

"It's at least a half hour's drive farther into the city. Now turn around."

"I—"

"Victoria, when a husband wishes to remove his wife's clothes, she usually lets him."

She gave him her back. "Even in a carriage?"

"*Especially* in a carriage."

He wanted to rip the peacock feathers from Victoria's back. He couldn't stand another item between him and his wife's smooth body.

Finally the feathers were gone, and he could feel the cool skin on the back of her shoulders. He kissed her there, running his tongue along her neck, kissing behind her ear, all while his fingers finally managed to undo the tiny buttons down her back. The lantern behind them swayed, chasing shadows across her creamy skin. He peeled the sodden gown down her body, and had her stand hunched over, to get the skirt off.

When everything was gone but her chemise, he whispered against her mouth, "Your drawers, too."

She released a little sigh that mingled with his own quick breaths.

"Hurry," he urged. "I'm impatient for you."

She stood again before him, leaning over him so that her head didn't hit the ceiling. When the carriage jostled from the uneven roads, she clutched his shoulders for balance. He could see her breasts hanging before him, bobbling gently with the motion, and he groaned, reaching up beneath her chemise himself for the tie of her drawers.

"I've thought of this all day," she whispered softly.

He didn't think he could get any harder, but he did.

"Well, I didn't exactly imagine the carriage," she added, "but—touching you, like you touched me."

When her drawers were gone, he pulled her forward so that she sat on him, straddling his thighs. His trousers were too tight, and he started to release them, when she put her hands on his.

"Let me."

Those two words were almost as arousing as her damp near-nakedness. He put his hands on the bench, barely realizing he was gripping the leather tightly. Didn't she know how she looked, her chemise translucent across her breasts? He liked her rising above him, and the way she worked so intently at loosening his cravat.

He put his hands on her waist. "We don't have much time."

"I know. I don't need all your clothes removed—just some."

He laughed. And then she was loosening the buttons of his shirt and waistcoat, pushing his evening coat wide open so that she could tug his shirt from his trousers. When her cool hands touched his stomach, he shuddered.

"You feel so warm," she whispered.

Her hands tentatively moved higher, and he held his breath, waiting. "Don't stop."

Her fingers caressed his nipples, and he pulled her hips against his and arched into her from below.

"I need to remove some more clothes," he said hoarsely.

Her fingers on his trousers were almost his undoing. He wasn't sure she would be brave enough to touch his erection, not yet, but just the thought made him groan into her mouth as he kissed her. He knew she'd made progress with his trousers when he felt less constricted. A sudden draft let him know he could pull her higher against him. Her hot moistness caressed the length of him, but he couldn't take her, not yet. With his mouth he tugged at the neckline of her chemise, exposing her breasts. Her flesh was cool and wet, and he tasted everything, from the puckered tips of her nipples to the hidden curves just beneath.

She was rocking against him, her head thrown back, her hands clasping his shoulders. When she cried out his name, he thrust up inside her, feeling the tug of her inner muscles, knowing that nothing else could ever feel this good. With his hands he guided her to ride him, with his mouth he worshipped at her breasts, until he felt the shudder of her climax all around him. He let go of his control and ground into her, his head thrown back, arching upward to take everything she offered.

As the world settled back into place, he pulled Victoria to his chest and held her there for a moment, stroking her damp hair where it hung in curls down her back.

She shivered.

"I'm a selfish bastard," he said abruptly, "using you without a thought to your comfort."

"I didn't even notice the chill until now," she protested. "You forget you're not exactly dry yourself."

He sat her up a bit—trying not to pull out of her—and leaned forward to reach around her. She laughed and clutched his shoulders. From beneath the far bench he pulled a blanket and wrapped it around her. With a sigh she hugged him and cuddled against his chest.

He moved within her, enjoying this connection, both physical and otherwise. He didn't try to think, didn't try to act as he thought he should. He just . . . existed.

Victoria experienced such a deep feeling of contentment. This was love, she thought, this wondrous feeling that one is sharing everything with the right person. She felt a part of him—and she still was—and wished the carriage ride could go on forever. Every turn of the wheels jostled them, so they rubbed pleasantly together. Was this incredible tenderness rare? Could David tell that? Or had he experienced all this before?

"We must be close to home," he murmured against her hair.

"Home." It was a whisper of promise, a prayer of thanks. He finally slid out of her, and she wanted to protest the return of such a solitary feeling.

He chuckled and sat her upright. "One of us has to be decently dressed. And since I'm the one who'll be doing the carrying, it had better be me."

"Carrying?" She slid from his lap, clutching the blanket tight around her shoulders, and watched him quickly fasten all his clothing. "I can put my gown on and walk."

"We barely got it off you. I'm going to wrap you warmly in that blanket and carry you up to a hot bath."

She didn't protest after that, just tried to keep her pleased smile to herself.

"David, what about my gown? Everyone will know I . . . removed it in the carriage."

"Leave it. We'll send Anna for it in the morning. And who will know at this time of night?"

David carried her up the front steps. Smith the butler opened the door just as Victoria leaned from David's arms to reach for it. She gave a gasp of surprise and pulled back inside the depths of the big blanket, feeling one of David's arms securely behind her back, the other beneath her thighs. Only her stocking-clad ankles and her shoes peeped out the far side.

She thought they might make it through the entrance hall, but the light was on in the library, and her mother peered through the doorway, retreated, and then pushed the earl's wheelchair before her. Both of their parents simply stared.

"She's fine," David said before Victoria could speak. "We got caught in the rain, and I don't want her to catch a chill."

His father let out a bark of laughter, and by the surprised look on David's face, Victoria knew that laugh hadn't been heard in this house in years.

"Set those damn nobles on their ears, I bet she did," the earl said.

She tried to hide her smile at the pleasure in his voice. What could she say? Probably not the truth.

She elbowed David, who was looking far too amused at her expense.

"Send for Anna," the earl said.

Victoria heard her mother chuckle. "I don't believe they'll need her."

David looked over his shoulder. "Tell her Victoria needs a hot bath."

In her bedroom, they found that Anna was already well prepared. The hip bath was surrounded by towels in front of the hearth, and the maid was arriving behind them with the first steaming buckets.

The footmen followed to fill the tub quickly, and Victoria groaned and sank as far into David's arms as she could, leaving just her eyes to peer out of the blanket.

Anna lit candles about the room.

"Anna," David said, "you can leave now. My wife is getting rather heavy."

"Of course, milord," the girl said, smiling. "Shall I come later to remove the bath?"

"No," he said, rolling his eyes.

"Very well, milord."

When the door had shut, Victoria gave a cry of

surprise as David set her on her feet and started stripping her of garments.

"I suggest, Lady Thurlow, that you take the quickest bath possible, because I will be watching you every minute."

She didn't think she had any more red left to blush, but she did. She stepped into the hip bath, sank into its heat, then stared with fascination as David began to remove his clothing. He stalked about the tub, watching her from every angle. She found herself using the soap in rather provocative ways she hadn't ever imagined before.

He couldn't seem to find the buttons of his shirt as she slowly washed her breasts.

He ripped a button from his trousers when she arched to reach her back.

He was finally naked and looming over her as she soaped between her legs.

"You're done," he said, in a voice she might once have thought menacing. "Stand up."

"But there's still soap—"

"Stand up."

She did. He had a bucket in his hands, and he poured fresh water down the front of her. The heat cascaded over her, and she sighed.

"Turn around."

He poured more down her back, then suddenly enveloped her from behind in a big, warm towel. With a powerful display of muscles, he lifted her and she was suddenly sprawled on her back in bed. He dried her off as if she were too delicate to help herself, and made love to her as if she were too fragile. More than once, Victoria had to wipe tears of happiness from her eyes when he wasn't looking.

She loved him so.

But again he went back to his own room when they were finished. Would he ever invite her in there—or into his heart?

In the morning, David went off to his railway announcement, looking as proud as if he'd given birth. Victoria fondly watched him go, and then toyed with her breakfast as her thoughts coalesced. Her marriage was beginning to succeed, but not at the pace she'd like. She was still not quite the Perfect Wife. She could slowly try to win over David's peers, one visit at a time, one dinner at a time, or she could host another party, only this time with members of the *ton*. She would not attempt something so formal as an evening event, which might remind too many people of the earl's parties.

She would do something different, like maybe a regular afternoon reception, with a theme such as . . . the arts. Something she could converse intelligently about! They could meet every few days. People could discuss their work, or the work of other artists, and maybe ladies would play or sing.

Not her of course. She would be too busy as hostess.

The first time she mentioned her idea to David, he seemed impressed with her endeavor, but could not promise to be able to attend. She understood—in fact, she wondered if it might be better that he *heard* what a glowing hostess she was, instead of seeing her flaws for himself.

Her invitations went out that day, for a reception to be held three days hence. She spent each day in between in a nervous state of planning, using every list-making skill she possessed. Her mother watched thoughtfully, but Victoria would not ask if Mama thought she was doing the right thing for her marriage. Victoria had set her goal on settling David's past, and she had to achieve it.

Her nights were spent in delicious abandon with David, and they were so vigorous in the efforts, she knew she would be with child soon. Better to hold her party now while she still could!

On the afternoon of the reception, the town house glowed with polish and sunlight. Even the servants seemed to be whistling, and though she was nervous, Victoria felt light at heart. The Fogges arrived first, both mother and daughter.

Miss Fogge went to the drawing room piano and stared at it. She looked over her shoulder at Victoria. "This is it, then?"

"Yes, but you must promise not to tell anyone,"

Victoria said, hiding her amusement. "Would you like to play it?"

"Oh no, I couldn't, my lady. But perhaps you would do me the honor?"

Victoria agreed to play, and soon Miss Fogge was singing. Victoria felt as if she'd found a new friend.

Maybe her only one, because no one else seemed to be coming.

After several songs, Victoria said, "Since this is a party to discuss the arts, shall we take a tour of the rooms? There's some lovely artwork in the library that the Bansteads have collected through the centuries."

She tried not to feel too disappointed. This was her first effort, after all. They happened to be on the staircase just above the entrance hall when the front bell rang. Smith answered the door, and Lord Wade and several men spilled in below them, all talking and laughing. They brought in fresh air and deep masculine voices, and Victoria knew her reception was saved.

Miss Fogge's mouth sagged open quite indecorously. "Mama," she began.

"Oh, hush, my girl." Lady Fogge's expression turned hopeful. "Lady Thurlow, you don't suppose most of these gentlemen are eligible."

"If I know Lord Wade, they're very eligible." Victoria knew exactly what he was doing— helping her reception the only way he could.

He looked up and saw her and grinned.

She smiled back with fondness.

Within a half hour, more people began arriving. Victoria was standing alone with Lord Wade when the rush began.

"You did this as well, didn't you," she said to him.

He spread his hands and shrugged his shoulders in innocence. "I brought my friends. And I might have mentioned at the club that we were attending your elegant affair. Several men might have heard me, but that is all."

"And they told their wives and daughters," she said. "Ah, Lord Wade, you don't know the effect you have. Some fine woman will be very lucky someday."

"Someday perhaps," he said with a grin, "but not anytime soon."

Though David tried to be home for the reception, he did not arrive until it was almost over. Guests were leaving as he entered, and he enjoyed hearing their compliments about his wife. He went up to the drawing room, and stopped in the doorway as he realized that Victoria was playing the piano. There were several ladies and gentlemen still gathered around her. Simon saw David and strolled over.

"So it was a success?" David asked.

"Yes, naturally," Simon said. "I think your wife puts guests at ease so well because she understands deep down how nervous most people feel in a new situation."

"Not these jaded people," David scoffed.

Simon shrugged. "Even these people. Perhaps it was not easy to enter your house after all these years. Ghosts, eh?"

David rolled his eyes, and together they turned back to watch Victoria play.

"She composed that, you know," Simon said.

David looked at him sharply. "She did?"

"You didn't know how talented she is?"

"No," he said slowly.

"You missed her singing. Her voice . . . ah, like the angels."

David spoke quietly. "I've never heard her sing. I never thought she would do something like that in front of strangers."

"But it's easier in front of strangers," Victoria said as she walked toward them.

David looked toward her, and he couldn't help his smile. He kissed her hand. "Simon tells me you are a complete success."

"Only because of him," she responded lightly. "He brought all his friends. Strange how single young women will flock to a house because of that."

Simon was grinning, Victoria was smiling, and

David felt . . . left out. Simon had been able to help Victoria. David wanted to be the one to do that.

"So if you'll sing to strangers," he said, finding it hard to speak lightly, "then you'll sing for me."

"Oh no, I couldn't. You're teasing me."

Simon was staring at him, and David felt as if it was his turn to blush. She would sing for strangers, but not for her husband?

She was called away to discuss a painting at the far end of the room. He watched her, and felt Simon's gaze on him. David didn't like that Simon guessed he felt hurt.

Why would Victoria reveal her passion in the bedroom, but not grant him something as easy as a song? He knew he didn't know everything about her, and for the first time it bothered him.

Did she feel the same? Was he hurting her, too?

She was challenging herself in so many ways, blossoming into a confident woman before his eyes. He liked that about her, but . . . what did it say about him? Was he stuck in the same old place, retreating from emotions he hadn't wanted to face for years? *Was* he obsessed with the past?

She was creating a new world for herself, and he was taking himself out of it, except in the dark of the night. Was that all he wanted?

Could he be falling in love with her?

* * *

Victoria awoke alone in the morning, but she could smell David on her skin. She lay still in the dusk before dawn, her eyes closed, trying to make sense of his mood last night. He had seemed so . . . urgent, his every movement passionate and intense. He hadn't wanted to talk, so she hadn't forced him. She hadn't told him she loved him, because she didn't know if she could say the words first, and risk his pity.

She was such a coward.

With song, she had revealed her emotions in front of strangers. But with David—

There was movement next to her in the bed and she froze, slowly opening her eyes.

He had stayed through the night.

She watched in astonishment as he sat up and stretched, his short hair tousled. She heard the bones in his back creak, watched as he looked over his shoulder at her. And then he smiled, and there was a pillow crease across his cheek that she could have gladly kissed.

"Go back to sleep," he murmured, leaning down to kiss her forehead. "I have an early appointment."

She let him go, still too amazed to put anything into words. But that had always been her problem. She was a writer at heart.

Of course she couldn't sleep. She rose and put on her dressing gown, and tried to distract herself by imagining what it could possibly mean that David had finally slept all night with her.

She would have to distract herself by thinking about her next endeavor. During the reception, it had come to her that every fear she faced turned out to be manageable. She needed to host a bigger event, one where David would be at her side, showing all of society that he was back for good. She would host a ball, an event to overshadow any memory of a scandal.

There were so many lists to make! She sat down at her desk and spread her journals around her and stared at them, but she knew deep in her heart that her excitement wasn't real, that she would use planning a ball as just one more excuse not to do something about her real problem.

Her marriage.

She needed to know how David felt about her. Why was she so afraid to say, *I love you*?

Maybe because there were so many other words left unsaid. Her mother had been right; as long as those forbidden words remained between them, there would always be a shadow of darkness in their marriage, a place both of them were afraid to go.

She had a chance for the kind of life she'd always dreamed of, back when only the fantasy of Willow Pond offered glimpses of a glowing future.

Fantasy was all she had as a girl—and the reality of Tom, there on the written page.

If she couldn't speak the words, maybe she could write them, and reach David the way she'd always reached Tom. She opened their childhood journal to a fresh page, and began to write.

She had to tell the truth to him—to David— even if he rejected her in the end.

Chapter 23

David arrived home before luncheon, and admitted to himself that he'd only done so because he wanted to be with his wife. Her mother was in the library with his father—again!—and they both looked up when he leaned inside.

"Is Victoria here?" he asked.

Mrs. Shelby lowered the book she'd been reading aloud. "I have not seen her since breakfast. Have you tried the music room? She spends several hours a day there."

He hadn't known that, and he felt like the worst of husbands. "I'll look, thank you."

But she wasn't in the music room, or anywhere

else in the town house. When he found Anna just sitting down to luncheon in the servants' hall, she came to her feet.

"Milord?" she said in a questioning voice, following him out to the corridor.

"Do you know where your mistress is?" he asked.

"Surely somewhere in the house, milord. She wouldn't go out without me."

Nodding, he let her go back to her meal. He went up to Victoria's bedchamber and stood uncertainly, feeling worry creep over him. Where could she have gone?

And then he saw their old battered journal left on the table by the door to his room. Instinct made him pick up the notebook and open to the final page. It was dated that day, surely written just that morning.

David,

I'm writing this to you because as usual, words fail me. I hope as you read this, you'll understand why I did what I did, and forgive me. I just wanted to cause you no scandal.

Inside David, worry exploded into fear, for the rest of the page was blank. Where had she gone, after writing such a thing?

359

He ran back down through the center of the town house, startling servants on every floor. In the library, he found only his father, and was about to leave when the earl called him back.

"Did you find Victoria?" his father asked.

"No."

David's expression must have revealed something, for the earl's face gathered into a frown.

"What did you do?" his father demanded.

David stiffened, but he refused to withhold the truth. When had his father become Victoria's champion? "I put conditions on our marriage from the beginning, demanding that she commit no scandal. Therefore she withheld something from me out of fear."

"I don't understand."

"I have spent my adulthood attempting to rebuild our name, Father, can't you see that? After everything that had happened, we were laughing-stocks. And when I couldn't marry someone of noble blood, I married Victoria, who has the grace and intelligence to rival any woman. But I didn't know what I had."

His father's hands were shaking as he reached up to wipe his face. "There is no excuse for my behavior after your mother died except grief too long withheld. I never thought you should hear this, but now I see that I was wrong not to explain things to you once you became a man."

"Father, you don't need to—"

"Yes, I do. For you see, David, during your mother's short life, I didn't know how to help her. She loved you so much that she wanted more babies, even though the physicians all said it could kill her."

David slowly sank onto a chair opposite his father and just stared at the old man.

"I tried to deny her, to help her understand that I needed her healthy more than you needed siblings. She didn't want to accept that, and I . . . I could deny her nothing."

"*She* . . . wanted more children?" David whispered the words, feeling the foundations of his childhood shake and reform all around him.

The earl nodded forlornly. "She wouldn't listen to me, and in the end, it killed her. And then like a foolish old man, I let my need for happiness outweigh a child's need for stability. David, forgive me for not seeing how unhappy you were with Colette's presence."

David could only nod. He'd spent years simmering under the weight of his anger toward his father, years of trying to repair the family name. And now he knew that his father had almost been destroyed by grief, and found comfort where he could. Colette had driven him away from his father, and David had let it happen.

"Can you forgive me?" his father asked.

David rose to his feet and crossed to the earl, putting a hand on his shoulder. "Perhaps we can forgive each other, Father."

The earl looked away and patted David's hand.

"Don't stay here," his father said. "Find Victoria."

David talked to the head groom, only to discover that Victoria had not summoned a carriage. But she certainly could have hired one. David questioned Anna again, who handed over the names of every person who had shown friendship to Victoria. It was a small list; it was sad to see that so few had understood Victoria's true nature.

Hell, he wouldn't even be on her list, not with the way *he'd* behaved.

He rode at breakneck speed to the Fogges' residence first, interrupting a luncheon of the family of three.

"Forgive my intrusion," he said, "but have you seen Lady Thurlow today?"

They hadn't, and something of his urgency must have communicated itself, because Lady Fogge walked him to the door, wearing a worried expression.

"My lord, surely she just forgot to tell you where she was going today."

"No, not even her mother or her lady's maid knows where she is."

"She'll be home soon."

"But I can't wait for that."

"Is something terribly amiss?"

He looked at the door, wanting to be gone, but not wanting to offend this woman who'd treated Victoria so kindly. "I fear my wife and I have had a misunderstanding, Lady Fogge. I must remedy it at once."

She smiled up at him, then patted his arm. "I'm certain you will. She is one to see and understand the truth."

"If only the same could be said about me," he said grimly. "My thanks for your assistance."

"Do let me know that all is well with Lady Thurlow."

He went to Simon's next, but Simon wasn't at home. Damn, the man could have helped with the search. But then David didn't need help when the list of Victoria's friends was so small. Several of the gentlemen heads of the household were home when he barged in. David didn't care what they thought as he asked about his wife. He saw several smirks, knew that he looked like a lovesick fool—

And he didn't care. Nothing mattered but the need to find Victoria, to make her see that *she* was all that mattered to him, not what other people thought of them.

But no one had seen her. At Banstead House Victoria's mother met him in the conservatory as if she'd waited at the windows to follow his progress home.

"Did you find her?" Mrs. Shelby asked.

David shook his head grimly.

"This is all my fault," she whispered. "I gave her counsel about your marriage, but I never thought it would affect her this way!"

"Mrs. Shelby, don't blame yourself. I'll find Victoria," he said forcefully, "and I'll make her see—"

"But do you love her?" she interrupted.

He calmed himself. "Since we were children."

She wiped at her eyes. "Then go find her and make it right. Because she must have loved you since then as well."

"Where should I look?"

"There was a place Victoria and her sisters would go when they wanted to be alone. I think they thought I never knew. They called it Willow Pond."

"Of course I know Willow Pond," David said, disgusted with himself for not thinking of it first. "She wrote about it often. It's in the far corner of your garden."

"She liked to think there—to dream," the old woman finished quietly.

"I promise you," he said with passion, "that she won't have to dream her happiness anymore."

Mrs. Shelby nodded and covered her mouth, and blinked her wet eyes. David left her there, striding outside and down through his garden. There was a small gate somewhere, rusted and never used, even by him. He remembered exactly where to climb the tall stone wall, and he dropped down to the ground on the far side. There were no sounds of gardeners come to chase him away, so he walked down the paths he'd once spied on from the nursery window.

He ducked beneath the low branches of the willow tree and saw Victoria immediately. She sat on a small bench, facing an ornamental pond long gone green with overgrowth. Her hands rested in her lap, and she was humming. She didn't hear him approach until twigs cracked beneath his feet.

The humming stopped, and her violet eyes opened and looked at him as if she'd known it was he all the time. Her smile was tinged with sadness.

"Hello, David. I was out for a walk and couldn't resist coming here."

"I was worried about you, especially after those few lines you wrote in our journal. I confess to being overwhelmed by panic. I looked everywhere, including at any house I thought you might go to."

"I didn't mean to worry you." A soft smile curved her mouth as she glanced down at her lap. "That must have been an interesting sight."

He stepped closer and she hugged herself, so he stopped. "I looked like a great foolish beast, searching for my wife."

"They didn't laugh at you," she said with distress.

"What harm could that do to me? All I cared about was what *you* thought of me, sweetheart."

She flinched at the endearment. What could be so wrong?

"But you saw what I wrote in the journal," she said in a sad voice. "I've been keeping a terrible secret. I knew I had to tell you, and that I had to do it in person, not by writing. That would have been the coward's way out."

He sat down beside her on the bench. "Then tell me, and we'll keep it together."

She sighed. "When you offered to marry me, you asked so little in return, only that I bring you no scandal. I failed you, David. I concealed an important fact about my family, all to spare my mother's pain and my father's memory." Her tone dropped to a murmur. "You see, he killed himself. My sisters and mother and I found him hanged by the neck in our stables."

He stared at her, aghast at what she'd had to go through, furious with a father who would harm his family so. It made his relationship with his own father seem almost harmless.

"My mother was near hysterics that anyone should know what he did, fearing that he would not be buried in consecrated ground."

It all was so clear now: Mrs. Shelby's terrible

366

sadness, the shadows in Victoria's eyes. Her own father had betrayed them, rather than stand up for his mistakes and help his family. And David was no better, insisting that everything revolve around him and his family.

"Victoria—"

"No, I must finish it all, or I'll never say it. We agreed not to tell a soul what we four knew. I could have borne this sin forever for my mother's sake—until I fell in love with you."

She said the words he longed to hear, but without the joy.

"I couldn't let this secret keep being a shadow between us. I married you violating the tenet of honesty you hold dear, and I would not blame you if you renounced our marriage."

"Victoria, stop!" He tried to take her hands, but she pulled away from him.

"Or if that would be too much of a scandal for you, I would gladly retire to the country, so that the *ton* will forget about me and not unearth the truth."

"Victoria, I gave you every reason to imagine my reaction to be so poor. I am deeply ashamed of myself, that I proved so untrustworthy—and so unworthy of your love."

"No, no, don't say that. I lied to you, about such an important thing! I chose my family over you."

"Do you think I blame you?" he demanded. "What was I to you at such a time? You had sworn an oath to your mother and sisters. It is my fault that later, as our friendship returned, that you didn't feel you could tell me the truth. I made you think you had to be perfect, when God knows I wasn't. I let so many things about my family's past affect my life. And it was all for naught."

Her voice was cautious. "What do you mean?"

"I was just a child, and thought I knew everything. I blamed my father for the deaths of my siblings, and for my mother's death in the end."

"David, you were so young."

"Don't excuse what I did. I began the ruin of my relationship with my father, when all along it was my mother who ignored her own health, my mother who needed to prove something by having more children."

She sighed and rested her hand on his knee. But he couldn't stop now.

"My father may not have been wise to have his mistress live with us, but he asks my forgiveness now, and it is a shame I could not grant it to him long ago. I didn't tell him everything that Colette had done, of course."

"You mean the scandalous parties?"

"That and . . . other things."

Victoria watched the struggle on his face, felt the pull of his emotions as if they were her own. She was so afraid to hope, so afraid that his words could not be true.

"Tell me, David," she whispered, taking his hand in hers and squeezing. "Let us have no more secrets."

"There have to be secrets between my father and me," he said tiredly. "In his own way, he loved Colette. How can I tell him that she spent so much time trying to seduce me?"

She inhaled sharply. "How old were you?"

"Seventeen, when it started."

"You could have written to me. Maybe I could have helped."

His beloved face softened in amusement. "My sweet Victoria, I could tell no one. Thank God my father finally allowed me to go off to Oxford. I don't know what I might have done to the woman, had she kept pressing herself on me." He shuddered. "She thought I would tumble her in my mother's bed. And my father wondered why I wouldn't attend the woman's funeral."

"I'm glad things are better between you and the earl," she said.

"They are—and it's because of you."

David turned to face her, their knees pressed together, their hands clasped. "I spent my adulthood looking at the past out of a child's eyes, instead of seeing that only *I* can decide how a scandal should affect me. And I hurt you in the process."

"David, do not berate yourself so."

"Of course you couldn't trust me, when I gave you no reason to do so."

"Please don't think my problems were because of you," she said, looking away from him. "It's taken me a long time to see that I really didn't trust anyone, except my sisters. Watching your struggle with your father made me realize how angry I was with my mother for shielding us for so long from their financial problems. She was caught in a terrible situation not of her making, and I blamed her for it. You see, David, you and I are not so different after all."

"Are things better between you?" he asked quietly.

"Yes."

A slow smile grew across his face. "Just as they are between my father and myself. So must we talk about them anymore?"

She smiled, feeling the small budding of hope in her heart.

"Ah, Victoria, sweetheart, you've endeared yourself to me with your very presence."

His tone was low and sincere, his words so very earnest.

"When I married you," he said, "I thought you were the answer to so many problems, as if you were an object created for my use, rather than a flesh and blood woman."

He gripped both of her hands now. His eyes,

with their pale color she once thought so frozen, now seemed to burn with sincerity.

"I used you," he said.

"But David, we both—"

"Yes, yes, I know I rescued you from a terrible situation, but I don't want you to feel like you owe me. Do you think you could love me, just for me?"

She inhaled through a throat thick with tears. "Oh David, I have always loved you," she whispered, trying to stop her tears, yet unable to. "From the time when you were just words and ideas and feelings, so full of energy and eagerness that I envied, to the man you are now, replete with so much goodness and courage that you would care for me and my family, regardless of our circumstances."

He closed his eyes, his face full of relief. "Victoria, I wasn't good. I was selfish."

"You could have given me money and assuaged your guilt. But you gave of yourself."

"Because it was you," he said, cupping her face. "You, the girl who listened to any crazy idea I had, who encouraged me when there was no one else to listen, the only one I felt comfortable talking to. You see the best in people, and that takes a bravery I admire. I may not have realized it at first, but I could not forget what we'd been to each other. I love you, Victoria. Promise me I won't lose you."

"Oh David!"

She threw her arms about him and he pulled her onto his lap, as if they both couldn't get close enough to each other. The kiss they shared held no secrets, no worries, and was full of a trust they finally had in each other.

Victoria broke the kiss first, resting her forehead against his and looking into his eyes. "I have one more requirement I didn't list at the beginning of our marriage."

His lifted one eyebrow. "You do?"

"My last and final wish is that I can sleep in your bed."

David groaned. "And I so value my privacy, too."

"Well, you must, because I've never even seen the inside of your room!"

He laughed and held her close. "Victoria, anything I have is yours. You only have to speak the words."

"And if I write them?" she asked in a teasing voice.

"Sweetheart, I cherish every written word we ever shared, but trust me, communication with our lips is far superior."

And he kissed her until she was breathless, and she believed his every word.

Epilogue

Dearest Victoria,

As you lie there sleeping, I confess that I have spent another hour staring at our son. I keep counting his fingers and toes, marveling at his tiny fingernails, his little nose, his eyes so full of your inquisitiveness. I never thought I could be more blessed with our marriage, but this result of our love, this precious gift, is more than I could have ever hoped for.

As I watched you grow big with our child, I could not speak my fears. I see now why you found it so much easier to write. I had not realized how my mother's death would haunt me as you struggled to give birth. But I can breathe easier as I give thanks to God for your health and our son's health. Perhaps we should not risk this again. Perhaps—

But of course, my lusty wife, there will be other babies, and God willing, we will both enjoy them for many long years to come.

And enjoy making babies, as well.

Your well-loved husband,
David